Love Finds You™

Under the
Mistletoe

Love Finds You™

Under the Mistletoe

Two heartwarming stories of Christmas past and present

AN APPALACHIAN CHRISTMAS

BY IRENE BRAND

ONCE UPON A CHRISTMAS EVE

BY ANITA HIGMAN

Doubleday Large Print Home Library Edition

summerside
PRESS™

Summerside Press™
Minneapolis 55438

**Love Finds You Under the Mistletoe:
An Appalachian Christmas**
© 2010 by Irene Brand

**Love Finds You Under the Mistletoe:
Once Upon a Christmas Eve**
© 2010 by Anita Higman

ISBN 978-1-61793-307-3

Scripture references are from The Holy Bible, King James Version (KJV).

Cover Design by Koechel Peterson & Associates | www.kpadesign.com

Summerside Press™ is an inspirational publisher offering fresh, irresistible books to uplift the heart and engage the mind.

Printed in USA.

Dedication

This book is dedicated to Anita Higman,
my coworker in this anthology,
and to Rachel Meisel, Summerside Press editor.
It was a pleasure to share this
experience with you.

—Irene Brand

This book is dedicated to the wonderful
folks in Noel, Missouri,
who made the time I spent there doing research
as pleasant and lovely as the surrounding
countryside.

—Anita Higman

Acknowledgments

My sincere appreciation to members of
the Owsley County Historical Society:
Delcie Hall, Wallace Edwards, Ella
Addison, Bertha Noble, Vicki Campbell,
Audrea Farmer. Special thanks to Delcie
for being our guide on a long tour of the
Buffalo Creek area, especially the Faith
Hill community; Wallace, who supplied
dozens of pictures of Booneville and
vicinity in the 1940s; and Ella and Bertha,
who went out of their way to find research
information in the Historical Society's
library. I would also like to thank Judy
Couch of Mistletoe, who talked with us
about her father, who was once the
postmaster. The abandoned Mistletoe
church, which is in her front yard, was an
important subject of conversation,
especially when she warned us to beware
of the copperhead snakes, which are

ACKNOWLEDGMENTS

summer residents in the church. I'm grateful also to many other local residents who were kind to us. Special thanks to my husband, Rod, who shared the research with me, who read my final draft for typos, and who entertained himself while I spent long hours at my computer.

—Irene Brand

Much gratitude goes to my editor, Rachel Meisel,
to agent Chip MacGregor,
to author Irene Brand,
and to publicist Jeane Wynn.
Thanks to each of you for your encouragement,
your help, and your friendship.
You are a wonder to behold!

—Anita Higman

Love Finds You Under the Mistletoe:
An Appalachian Christmas

BY IRENE BRAND

Chapter One

....

Its driver whistling merrily, the antiquated bus climbed a hill into the small Kentucky town on a sunny September morning. With brakes squeaking and the engine groaning like a sick person gasping for a final breath, the bus eventually ground to a halt before a two-story building. Opening the door, the driver shouted, "Booneville. All passengers get off."

Julia Mayfield gathered her bags, lifted her nephew, Bobby, into her arms, and exited the bus. In a voice hoarse with frustration and fatigue, she asked the driver, "Is there any other public transportation available here?"

The driver pointed to a gasoline station across the street. "You might hire a taxi over there."

Julia thanked the driver and walked toward the small building he'd indicated. She hadn't wanted to take this trip. Now that the war had ended, she had plans for the future that didn't include honoring her sister's dying request.

Shifting Bobby to her left hip, Julia walked into the gasoline station. The only occupant of the building was bending over the engine of a car. When he became aware of Julia's presence, the black-bearded man straightened, took off his cap, and spit a mouthful of tobacco into an oil drum. "Howdy, ma'am. My name's Alex. What can I do for you?"

"I need transportation to Mistletoe. The bus driver thought you could help me."

Alex shook his head. "'Fraid not, ma'am."

"You have a sign in your window, 'Taxi for hire.'"

"That's a fact, ma'am," he agreed. "I've got *one* taxi. A man rented it this morning and took off for Louisville. He won't be back till day after tomorrow."

"I can't wait that long," Julia persisted. "Is there another taxi stand?"

"Nope. Autos are scarcer than hen's teeth around here."

Confronted with another delay in her plans, Julia sat cautiously on a rickety chair and let her nephew stand beside her. Grasping at straws, she asked, "Is it too far for me to walk?"

If she hadn't been so tired and discouraged, Julia might have laughed as the man's mouth dropped open and his faded brown eyes widened in amazement.

"Walk! Why, lady, hit's nigh on to eighteen miles from Booneville to Mistletoe."

Bobby looked up at her, and his blue eyes glistened with tears. "I hungry."

Julia lifted him to her lap. "I know you are, sweetie." She took some cookies wrapped in waxed paper from her purse. "Nibble on these until I decide what to do."

Perhaps sensing her distress, Alex said kindly, "Wish I could help, ma'am. Looks to me like you're between a rock and a hard place."

"Yes. That states my situation exactly," she replied in a cynical tone.

Alex's faded eyes squinted in thought. "Just a minute," he shouted. "I might find you a ride after all."

He rushed outside into narrow Mulberry Street and waved down a dilapidated Ford pickup. Judging from his gestures, Julia assumed Alex was talking to the driver about her. Placing Bobby on the chair, she stood and anxiously watched the exchange between the two men. The driver parked his pickup and came into the service station with Alex.

"Ma'am, you're in luck. This is Tom Morriston. He carries the mail to Mistletoe. He'll give you a lift."

Mr. Morriston, a small, wrinkled-faced man with gray hair and a winning smile, extended his right hand. "Howdy, ma'am."

She took her benefactor's hand. "Oh, thank you, sir. I'm Julia Mayfield."

She motioned to her luggage in front of the bus station. "If you can't take all of my suitcases, perhaps I can store them at the station."

He glanced out the window. "I can haul all of them, ma'am. It looks like you've come to stay a spell. You got kin in Owsley County?"

Julia shook her head, unsure how to explain her reason for visiting Mistletoe. She ruffled Bobby's brown curls. "This is Bobby, my sister's son."

The mail carrier chucked Bobby under the chin. "Hi there, Bobby."

Her nephew was a friendly boy, and he welcomed the mail carrier's attention. His eyes sparkled, and he wiggled like a playful puppy.

"Hit'll be about an hour before I start home," Mr. Morriston said. "I can pack your things in the truck now."

"If there's a restaurant close by, Bobby and I will eat lunch and wait there until you're ready to start."

He nodded his head. "You'll need to eat. Hit'll take two or three hours to reach where we're goin', but we'll get there before dark." He scratched his head. "Probably the best place for you to eat is the Wilder Hotel. I'll show you where it is, and then I'll tend to my town chores."

"Thank you very much," Julia said. "I'll

take the small suitcase with me, so I can change Bobby's clothes while we wait."

An hour later, Julia and Bobby were bouncing along in Tom Morriston's pickup truck on their way out of Booneville. Bobby snuggled against Julia and almost immediately went to sleep. A few miles out of town, the uneven pavement gave way to a rough, graveled road. While she gazed with interest at the rugged, wooded landscape, Julia wrapped a protective arm around her nephew to keep him from rolling off the seat.

Although the train had traveled through several mountainous regions on the journey from Baltimore, Julia had devoted her time to Bobby instead of looking at the scenery. Her home in Maryland was located near Chesapeake Bay, and compared to the flat land she was accustomed to, these rugged Appalachian Mountains seemed intimidating and mysterious. Giant sprawling oaks, a variety of maples, and other trees Julia didn't recognize intermingled with cedars and pines.

Time passed more quickly than Julia

had anticipated, for Tom Morriston was an interesting companion and a goldmine of information. They were soon on a first-name basis, as the mail carrier asked her to call him Tom.

"People have been livin' here since the days of Dan'l Boone," he'd explained. "My pappy moved to Kentucky soon after the Civil War. I was born in these mountains. Except for the years I was away durin' the First World War, this has always been my home."

"Tell me about the town of Mistletoe. How did it get its name?"

"Hit's not a town, Julia—just the name of our post office. The way I hear it, the government man who came to establish the route asked what to call the post office. Somebody looked up at a clump of mistletoe clingin' to an oak tree and said, 'Let's call it Mistletoe.'"

Disappointed that there wasn't a more romantic story behind the name, Julia laughed quietly. "I've been interested in mistletoe ever since I was crowned Queen Mistletoe in a Christmas pageant when I was in the fourth grade. The little boy who played the king waved a sprig of mistletoe over my head and kissed me. That was my first kiss."

Tom guffawed and glanced toward her, admiration in his eyes. "I bet you've had plenty of kisses since then."

Julia shook her head. "Not as many as you might think." She changed the subject. "You say that Mistletoe isn't a town— surely there are stores, a restaurant, a hotel, or a boardinghouse?" She tried to keep the desperation out of her voice.

He shook his shaggy head. "Nope. The only public buildings are the church and Rockhouse School. About seventy families live in the hills and hollers of Buffalo Crick, and they get their mail on the Mistletoe route. The post office is in one room of the postmaster's home."

Julia experienced momentary panic as her thoughts rioted. If she couldn't stay with the Waldens, where could she find lodging? Her personal comfort wasn't an issue—during the past three years, she had slept in many uncomfortable beds— but she must find a place for Bobby. Perhaps sensing her agitation, the child stirred in his sleep. Julia patted his back, and he didn't waken.

Suddenly Julia's concerns about where they'd spend the night faded into the background. Tom made a sharp right turn on a steep, rocky road, which twisted downhill like a serpent, and her nerves tensed immediately. At every curve she expected the old truck to plunge into the deep hollow, and her breath seemed to have lodged in her throat. To add to her concern, two deer leaped out of the woods and crossed the road. Tom braked sharply and missed them by a hairbreadth. By the time they'd reached a narrow creek valley, her chest felt like a volcano on the verge of erupting.

"This is Buffalo Crick," Tom volunteered calmly as Julia struggled to breathe. "In dry weather this road's not too bad, but we've had a wet spring, so it's full of chuckholes. We'll be fordin' the crick off and on the rest of the way."

Julia soon lost count of how many times the road ran through the stream, but they were in water more than on dry land. Except for occasional clearings where isolated houses and outbuildings stood, the forest pressed in on both sides of the muddy road. She felt smothered and wondered how soon this nightmare would be over. Occasional shafts of sunlight filtering through the trees afforded some respite, but for the most part it was a nerve-wracking ride.

Perhaps sensing Julia's reaction to her surroundings, Tom stopped chatting and devoted his attention to driving. Several times the truck mired in mud holes, and Julia held her breath until Tom maneuvered the vehicle to safety. She sighed in relief when Tom flashed a smile in her direction and said, "Hit's only five more miles to Mistletoe, and we've got only one more crossin'."

Bobby stirred again and whimpered several times before he opened his eyes. Julia had hoped he would sleep until they reached their destination, but she lifted him to her lap. "We're almost there, Bobby. You can look out the window for the rest of the way."

"Why?"

Julia cringed inwardly, having lost count of how many times she'd heard that question since they'd left Maryland. Suspecting that she had only one nerve left, she forced herself to say lightly,

"Because the tall trees are beautiful, and there's mistletoe growing in them."

"Why?"

Before she could think of an answer, they rounded a curve, where about a foot of water covered the road. Tom slowed the truck to a crawl. The water seemed swifter here than it had at the other crossings, and Julia tensed immediately. The truck eased slowly into the water, but after they moved forward slightly, the vehicle bumped against something rigid. With a thud it veered sideways, and the engine died.

"Of all the luck," Tom muttered. "I must have hit a rock and busted a tire. This would have to happen when I had passengers! You stay put, miss."

Considering their surroundings, Julia had no intention of moving. They were in the middle of the creek, which splashed gently on the truck's bottom. She couldn't see any way out of this predicament, but in spite of her inner turmoil, a myriad of birdsongs in the surrounding woodlands brought some peace to her heart.

"Flat tire or not, I'll try to drive this vehicle to dry ground. Hold on!" Tom started the truck, gunned the engine, changed into a low gear, tried to move forward, and then quickly switched into reverse.

He rocked the truck back and forth several times, but if it moved as much as an inch, Julia wasn't aware of it. Bobby, however, seemed to think they were playing a game. He swayed back and forth with the truck as if he was on a teeter-totter, yelling, "Whee! Whee!"

Julia was pleased that *someone* was having a good time. Panic like she'd never experienced coursed through her mind and body, and she struggled to keep her fragile control. For the hundredth time since leaving Baltimore, she asked herself if this trip had been necessary in the first place.

"Stuck tighter than the cork in a jug," was Tom's calm opinion after he'd tried repeatedly to drive the truck to dry land. He pulled a pair of gumboots from behind his seat, rolled up his overalls, kicked off his shoes, and pulled on the boots. "I'll have to get some help. There's a farm a little ways up the road. I'll walk there and borrow a mule or horse to pull the truck to land."

Julia stifled a groan. "What are we supposed to do?"

"Oh, you'll be all right. The water's fallin' now. I'll be back as quick as I can."

"This water looks deep and swift," Julia observed. "You be careful!"

"Now, don't you fret! Old Tom has been in worse trouble than this."

Fearing that he might topple over, she watched tensely as Tom stepped into water above his knees. He steadied himself by holding on to the truck door. "You're right, miss. It's plenty deep. My boots are full of water already."

"I feel so helpless sitting here." Her stomach churned with worry and frustration. Julia was a woman of action, and it went against the grain to be in a situation she couldn't handle.

"If you're a prayin' woman, you might ask the good Lord to send help."

If rescue depended on her prayers, Julia thought wryly, they were in trouble. Although she had once been on speaking terms with God, she wasn't any longer.

Experiencing three years of war firsthand had caused her to doubt that God was concerned with the problems of His people.

The situation was desperate, however, and knowing that God had once answered her prayers, Julia lowered her chin on Bobby's head and closed her eyes. "God, I can't bear much more," she cried aloud. "I'm at my wit's end. Please help us out of this nightmare."

When she lifted her head, Tom still stood beside the truck, his mouth hanging open, his eyes wide with astonishment. "Miss, that's powerful prayin'."

Having no idea what he meant, her gaze followed his pointing finger. A man on horseback loped toward them. Julia breathed silent thanks for answered prayer, strengthened by the assurance that God hadn't cast her aside. "Do you know him?"

"Sure, I know him. I know everybody in this holler." He lifted his right hand and hailed the approaching rider. "David, you're sure a sight for sore eyes!"

The man swung from his saddle in one fluid movement, and Julia took a quick breath. A shaft of sunlight glimmering through the grove of sycamore trees spotlighted the newcomer, and she stared at him in disbelief. She had seen hundreds of handsome men in the past three years, none of whom had been as pleasing to the eye as this stranger. In a cursory glance she took in his tall, powerful, well-muscled body. He was bareheaded, and his black hair gleamed like ebony in the sunlight. Jet black eyes shifted from Tom to Julia, and when their eyes met, a sudden warm glow radiated from her toes to the top of her head.

Chapter Two

Tom walked to the creek bank and shook
hands with the rider. Leaning against a
tree for support, he emptied water from
his boots. Then he gestured toward the
truck. "David, I've got a flat tire and I'm
stuck in the mud. Can you pull us out?"

"I think so, but I'd better rescue your
passengers first." He lifted the bridle of
the gray horse and eased slowly into the
water. Before he reached the side of
the truck, Tom called, "My passengers
are Julia Mayfield and her nephew,
Bobby. Ma'am, meet David Armstrong."

Julia acknowledged the introduction,

and as David reined his horse close to the truck, she noted again that he looked too perfect to be real.

"I'll take the boy to safety first and come for you." His voice, deep and compassionate, conveyed genuine concern over their predicament.

Bobby pulled back and hid his face on Julia's breast. "No."

David flashed his even white teeth in a smile. "No reason to be afraid, Bobby. My horse wants to take you for a ride."

Bobby glanced up at Julia. "Horsey?"

"Yes, just like the one you play with at home, only a lot bigger," she encouraged, with a grateful glance toward their rescuer.

"Open the door, and I'll reach in for him."

Bobby whimpered piteously and cringed against Julia, but he relaxed somewhat when she said calmly, "It will be fun. You'll see."

Perhaps the man's irresistible smile made Bobby more confident, for he lifted his hands without further protest. David took the boy in his arms. Guiding the horse with his knees, he delivered Bobby to Tom, whirled the horse, and again splashed through the creek toward the truck.

In a deep, calm voice, he asked, "Do you want to ride astride behind me? Or I can hold you in front like I did the boy."

Julia glanced at her short, narrow skirt, envisioning what a spectacle she'd make astride a horse. "You'd better take me the same way you did Bobby."

David moved behind the saddle and leaned toward her. "Step out of the truck, and I'll lift you."

Julia suddenly understood Bobby's fears. As she stepped on the narrow running board, the muddy water lapped at the soles of her shoes, and a quick glance at the swift-flowing stream made her feel dizzy. She was no lightweight. Could this man lift her, or would she fall into the creek?

She raised her hands, and his muscular arms wrapped around her waist. He lifted her without noticeable effort and cradled her gently on the saddle with his left arm, guiding the horse with his right hand. When they left the creek bed, David carefully lowered her to the ground.

"Thank you."

"My pleasure, ma'am."

Bobby's shoes were already muddy, so Julia let him explore the area while the men prepared to tow the truck to land. Tom walked into the water, took a long chain out of the truck bed, connected it to the front of his vehicle, and tossed the other end to David. He fastened the chain to his saddle and stepped to the horse's head.

"Wait until I get behind the truck," Tom said. "I'll push and help the horse a little."

Watching as David calmly encouraged the large gray horse to pull the truck, Julia was impressed by his patience. He gently urged the horse by patting its neck and speaking softly. "Come on, Clyde, pull a little harder. You can do it." Within a short time, the pickup was out of the water and parked beside the road.

"We'll leave the truck here till mornin'," Tom said.

"What about my suitcases?" Julia protested. She could manage with the clothes she wore, but she would need changes for Bobby.

"How many do you have?" David asked.

"Three."

"I'll strap one behind Clyde's saddle, and I'll carry the other two."

David reached inside the truck bed and removed her luggage as well as a small mailbag. He turned to Julia. "You and the boy can ride. Tom and I will walk."

Considering the width of the saddle and her narrow skirt, Julia shook her head. "Thank you, but Tom's clothes and boots are wet, and he must be uncomfortable. Why can't he ride and carry Bobby? I'll walk and help with the luggage."

David lifted his eyebrows speculatively. "It's over three miles to Mistletoe."

"That's all right. I'm used to walking."

Tom argued stubbornly but finally agreed to ride the horse and hold Bobby in front of him. Julia guessed that Tom probably had grandchildren, for he soon gained Bobby's confidence. The child snuggled against him and put one chubby hand on the reins. It was obvious that Bobby was more at ease with the mail carrier than he was with her.

She changed from black patent pumps to flat-heeled walking shoes. Against David's protest, she insisted on carrying the medium-sized case, leaving him with the larger one. They walked a mile or more in companionable silence until David cleared his throat hesitantly. "Normally I don't meddle in a stranger's business, but I am curious to know why you're visiting Mistletoe."

Julia had been wondering how she would go about finding Bobby's family. She was acutely aware that the afternoon was waning, and she didn't know where she could spend the night. Perhaps David was the one to advise her.

"Do you know where the Walden family lives?"

David sliced an astonished glance in her direction. "You've come to visit *them*?"

She nodded. "I didn't intend to *stay* with them, but I may have to. Tom said there isn't a hotel in Mistletoe."

"Do the Waldens know you're coming?" David persisted.

Julia shook her head.

"Well, Miss . . ." He looked at her left hand. "It is Miss Mayfield?"

"That's right. I'm not married. Bobby is my nephew."

"Ever since Mr. and Mrs. Walden

received word that their son, Robert, was killed in the war, they seldom leave the house," David explained. "Their door is closed to all visitors."

Startled by this information, Julia stopped in her tracks. Her mind reeled in confusion.

"You won't be welcomed by the Waldens," he continued. "I don't mean to pry, but before we reach their house, I should know what brought you here."

"Bobby is their grandson," Julia said.

David stopped abruptly and stared at her in disbelief.

* * * * *

They continued walking slowly as Julia explained, "My sister, Margaret, worked in Washington, D.C., during the war. She met Robert Walden shortly before he was shipped overseas to the Pacific battlefront. They had a quick courtship and were married a few days before he boarded a train for the West Coast." Julia stumbled and quickly righted herself. "Soon after their baby, Bobby, was born, Margaret became ill. She had strep throat as an infant, which led to rheumatic fever, and she'd suffered health problems the rest of her life. When Bobby was about a month old, she developed an infection in the lining of her heart and died."

The woman was facing a big problem, and David didn't know how he could help her. He waited for further explanation.

"Margaret received word that Robert was missing in action, and when she knew she was dying, she wrote a letter asking me to bring Bobby to Mistletoe to meet his paternal grandparents. I was away from home during most of the war, so I never met Robert. I thought my parents should have brought Bobby before I came home, but that's another story."

In the gathering dusk, her face seemed to register irritation, and David detected a note of bitterness in her voice. Sighing, she continued. "Margaret was my only sibling. I'd always done what she asked me to do, and this was the last thing I could do for her. But I don't think Robert ever knew he had a son, so I doubt his parents know about Bobby."

"They may not even know that Robert was married. If they did, they've never told anyone."

"This is the most frustrating thing that

has ever happened to me. Normally I'm an organized person, so I can't believe I undertook this trip without some advance preparation."

Although he thought it was hopeless, David decided to help her. "Robert and I were best friends, and they'll come nearer talking to you if I'm along."

"I'd appreciate your help. The sooner I can make contact with the Waldens, the better. I didn't expect to be away from home more than a week, but it's been that long since I left Baltimore."

David noted the weariness in her voice. He sensed that Julia was an independent, self-sufficient woman, and the fact that she didn't protest when he took the suitcase she carried convinced him of how tired she really was. He slowed his stride and covertly watched her.

She was of medium height with a strong body, and she walked with long, purposeful strides. Sunrays filtering through the trees highlighted coppery tints in her short, wavy auburn hair. When she had stood on the truck's running board looking up at him, he'd noticed that her hazel eyes, with sweeping dark lashes, gleamed from a strong but beautiful face.

David was convinced that Mr. Walden wouldn't allow Julia to enter the house, and he wondered what he could do with her and the child. No one in the Mistletoe community took in boarders. He lived alone, so he couldn't invite them to stay at his house. The only alternative was to take them to his grandmother's.

When they neared the Walden house, David called to Tom, who'd kept Clyde at a slow pace. Tom halted the horse, and with Julia's permission, David explained her presence in Mistletoe.

"Well, I've never heard the like," Tom said in surprise. "I had a notion that there was something familiar about this boy. Let me see your fingers, sonny."

Bobby lifted his hands. Chuckling, Tom pointed to the two middle fingers, which were the same length on both hands.

"It's the Walden birthmark, all right," David said.

"I don't understand." Julia's brilliant hazel eyes questioned him.

"In almost every generation, the Walden men's fingers are like that," David explained. "Robert's fingers weren't even, but his father's and grandfather's were."

"He favors the Waldens," Tom said. "Even his curly light hair and blue eyes."

"Then his grandparents will surely want to see him," Julia said, eyeing David hopefully, but he didn't respond.

"Tom, you take my horse and stable him at your house. I'll try to persuade the Waldens to see Miss Mayfield and Bobby. If they refuse, I'll take them to spend the night with Granny."

"You want me to take the suitcases?" Tom asked.

"I'll need the small one with Bobby's things," Julia said.

David handed the case he carried to Tom and took a deep breath, dreading the reception they might receive at the Waldens.

Chapter Three

As they'd walked, the mountains had seemed to press in on each side of the road, and the shade was so deep that the sunlight couldn't penetrate through the trees. Julia felt isolated, as if the outside world no longer existed. She stifled momentary panic that threatened to overcome her.

The Walden home was in a clearing on the mountainside. Although it looked rundown and neglected, the house seemed to be a larger, better-constructed residence than the others Julia had seen along Buffalo Creek.

David set the suitcase outside the picket fence and took Bobby into his arms before climbing the steps to the porch. The blinds were pulled, and an oppressive silence surrounded the residence. Julia stayed close to David, trying to draw strength from his rock-solid presence.

He knocked on the screen door several times. No answer. He pounded on the door frame with his fist. Anyone in the house could have heard it, and although she didn't think she *could* feel any worse, Julia's emotions plummeted.

When there was no response, David called loudly, "Mr. Walden, it's David Armstrong. I *must* speak to you."

Julia didn't hear a sound until the hinges squeaked slightly and the door opened about five inches.

"What do you want?" a man muttered in a harsh, raw voice.

"I have someone who wants to talk to you," David said, gesturing for Julia to come to his side.

On trembling legs, she stepped forward and took her sleeping nephew from David's arms. She shook Bobby gently to awaken him. The waning twilight revealed a white-haired, whiskered man with a vicious expression on the stony mask of his face.

"Mr. Walden, I'm Julia Mayfield. My sister was married to your son, Robert," she explained in a shaky voice. "She died two years ago when their son was a month old. Her deathbed wish was for me to bring your grandson to meet you." She thrust her nephew closer to the screen door. "This is Bobby."

The old man gasped, and a keening wail escaped his lips. "Go away, go away!" he shouted. "You lie. I'll kill you if you ever come here again. I'll kill you." Wailing like a banshee, he slammed the door, and a key turned in the lock.

Julia staggered backward, stunned not so much by what Mr. Walden had *said* as she was by the venom in his voice. Although she'd never fainted in her life, sweat spread over her body, and her eyes refused to focus. Bobby started crying, also apparently frightened by his volatile grandfather.

David quickly took Bobby and put his arm around Julia to steady her.

"Come, sit down," he urged. While he

murmured soothingly to Bobby, David guided Julia off the porch and held her while she slumped on the top step.

"We have to get away from here," she muttered. "You heard what he said."

Julia couldn't stop trembling. Still holding Bobby in his left arm, David pulled her toward him and cradled her head on his right shoulder.

In spite of the warmth and tenderness of his friendly embrace, Julia had never felt so alone in her life. Twilight was creeping into this isolated hollow. She was among strangers. She'd never before been solely responsible for the care of a child. A man had just threatened to kill her, and another man, whom she'd met only a few hours earlier, was holding her in his arms. Things like this didn't happen to Julia Mayfield. Surely she would wake up soon and realize it was only a dream.

* * * * *

David knew he had to take Julia and Bobby to safety right away. Mr. Walden might be aiming a shotgun at them this very minute. It wouldn't be the first time he'd used a gun to drive trespassers off his property.

Julia didn't look like she was in any condition to walk, and he couldn't carry both her and Bobby too. When Julia took a deep breath and stood, David decided that he had apparently underestimated her strength.

"I don't think he was joking about shooting us, so we'd better move on. I'm sorry to have caused you all of this trouble, Mr. Armstrong, but I have no choice except to impose on you further. If your grandmother will let us stay with her tonight, I'll make arrangements to return to Maryland tomorrow."

"It's no trouble, miss," David assured her. "Granny likes to have company. It's not too far now. She'll welcome Bobby and you."

Bobby stirred in his arms, but the boy didn't say anything so David figured he was napping again. Nightfall came rapidly in this deep hollow, and David wanted to reach Granny's house before dark. He doubted that Julia had ever been in such an isolated area, and at night, these mountains could be intimidating to a stranger.

His admiration for Julia Mayfield

increased steadily during the rest of their journey. She matched his stride step for step, and if she wanted to walk more slowly, she didn't mention it. Slanting a sidewise glance toward her, he saw that her chin suggested a stubborn streak. Drops of moisture clinging to the smooth forehead of her oval face had dampened a few tendrils of her hair, which gleamed like gold in the fading sunlight.

David's wife had died a few months before he'd enlisted in the army. During the war, he'd focused on his job and pushed personal needs into the background. Suddenly it struck him like a sledgehammer that he had been lonely. Without realizing it, he'd longed for a companion to walk beside him, rejoicing when life was good but never faltering when bad times came their way.

He sensed that Julia Mayfield was that kind of woman, but he surmised that she was as far out of his reach as the moon and the stars. She would probably leave Mistletoe tomorrow, and he would have nothing but the memory of a few fleeting hours of her company.

They came to a small clearing along the

creek where a church and a schoolhouse were located. "I suppose this is Mistletoe," Julia commented with a bitter laugh.

"This is it, ma'am. I'm sorry to disappoint you."

"I wish you'd call me Julia."

"Sure," he agreed. "Folks around here mostly go by first names. I'm David. As for my grandmother, just call her Granny. Everybody in these parts does."

"Are we close to her house? If not, I'd better carry Bobby. For a two-year-old, he's quite a load. I've been lugging him around for the past week, so I know how heavy he can be."

"I'm all right," David assured her. "After carrying a heavy duffel bag all during the war, Bobby seems light as a feather." Pointing, he added, "See the log cabin in the hollow straight ahead? That's Granny's house."

* * * * *

This will be a first, Julia thought humorously. During the war years she'd slept in a lot of different places but never in a log cabin. As she walked steadily beside David, she surveyed the area he'd indicated.

The cabin had the splendor and patina of long years of habitation. Several rocking chairs stood invitingly on a porch that ran the length of the cabin. In the pale light shining from the windows, Julia saw a black hound unwind lazily from the porch and, with tail wagging, run toward them. Barking joyfully, a pup followed the older dog. David spoke quietly to the animals. The barking ceased, but the dogs stuck close to David's heels as they crossed a small level field to the cabin site.

Julia's heart was touched by the beauty and serenity of the rustic dwelling. When they drew nearer, a tall, gaunt, gray-haired woman stepped out onto the porch and raised her hand in greeting.

"Hey, Granny," David said when they reached the porch. "I've brought Julia Mayfield and her nephew, Bobby, to spend the night with you. They're from Maryland. Julia, this is my grandmother, Elizabeth Armstrong."

Without asking questions, Granny said, "Well, come on in! You're just in time for supper." Reaching for Bobby, she added, "Give me that precious baby."

Julia swallowed with effort, and tears threatened to overflow her tired eyes. All of her life she'd struggled with the feeling that she was unappreciated and taken for granted. At this backwoods home, she had never felt more welcome in her life.

Bobby stirred when Granny took him from David's arms, and Julia was sure he would start bawling. Instead, he yawned and settled contentedly in Granny's long arms as she led the way into the cabin.

"I hungry," he said.

"Well, bless your little heart," Granny replied, fondly patting his bottom. "I'll soon take care of that. David, bring Julia in the house."

Julia's first impression of the cabin's interior was that it was cozy, huge, and cluttered. The room they entered spanned the entire width of the cabin. A massive stone-faced fireplace took up most of the space along one wall. Several steaming pots stood on an iron cookstove. An oil lamp on the mantel, and a larger one on a corner table, bathed the cabin in soft light. Benches instead of chairs surrounded a long wooden table.

"The light in here probably seems a

little dim to you," David said. "We don't have electricity in the hollow yet. Now that the war's over, I figure we'll soon have power. I got used to electric lights and appliances while I was in the army, and it's been rough to go back to the old-fashioned ways."

An oak bed with a high backboard and multicolored quilt stood in one corner of the room. Various chests and chairs were scattered haphazardly around the walls. A mantel clock struck six, its quiet, melodious tones adding to Julia's feeling of stepping back into a former time.

Granny kissed Bobby's soft cheek and handed him to Julia.

"David, you go feed the livestock while Julia and Bobby freshen up. Supper will be on the table soon."

After David left, Granny opened a door into another part of the cabin and set Julia's suitcase on the floor of the small room. "You and the boy can tidy up in here," she said. "There's a wash pan and other necessities in this room." She struck a match to light a lamp on the dresser. "When you're ready, come into the kitchen."

The door closed behind Granny, and Julia looked around helplessly. She had used primitive bathing facilities when she'd camped with her parents. As a child it had been fun, and she had considered it quite an adventure, but she hadn't had a two-year-old with her then.

Believing she could stand anything for one night, Julia gritted her teeth and poured a small amount of cold water from a bucket into the pan. She bathed Bobby and removed his muddy shoes before she dressed him in clean clothes. She placed him in the middle of the bed, and with a startled cry, he sank out of sight. Julia had heard of feather mattresses, but this was the first time she'd seen one.

"Auntie!" Bobby screamed, reaching for her.

She sat on the side of the bed. "It's all right. This is softer than your bed at home, but you'll like to sleep in it." She bounced up and down on the bed. "See."

Bobby crawled to Julia's side. Still on his knees, he bounced like a ball on the soft bed. "Whee!" he cried, and his blue eyes sparkled.

"Be careful." She eyed the almost two

feet between the bed and the floor. "Stay in the middle of the bed."

"Why?"

"Because I don't want you to fall on the floor." She swatted him playfully on the rear. "Behave now, while Auntie gets ready."

After disposing of Bobby's bathwater in a bucket, Julia poured fresh water into the wash pan and tried to improve her own appearance by washing her face and hands, combing her hair, and straightening her clothes. That was the best she could do until she got the other luggage.

She heard David's voice in the other room, and a soft knock sounded on the door. "Miss," Granny said, "we can eat whenever you're ready. But take your time."

Julia opened the door. "We're ready." She lifted Bobby to the floor and led him to the next room. He made a beeline for Granny and held up his hands.

"If you're not a sweetheart," Granny said. "I need another grandbaby to love." She lifted Bobby into her arms and hugged him tight. He put his arms around her neck and kissed her wrinkled cheek.

Julia cast a helpless glance in David's direction. "That's the advantage of being a mother, I guess. I've been home for a month, and he's never once kissed me. I must not have any maternal instincts."

Granny settled Bobby into a well-worn wooden high chair. "Don't you fret about that. I have four livin' kids of my own, and I've mothered lots of other young'uns. David is one of eleven grandkids so I've had plenty of practice. Hit takes experience to deal with little tykes."

"Granny isn't happy if she doesn't have a baby to fuss over." David pointed to one of the benches. "Go ahead and be seated."

After Granny strapped Bobby in the high chair, she took three dishes out of the oven and placed them on the table. She removed the lids as she said, "We're having pork sausage, mashed 'taters, green beans, and cabbage slaw." She opened the oven door, lifted out a heavy iron skillet, and upended a large corn pone on a stoneware plate.

David reached for a cup beside Julia's plate. "Do you like coffee?"

"Yes, but I've been drinking more

coffee than usual the past week. If it's not too much trouble, I'd rather have water."

"No trouble at all." David stood and walked to an aluminum bucket on a cabinet. With a dipper, he filled a large glass for Julia. He took a pitcher from a cupboard and poured a glass of milk for Bobby.

Granny sat at the head of the long table with David opposite her. She pulled Bobby's chair close to her. "You eat hearty now," she told Julia. "I'll take care of this little angel. David, ask the blessin'."

"Our Father," David began, in the voice of a man who's in close fellowship with his Maker, "creator of heaven and earth and all of us living on the earth, cleanse our hearts so that our works will be acceptable to You. Thank You for protecting Julia and Bobby on their long journey and for bringing them to us. I'm grateful for Granny and the food she's set before us. May our lives always glorify You. Amen."

Julia had noted the strange vernacular of the older people she'd met, but although David spoke slowly, almost in a drawl, his grammar was better than the others'.

Until David passed a large platter to her and she smelled the tempting aroma of sage-flavored pork, Julia hadn't realized how hungry she was. The rest of the food was equally appealing to her taste buds, and as she ate, her body and spirit felt revitalized.

When David insisted that she have second helpings, Julia shook her head. "I didn't know that I was so hungry. Train fare isn't very good, and when we stopped overnight, I was so nervous about the outcome of this trip that I couldn't eat much. This is the best food I've had since I left home." She looked at Granny. "Did David tell you why I'm here?"

Nodding her head, Granny said, "Yes. I'm sorry that you had such a long trip for nothin'. Oscar and Mamie Walden have been tetched in the head since they got word that Robert was dead."

"My sister received a telegram that he was missing in action, but never an official notice of his death."

"That's what his folks heard first, but then they got another letter sayin' he'd been killed in action," Granny explained.

"Dad tried, unsuccessfully, to call them

a few times to tell them about Bobby. Tom told me there aren't any phones here in the hollow, but we didn't know that."

They finished supper with a slab of apple pie topped with fresh sweet cream. Granny wiped Bobby's mouth and hands with her apron and lifted him from the high chair. "I'll tidy up the kitchen after you've gone to bed," she said to Julia. "Let's sit on the porch and relax in the cool of the evening."

David held the door open, and Julia followed Granny and Bobby to the porch. "Take a chair," Granny said as she lowered her body into a wooden rocker. David sat on the steps and leaned against a porch post. Julia relaxed in the chair next to Granny so she could take Bobby when he got restless, as he usually did when night came.

Granny laid Bobby on her chest and leaned his head on her left shoulder. "David," she said, "if you played your guitar, it wouldn't be long until this little one would go to sleep."

"The guitar is over at my place, but I'll get my banjo." David stood and walked into the cabin.

"My mother says that Bobby hasn't slept well since he was born. He seems afraid of the darkness. She keeps a light in his room, but he always wakes up a time or two every night."

Granny smiled as she slowly and quietly rocked back and forth. David came from the cabin with a banjo, sat back down on the steps, and strummed the strings softly as he glided from one tune to another. Julia recognized a few folk medleys, and her heart was touched when David played "What a Friend We Have in Jesus."

She sang and hummed along with him, for although it had been a long time since she'd heard the hymn, she remembered some of the lyrics. "O what peace we often forfeit, O what needless pain we bear, all because we do not carry everything to God in prayer."

After a few months in Europe with the Women's Army Corps, Julia had decided that God wasn't doing what He was supposed to do. If He was, why did He allow the malicious destruction of millions of Jews and the atrocities visited upon them and other innocent people by the

Nazis? Why didn't He intervene before thousands of Europeans and Americans paid the supreme sacrifice? Julia had lots of questions, but it had been two years since she'd believed that God had all the answers.

When she couldn't believe that God would or could deal with the world situation, she'd stopped her daily communion with Him. Listening to David's quiet music, the squeak of the rocking chair as Granny moved back and forth, and Bobby's soft breathing as he slept, Julia wondered if she had been wrong. Was God in control after all?

Whatever the answer, a white mist seeped into the hollow, and nighttime settled quietly but relentlessly over Mistletoe, and Julia sensed a peace she hadn't known for a long time.

Chapter Four

David knew he should go home, but he
didn't want to leave Granny with the
responsibility of guests he'd invited to her
home. It wasn't that Granny wasn't equal
to any occasion, but she'd already
passed her seventieth birthday, which
was old for a woman in these mountains.

As he gently strummed the strings,
Julia's head drooped lower and lower,
and he knew she was asleep. Quietly he
stepped inside the cabin and hung the
banjo on the wall. When he returned to
the porch, Granny glanced his way. David

spread his arms wide in a gesture as if to say, "What do we do now?"

In the semi-darkness, he saw her slow smile. She reached out her left hand and touched Julia on the shoulder. Julia jumped, and a soft gasp escaped her lips.

"Oh. I—I didn't intend to go to sleep." She shook her head. "So much to do. How often does Tom Morriston go into Booneville? I must make arrangements to go with him."

"Honey, don't start borrowin' trouble," Granny said. "We'll figure out what you can do in the mornin'. Hit's a mite early to go to bed, but you've had a long day. You're wearied to the bone. After a good night's sleep, it'll be easier to decide what to do. Bobby can sleep with me tonight."

Julia stood quickly. "Oh, no. He's my responsibility. He's always restless at night, and I don't want you to lose sleep."

"You need rest more than I do." Granny's tone didn't allow any argument. David had heard that tone often enough in his youth, and he grinned, knowing that Julia would do what Granny said. "Bobby is sound asleep now, and I'll be surprised if he wakes up all night. If he does, I'll know what to do for him."

Knowing that Granny could meet Julia's needs more than he could, David said, "I'm going home now. I'll be back tomorrow morning."

"Do you live far away?"

He shook his head. "Just a short distance up the hollow."

Julia laid her hand on his forearm, and his flesh tingled at her touch. "Thanks for what you've done for me today. I felt completely lost. You'll never know how much I appreciate your help."

Covering her hand with his own, David was surprised at the proprietary feeling he had for Julia. "Try to get a good night's sleep. Your troubles won't seem so bad tomorrow."

* * * * *

Watching David's purposeful stride as he walked away, Julia hoped his prediction was true. Right now she didn't believe she could possibly feel any worse.

"I shouldn't have made this journey," she murmured, more to herself than to Granny, "but I thought I was doing the right thing."

Still holding the sleeping child, Granny stood and motioned for Julia to precede her into the cabin. "God has a way of intervening in our lives. If He put the idea in your head to come here, it was the right thing to do."

Julia shook her head. "I don't think the idea *was* orchestrated by God. I wasn't at home when my sister died and left a message for me to bring her son to Mistletoe. Bobby was two years old when I first saw him. I've never been around children, and I resented it because she didn't ask Mother and Dad to bring Bobby to see his other grandparents." She sighed. "I've tried, but the Waldens chased us away, threatening to kill me. I've done all I can do."

"Maybe." Granny laid Bobby in the middle of the large bed and spread a quilt over him. The child fretted momentarily then turned on his side without waking. Granny put her comforting arm around Julia's shoulders. "In the first place, I don't think Oscar Walden would have shot you. Normally the Waldens are kind, good people, but Robert was their only child. His death took away their common sense."

Julia was too tired to defend her opinion of the Waldens. She said good night to Granny and walked into the small bedroom, leaving the door ajar so she could hear Bobby when he cried. She took off her shoes and lay across the bed without undressing, wishing she could go to sleep right away and forget the nightmare that surrounded her. She'd heard that when troubles surrounded one on every side, the only way to look was up. She'd reached that point.

Julia lay awake long after Granny called good night and extinguished the lights in the main cabin. Darkness was complete, and she couldn't hear a sound. In the quietness of the night, a still, small voice filtered into her conscience. *"My child, you'll never wander so far away that I can't protect you."*

Breathless, Julia bolted upright. Had she imagined it? Was it a dream? She remembered the incident that afternoon when Tom had asked her to pray and she'd called on God for the first time in months. David had shown up immediately, but she'd considered that a coincidence rather than an answer to prayer. Suddenly she recalled a Bible story describing the disciple Peter about to drown. He called out for help and Jesus answered immediately. Was it possible that after all the months she'd turned a deaf ear to God's voice, He had been patiently waiting for her to return to Him?

* * * * *

The smell of frying bacon wakened Julia, and for a moment she didn't know where she was. Why was she in bed with her clothes on? Suddenly the difficulties of the past week flooded her mind, and she groaned. She pulled the quilt over her head, wondering if she had the stamina to face the day. It shouldn't take long for Tom to change the tire on his truck, and when he did, she would return to Booneville and take the first bus northward.

For a moment she luxuriated in the comfort of the feather mattress that had wrapped around her like a blanket. Julia dreaded the return trip—first the drive to Booneville over that treacherous road, then the bus changes on the way to Lexington, where she could finally board a train for Maryland. However, she hadn't spent three years in Uncle Sam's service without learning that she had to take the bitter with the sweet. The fact that this situation in Mistletoe was about the bitterest pill she'd ever swallowed wasn't going to stop her. Margaret had wanted Bobby's grandparents to see him. She'd shown the child to his grandfather, and perhaps his grandmother had been peering from the shadows. Their rejection of the boy wasn't her fault. She could leave Mistletoe with a clear conscience. That decision made, she got out of bed and washed her hands and face before she went into the main room of the cabin.

Granny was working at the kitchen stove, and she turned. "Mornin', Julia."

"Good morning." Julia looked around for Bobby.

He was sitting in the high chair, chewing on a biscuit. With a wide smile, he said, "Hi."

"Hi, yourself." She bent to kiss his cheek. "Did he give you any trouble last night? I'm ashamed that when I finally went to sleep, I didn't hear anything."

"He only roused once and went right back to sleep," Granny assured her. "Breakfast is ready. Go ahead and sit down."

The outside door swung open, and David entering carrying her suitcases.

"Oh, thank you," Julia said.

"It wasn't any trouble. When I left here last night, I went to get your cases from Tom. They've been at my place all night."

"What time does Tom go to Booneville? I'd like to go with him."

"He's already gone."

"Oh." Julia was overcome by a wave of disappointment. She glanced at the mantel clock. "It's only seven o'clock."

"He borrowed his son's car and left early since he's got to pick up a new tire. It's not easy to find auto parts in Booneville, and he may have to go on to Beattyville, which is twenty miles farther. Either way, it's a long drive."

"I know," Julia said wryly. She couldn't keep disappointment out of her voice. "Is there anyone else who can take us to Booneville?"

"I have a car," David said, "and I'll take you. There's bus service six days a week, but I don't know anything about bus connections to Lexington."

Granny set a plate of grits and eggs in front of Julia. "Hit's not my place to give you advice, but why don't you stay with us a few days? You're wore to a frazzle now, and it'll be good for you to rest up before you start another long trip."

Bobby chortled and held out his arms to Granny. She lifted him from the high chair and hugged him. "Besides, I'm gettin' right fond of this little tyke. I'd hate to see you take him away so soon."

As she watched Bobby settle contentedly on Granny's lap, Julia's shoulders slumped in defeat. "I can't understand it. For a month I've been trying to get close to Bobby, but he's fretful with me most of the time. He's content with Mother and Dad, just as he is with you. What am I doing wrong?"

Granny's faded brown eyes were compassionate as she patted Julia's arm. "I suspect you're tryin' too hard. You're afraid you're gonna make a mistake. The boy senses that, and it makes him fearful too."

"Then I need to take him home to

Mother and Dad. So whenever it's convenient for you to take me, David, we can start."

"I can take you today if you want to go, but I agree with Granny. You ought to take it easy for a few days. That is, unless your folks are expecting you home."

Julia shook her head. "For all they know, the Waldens might have asked us to stay for a visit. They won't worry unless they don't hear from me for a week or two, but I dread the trip home. I'd just as soon get it over with."

"At least stay until Monday. Granny will look after Bobby, and you can rest. Who knows, the Waldens might decide that they want to see the boy."

Julia shuddered. "I won't put Bobby or myself through another experience like we had last night. Even if he's only two, Bobby must have sensed Mr. Walden's hatred."

Julia finished eating the food on her plate, then stood and walked to the window that overlooked the valley. Two sleeping hounds sprawled on the porch floor. A flock of sparrows flitted from the top of a maple tree, landed on the lawn, and searched for food. Sunshine sparkled in the small creek that wound its way from the mountainside. The solitude and tranquility of this place appealed to Julia. Perhaps she should accept the Armstrongs' invitation.

Impulsively, she turned around to face Granny and David. "All right, then. If you're sure we won't be too much trouble, Bobby and I *will* stay through the weekend." She grinned. "I feel as if I could sleep in that featherbed for a month."

A dazzling smile spread across Granny's wrinkled face, and her eyes sparkled with pleasure. "That's just fine. I love company. I'll take care of Bobby, and David can show you around Mistletoe." She laughed. "Not that there's much to see. And you can go to church with us tomorrow."

"It's good that you're here to see our mountains in autumn." David was obviously as pleased as his grandmother that she had agreed to prolong her visit. "Winters can be pretty rough, but from

May through November, it's hard to beat living in Owsley County."

"I daresay you're prejudiced," Julia said, a touch of humor in her voice.

"Maybe, but I saw a big part of the world when I was in the army. I still say Kentucky is a good place to live."

"I think Maryland is a good state too, but I'm willing to be persuaded about Kentucky's good points," Julia conceded.

"Then why don't you take it easy this morning, and we'll go hiking this afternoon."

Julia sighed. "I can't take it easy. I need to wash Bobby's clothes. That's something else I'm learning—a baby goes through a lot of clean clothes in a day's time."

"I figured you'd need to do some washin'," Granny said. She motioned to a large boiler on the stove top. "I het up some water, so we'll do the washin' as soon as I feed the chickens and gather the eggs."

"I'll wash the breakfast dishes if you'd like," Julia volunteered.

"That'd be a big help." Granny emptied a teakettle of hot water into a large metal dishpan and set it on the side of the table. She handed Julia a bar of soap.

"Hit's homemade."

Julia lifted the soap to her nose. "Mmm! It smells good."

Granny was obviously pleased. "It's scented with dried rose hips." She laid a large cloth on the table and poured another pan of water for rinsing. "Hit's nice to have someone around to share the work. I miss my girls, who live over in the next county."

"How many children do you have?"

"I have four livin' young'uns. My oldest boy, Millard, lives up the road a ways with his family, and of course David's here with me. But the rest of 'em moved away durin' the war. They found life was easier outside of Owsley County, so they won't come back to live. We also had four babies that we laid to rest over there in the graveyard." She gestured toward the forest across the road. "My man died ten years ago."

Julia was surprised that Granny spoke so casually about her children's deaths, especially when, with a shake of her gray head, she added in a resigned voice,

"The Lord giveth and the Lord taketh away."

* * * * *

Being accustomed to cold and hot water from a faucet for laundry, dishwashing, and bathing, Julia's movements were awkward as she washed the dishes in soapy water, transferred them to another pan for rinsing, and dried the heavy stoneware on a snow white feed sack. She'd finished her task by the time Granny returned.

"You done good," Granny complimented. "We'll do the washin' out on the back porch. Gather up your dirty clothes and bring them to me." She picked up Bobby. "I've got a pen in the backyard to keep him from being underfoot while we work. It's a mite cool this mornin', so he might need a sweater."

During her years in the WAC, the Women's Army Corps, Julia had sometimes poured water in a hubcap to wash her hands and face. She had washed her clothes in woodland streams. She had slept on army cots, on the floor, and even on the ground many times, so she had some experience in rough living.

During those times, she hadn't dreamed that the experiences would prepare her for a weekend in backwoods Kentucky.

Wringing water from the garments with her hands, Julia hung them to dry on the clothesline strung from a porch post to a gnarled maple tree in the backyard. She had lost some of her modesty during the war years, but it was discomfiting to hang her underwear in plain view of David, should he wander by. Still, she was grateful for this opportunity to have clean clothes for Bobby and herself on their return trip to Maryland.

After she and Granny finished the washing, Julia took Bobby from the pen and watched him as he played in the yard. She followed the boisterous boy as he examined the rocks and the flowers growing around the house. He tried to catch sunbeams filtering through the foliage of the oak trees that bordered the mountainside behind Granny's well-kept yard.

She admired the clumps of mistletoe in the trees and marveled at the strange turn of events that had brought her— someone who'd been interested in the mistletoe plant since childhood—to an area by that name.

Julia's longtime fascination with mistletoe had taught her some strange things. For instance, the legend that Jesus was crucified on a mistletoe tree, and as punishment for the Savior's crucifixion, the plant was forbidden to ever again take root in the ground. Perhaps that was the main reason people in medieval times had deemed the plant bad luck. Other groups throughout history had considered mistletoe a good luck charm to be hung over doors to keep demons out of their houses, and enemies often signed peace treaties under mistletoe trees. Regardless of all the folklore, the plant had long been valued for its medicinal properties.

Julie was distracted from her thoughts when Bobby stopped before her with two roses in his hand. "Here." He thrust the pink flowers toward her. She probably should have scolded him for picking the blooms, but she didn't want to hurt his feelings, and his sweet gesture touched her. Besides, she was sure that Granny wouldn't miss a few flowers.

"Thank you, Bobby." She smiled. "It's been a long time since a gentleman has given me flowers."

"Well, that's a shame," a masculine voice said behind her.

Julia whirled and saw David approaching. She sensed a rare blush creeping into her cheeks. He stooped and pulled Bobby into his arms and tossed the boy into the air. Bobby turned frightened blue eyes on Julia, but when David caught him and swung him upward again, the boy laughed gleefully.

When David put him on the ground, Bobby cried, "'Nutter time! 'Nutter time!"

Laughing, David lifted Bobby again and again while Julia watched with pleasure. David wore a denim shirt and dust-stained overalls. He was bareheaded, and his dark hair was damp with sweat.

In spite of Bobby's continued protests, David put him on the ground. "That's enough for now."

Bobby must have sensed the finality in David's voice, for he trotted off after a robin that stood with head bent sideways, apparently listening for a worm.

"What've you been up to this morning?"

David asked Julia as they followed the energetic boy.

"Granny and I have been washing clothes."

"I've been working too. I sowed turnip seed and crawled on my knees to pull weeds from the strawberry patch."

"Isn't there an easier way to do that?"

"Not that I know of." David smiled. "But if you think of a way, let me know."

Bobby was wandering toward the woods, and Julia called to him to stop.

Bobby kept running. "Why?"

"Because that bank is too steep for you to climb!" she called. Bobby continued on his way, paying no heed to her words. She hurried to stop him before he took a tumble.

"Strawberries are a good cash crop," David explained when he'd caught up to her, "but they take a lot of work. I sell most of them in Booneville, but if the yield is big, I've even shipped them to Lexington and Louisville." He picked Bobby up. "Let's see what Granny fixed for dinner."

Bobby squirmed, trying to get out of David's firm grasp.

"Do you take all of your meals with her?"

"I eat dinner and supper here most of the time. Granny is used to a big family, and she doesn't like to eat alone. If I didn't eat with her, she would never fix a full meal for herself. I buy most of what we need from the store to pay my way."

Although she hadn't known him long, Julia was convinced that David was a caring, thoughtful man, and she wondered why he hadn't married. She herself had fixed ideas about what she wanted in a husband. It seemed rather ironic that, when she'd seen so much of the world and its people, she would find a man in this backwoods community who met most of her lofty standards.

Realizing that David was gazing intently at her, as if waiting for an answer, she stammered, "I'm sorry. Did you say something?"

"Do you want to take a walk this afternoon?"

"I'd like that," she said, "but we can't go too far with Bobby."

"Granny will keep him. If not, I'll carry him."

Julia smiled. "In that case, I'd love to go."

The possibility of having a few hours' respite from her nephew's care appealed to her. As she entered the house, glancing sideways at David's handsome countenance, she relished the idea of this opportunity to learn more about him.

Chapter Five

The more David saw of Julia the more
she impressed him, but he sensed that
she carefully guarded certain aspects of
her life. For one, why was she hesitant to
comment on her war experiences? There
was much classified wartime work that
had to remain secret, and that could be
why Julia was evasive. He should be the
first to understand that it wasn't any of his
business what Julia had done in the past.
There were corners of his life he wouldn't
discuss either.

People in Mistletoe didn't take kindly to
strangers asking personal questions, so

he wasn't going to be inquisitive, but that didn't keep him from wondering. Perhaps when he knew her better, she wouldn't seem so mysterious. His sleep had been restless, and every time he'd awakened, Julia was in his thoughts.

For more than five years David had avoided women, and it annoyed him that Julia had captivated his mind so quickly. He had enough to trouble his conscience without being tempted to break a vow he'd taken in all sincerity. Before he'd left his home this morning, he'd taken a picture of his "dream woman" from his billfold and looked at it for several minutes. During the war this picture had served as a reminder of what might have been, but it hadn't filled the emptiness in his heart.

While they waited for Granny to put the food on the table, David saw Julia glance down at her skirt. It was the same one she'd worn yesterday.

"Is it all right if I change into pants?" she asked. "I noticed that the women in Booneville wore dresses as Granny does. I don't want to do anything to offend her."

"It's okay. We'll be walking over some

rough places, and pants are more practical. I saw servicewomen wearing them, so I'm used to it. But generally speaking, almost all women around here wear dresses to church and when they go to town."

"Then I'll wear pants for hiking and a dress the rest of the time."

After dinner Julia went into the bedroom and soon returned dressed in sturdy brown shoes, a pair of khaki pants, and a green plaid long-sleeved shirt. A black hat was perched on her auburn hair. David handed her a walking stick he had made from a small twisted tree.

"Most of my walking has been on level ground," she said, "so this will come in handy when I'm climbing the mountain."

Carrying Bobby on her hip, Granny followed them to the door. "Have a good time!"

"Bobby go?" he begged.

"Not this time," David said. "You stay with Granny while I show your aunt around Mistletoe."

Julia kissed Bobby's cheek. "Be a good boy for Granny."

Bobby waved. "Good boy. Bye-bye."

Julia followed David as he plunged down the steep bank into the hollow behind Granny's house. When he reached a narrow dirt road, he stopped and waited for her. A small creek ran beside the road, its clear water bubbling over a colorful, rocky bed.

"We'll stop at my house first, then climb the mountain, come down on the other side, and circle back to Granny's house. That'll probably be enough walking for today." Observing how she matched his stride, David knew that Julia wasn't any stranger to walking.

"The other side of this creek is the border of our land," he continued. "My ancestors came to Kentucky from Virginia before the Civil War and settled along the right-hand fork of Buffalo Creek. Some of the family kept moving westward, but my great-grandfather liked this country, so we're still here."

"You mentioned that you did a lot of traveling during the war. Didn't you see any other place where you would like to live?"

"Oh, I saw a lot of pretty country, but I never considered not coming home to

Kentucky. Our mountain region isn't prosperous, and if I'd wanted to get rich, I'd have gone someplace else. The way I see it, though, it's like rats leaving a sinking ship. If all of the young people leave, it's going to make it harder for the ones who have to stay." He darted a look at Julia, but he couldn't tell what she was thinking. "I suppose you think I'm stupid."

She shook her head. "No, not at all. I admire you for your concern."

David felt his face flushing, but just then they rounded a bend and had a view of his house. "That's where I live."

A fan-shaped clearing at the base of the mountain was the site of a large log dwelling. Situated in front of a grove of maple and beech trees, the house had two dormer windows. A porch, facing the valley, was built along the front.

"Why, David, it's beautiful! When did you build it?"

David was proud of his home, and Julia's praise pleased him. "Right after I came home from the army. There was an old cabin on that spot, but I tore it down to make room for this one. I cut the logs off of our property. An older neighbor knew how to build a log house, and he helped me."

Walking slowly, they approached the house. When they reached the front porch, David said, "Come in and look around."

David had designed the floor plan to be similar to Granny's, with a combination kitchen and living room along the front and two bedrooms behind them. "I have an unfinished extension behind these rooms, where I eventually intend to install a bathroom," David explained. "There's a good spring on the mountainside, and I'll pipe water into the house by gravity. Someday, I'll have two rooms upstairs."

Julia walked through the house and seemed impressed by what she saw. "You're a good housekeeper."

"I can't take much credit for that. My cousin, Nellie, comes in once a week and straightens up everything. She was here yesterday."

They stepped out onto the porch again, and Julia pointed to another dwelling almost hidden in a clump of evergreen trees on the other side of the creek. "You've got a close neighbor."

"Well, yes and no. A lawyer from Louisville bought that property about twelve years ago for a summer residence. He built the house then. He drilled a well and bought a gas generator, so the house has electric lights and running water, complete with a bathroom. After his wife died, he stopped coming. He's leased it a few times, but it's vacant this summer. He wants to sell the property, but the price is too high. If people have that kind of money, they don't want to live in Mistletoe."

"Why didn't you buy it instead of building?"

"I'd have liked to, but I couldn't afford it. Granny gave me the land for my cabin, and I'm building as I have the money."

David led her out of his house. He wasn't sure why her admiration of his cabin had so pleased him, but now he was eager to show her the best scenery in the hollow.

* * * * *

After they passed several patches of cultivated land, they climbed steadily for half an hour or more, and Julia found it difficult to breathe. David walked in front of her, and he turned his head frequently to check on her progress. "If you can hold on a little while longer, we'll stop and rest."

She nodded, unwilling to use any extra breath for talking. By the time they stopped, she'd gotten her second wind, and her breathing was more regular. They were near the top of the mountain, and they sat on a rocky ledge and looked down into a deep ravine. A well-traveled trail wound its way downward through the creek valley.

"I don't mean to meddle in your affairs, David, but what do you *do*? After you've seen life outside of these mountains, I can't believe that you'll be content to raise turnips and strawberries the rest of your life." David laughed, and Julia felt her face warming. She turned her head. "I'm so sorry. What a terrible thing for me to say!"

"Hey." David moved closer and turned her head to face him. "It's all right. I'm flattered that you looked beyond this rough exterior and saw more than a hillbilly. Not that it's a disgrace to be a hillbilly."

"There isn't anything wrong with

farming, either. If you've found your calling, so be it."

"Actually, I'm enrolled at the University of Kentucky in Lexington, and my farming is a way to make some extra money. I took the summer off to catch up on work around the cabin. I'm already registered for the fall semester."

"Really? I'm impressed." She was deeply interested that he was pursuing his education. "Tell me more."

David chuckled. "Well, after I finished high school, Granny arranged for me to attend Berea College. You've heard of it?"

Julia shook her head. "I don't think so."

"The college was established before the Civil War by an abolitionist. He wanted to educate black and white students who were too poor to pay college tuition. It was one of the first non-segregated colleges in the South—and one of the few to accept both male and female students in the mid-nineteenth century."

"Oh, I believe I *have* heard of it. No tuition is charged, but students have to work to pay their way."

David nodded. "It was a godsend to me, since we didn't have any money for college. I attended two years. About that time I—well, something happened that made me want to get away from home. It was obvious that we were going to war, so I enlisted in the army."

Julia was curious but didn't pry. "So why didn't you return to Berea instead of the university?"

"I'm going to college with assistance from the GI Bill, so I wasn't eligible to continue at Berea. I schedule my classes on just two days so I don't have to stay in Lexington all week. I have one more year, and then I'm hoping to teach in the high school at Booneville."

Julia couldn't understand why David's answer filled her with such a sense of peace and warmth. This time yesterday she'd never even heard of David Armstrong. Why did it matter to her what he did with his life? David took Julia's hand to help her to her feet, and she was poignantly aware of the warmth of that impersonal grasp. When he started down the narrow trail, motioning her to follow, she knew that from now on, no matter where she was, she was going to be interested in what David Armstrong did with his life.

It wasn't until they'd walked down a long stretch of trail that Julia recalled David's comment about enlisting in the army because he'd wanted to leave Mistletoe. He seemed to have no desire to live any other place now. So what had caused his former disillusionment?

Chapter Six

Tom Morriston was sitting on the porch
with Granny when David and Julia
reached the cabin. He was bouncing
Bobby on his knee, and Julia marveled at
the child's laughter. She'd never known
her nephew to be so happy. Could it
be that the blood of his ancestors flowing
through his veins caused him to sense
that he had come *home*? She wished
fervently that Robert was alive to claim
his child.

"Auntie!" Bobby squealed when he saw
her approaching.

"Hi, Bobby, and you too, Tom." Julia

sighed when she sat in a rocking chair. Their strenuous walk had lasted almost three hours, but until this moment she hadn't realized how tired she was.

Bobby scooted off of Tom's lap and came running toward her. She held out her arms, and Bobby crawled on her lap.

"I've got my truck fixed," Tom said, "so I can take you with me Monday morning if you're still of a mind to go. Granny says she's tryin' to convince you to stay on a spell."

Julia sensed that David watched her closely, waiting for her answer. "I need a few days of rest, but I'll plan to leave Monday. I don't see any reason to stay any longer. Have you heard how Mr. Walden carried on when we stopped there?"

Tom nodded. "Yep. David told me when he fetched your suitcases. The man is tetched in the head. A lot of families in Owsley County lost sons in the war. I reckon they miss their boys too, but they're going on with life." He unlimbered his sparse frame from the rocker. "Well, I've got to move on. If I don't hear different, I'll plan on pickin' you up at eight o'clock Monday mornin'. Maybe I'll see you at Sunday meetin' tomorrow."

"Sure, we'll bring her with us," Granny said. "No need to be in a hurry, Tom."

"Thanks, Granny, but I've got chores to do."

Bobby squirmed on Julia's lap. "Bobby go?"

"Not this time, buddy," Tom said, ruffling Bobby's curls.

Bobby started to whine until Julia said, "You haven't told me yet what you and Granny did this afternoon."

Chattering so fast Julia couldn't understand what he said, Bobby waved to Tom as he stepped off the porch and walked away.

After supper, Julia again sought a comfortable rocker on the porch. Solitude was one of the things she had missed most during her years in the WAC, and she'd often daydreamed of finding a place of absolute peace and quiet. Well, she'd found quietness in Mistletoe, but not peace of mind. David had gone to his cabin, and Granny had walked up the road to visit her son Millard and his family.

Julia had been sitting on the porch for

more than an hour, and during that time, she'd seen three people. A man and woman walked off the mountainside opposite Granny's house and turned toward the church and post office. She noticed that the woman walked several steps behind her husband. Then a boy rode down the hollow on an antiquated bicycle with a hound running beside him. Otherwise, she'd spent an uninterrupted hour.

Before she left, Granny had pulled the playpen to the front yard and put Bobby inside. Julia gave him a set of blocks, and Granny brought him an old catalog from the cabin.

"If he's like most young'uns, he loves to tear up paper. That and the blocks ought to keep him busy for a while."

The playpen was soon littered with pieces of paper, but so far, he hadn't tried to eat any of it. The two hounds dozed in the yard not far from Bobby's pen. Tired of tearing paper, Bobby stood, picked up his blocks, and threw them at the dogs. Fortunately his aim wasn't good, and the dogs dozed on.

Julia's mind swam with thoughts of the past and plans for the future. Physically she felt drained, hollow, and lifeless. She roused from the numbness that seemed to weigh her down when Bobby called, "Auntie! Play with me."

She sighed, stood, walked down the steps, and lifted Bobby from the pen. "Let's walk out to the barn and see the animals."

"Doggies come too?" he asked.

"If they want to, but they look like they'd rather sleep."

Julia took Bobby by the hand, but he soon pulled away to investigate everything that interested him. He broke into a run when he saw a hen and her chicks scratching in the yard. The hen flew at Bobby with outspread wings, and he ran back to Julia. Then the hen clucked to her chicks, and they fled to the safety of her wings.

"Bad chicken. I scared."

"And so you should be," Julia said. "She wasn't very nice. Maybe you can pet the calf."

When the cow and her calf didn't seem

friendly either, Bobby started sniffing. Julia finally picked him up and walked back to the cabin.

"Maybe if David takes you to the barn, the animals will let you touch them. They don't know us very well. Let's get ready for bed."

After settling Bobby down for the night, Julia retired to her room. Remembering what David had mentioned about church clothes, she took a black skirt and a long-sleeved multi-colored rayon blouse from her suitcase before she went to bed. She arranged the wrinkled garments on a wire hanger and hung them on a wooden peg beside the door. Considering Granny's long, plain dresses with voluminous skirts, Julia had a feeling that her knee-length, fitted skirt wouldn't be appropriate for the local church, but she didn't have a simpler garment.

She didn't want to go, but Julia had surmised that anyone living under Granny's roof went to church on Sunday. She didn't expect to be impressed by the local meeting, but she wouldn't insult her hostess.

When she left the bedroom the next

morning, Julia stood before Granny for inspection. "I don't want to be an embarrassment to you and David. If my clothes aren't appropriate, Bobby and I will stay here."

Granny's faded brown eyes regarded Julia's garments with a speculative gaze. "Well, the skirt is a mite short," she said, "and that blouse would look a fright on me, but it seems all right for *you* to wear. Besides, the Bible says that God looks on the heart, not what we look like on the outside. I believe you've got a good heart. People are gonna stare at you no matter what you wear, but don't take it personal. They always look at strangers."

* * * * *

The door opened and David walked in and took his banjo from the wall. Julia was standing with her back to the door. He stopped dead in his tracks as he recalled an incident that had happened four years earlier, which he remembered as well as if it were yesterday.

He'd been riding a troop train as it slowly approached Washington, D.C., on his way to overseas deployment. On the banks of the Potomac River, a woman stood with her back to him, gazing upward toward a grove of trees. The woman wore a blue coat, and a white scarf was tied around her head. While he'd watched, she'd taken off the scarf and her reddish hair had gleamed in the sunlight. Perhaps because of the sadness in his heart and the loneliness and fear he felt, he took a picture of the woman.

David wasn't leaving a sweetheart or wife behind, so throughout the war, whenever he was homesick, he'd look at the picture of his "dream woman" and pretend she'd be waiting for him when the war was over. Although he knew it was ridiculous, he stopped in D.C. on his way home and revisited the area where he'd taken the photograph of the woman of his dreams. He was disappointed but not surprised when he didn't see her there.

His mind came back to the present when Julia turned to face him, and he was reminded again of how beautiful she was. Scanning her from head to toe, he whistled!

"David!" Granny reprimanded him. "She's already frettin' whether her clothes are passable. You didn't help any."

"Of course her clothes are all right." He hoped his smile would ease her mind. David wanted Julia to like the people of Mistletoe, and he hoped that they would look beyond the differences in her lifestyle and like her as much as he did.

Bobby toddled out of the bedroom, and David lifted him into his arms. "Let's go, buddy."

"Es go, buddy!" Bobby mimicked. All of them laughed, and David hoped that Julia had dismissed the uncertainty about her clothes. As long as she was Granny's guest, she would be welcomed.

* * * * *

The bell ringing in the church steeple greeted them as they walked toward the road. A cool breeze wafted up the hollow. The sun was shining, and songbirds in the willow trees along the creek seemed to compete for the title of loudest and most melodious. Julia breathed in the fresh air, and for a moment she forgot the past and the future and enjoyed the present beauty of God's creation.

A family of five waited in the road for them. The man carried a fiddle. Granny introduced Julia to her son Millard, his wife, Hattie, and their three children. Their oldest daughter, Nellie, was a slender girl of medium height. A mass of honey-colored hair capped her head, and blue eyes shone from a pretty, oval face. Julia liked her at once.

Nellie reached her arms toward Bobby, and the grinning child willingly transferred from David to the girl. She hugged him close.

"Who're you?" he asked.

"I'm Nellie," she said, giggling. "Who are you?"

"Bobby."

Nellie bounced him up and down as they continued walking, and Bobby crowed with pleasure, enjoying the attention. Julia wished Bobby would respond to her so easily. Somehow she had to get over her fear of incompetency when caring for her nephew.

Her eyes must have mirrored her frustration. Granny sidled next to Julia and said quietly, "Don't fret about it. Nellie helped raise her brother and sister, so she knows how to take care of a young'un."

"I didn't know my feelings were so

obvious," she apologized. "I've never felt so inadequate."

"I don't suppose you've been around babies much."

"Not at all. I was older than Margaret but only by a year. Except for the past month, I've never lived in a household with a baby."

"That'll change when you get one of your own," Granny assured her. "Do you have a special feller waitin' for you back in Maryland? Is that why you're leavin' us so soon?"

Conscious that David had turned quickly when he heard the question, Julia responded in the negative, but she didn't think it was necessary to elaborate that she'd never had a "special feller" in her life.

The small party reached the church, and Julia chose a back seat near the door. At her home church, Bobby spent the worship hour in the nursery, and she didn't know how he would react to these new surroundings. If he became restless and she had to take him outside, she could do it without disturbing the other worshipers. Julia was pleased when Nellie sat beside her, and Bobby seemed content as long as he could switch from her lap to Nellie's and back again.

Julia estimated that seventy or more people could be seated in the church, but the pews weren't more than half-full. She frowned when she noted that men sat on the right side of the aisle, women on the left. She'd also noticed that Hattie had walked a few paces behind her husband as they came to church. Didn't these mountaineers know they were living in the twentieth century?

Pastor Kenneth Brown was a tall, plain, full-bearded man dressed in an open-necked plaid shirt and bib overalls. His wife, Sadie, was short and shaped like a partridge. Her hair was twisted into a knot at the nape of her neck, and she wore a black dress—not the kind of clothing Julia was accustomed to in the pastoral family. She'd learned not to judge by appearances, however, and she looked forward to hearing the preacher's message.

She anticipated that the worship hour would provide an opportunity to reflect on whether this trip had been necessary. At one time she'd believed that God directed her life and activities, but if so, why had He sent her to Mistletoe?

Instead of the majestic organ music associated with her childhood worship, Julia's ears were soon greeted with a cacophonous musical blend of David's banjo, Millard's fiddle, Tom Morriston's guitar, and the piano chords of Sadie Brown. After a full five minutes of instrumental music, Pastor Brown swung his arms and kept time with the music as the congregation belted out the words of "He Will Set Your Fields on Fire." Accustomed to traditional hymns, this type of music—if it could be called such—grated on Julia's nerves.

With a loud squeal, Bobby clapped his hands over his ears and turned a frightened face toward Julia. "Boom! Boom!" he shouted, and Julia suppressed a smile.

"It's all right," she whispered. Julia pointed to Nellie, who didn't hold a songbook but was singing merrily, her long-lashed blue eyes glowing with inner satisfaction. "They're singing."

"Sing?"

"Yes."

Bobby opened his mouth and tried to imitate Nellie as she sang fervently.

"From the blessed Lord and His
    own true word
But still you say retire.
Leave the downward path, kindle
    not His wrath
Or He'll set your fields on fire."

Is there no end to the verses of this song? Julia wondered how long she could endure the clamor. She admired Nellie's strong, contralto voice and was amused by Bobby's efforts to mimic her. Recalling the old adage, "When in Rome, do as the Romans do," Julia flung dignity to the wind and sang with the congregation as they repeated the same lyrics over and over.

"Now, my friend, if you desire
You may join the heavenly choir
And rejoice with Him, free from
    every sin,
When He sets this world on fire."

AN APPALACHIAN CHRISTMAS

After half an hour of music and testifying, the congregants stirred to greet one another by hugging or shaking hands. At the beginning of this fellowship time, Granny came to stand beside Julia and introduced her to everyone who came to shake her hand. Granny's comment was simple: "This is Julia Mayfield and her nephew, Bobby. They're stoppin' with us a few days."

When the pastor asked for announcements, his wife stood. "It might seem like a long time until Christmas," Sadie Brown began, "but the weeks will pass before we're ready. It's time to start making comforters and lap robes as Christmas gifts for the residents in the old folks' homes in Booneville and Beattyville. We'll meet at our house on Tuesday afternoon."

Two announcements followed, and then the preacher called for another song. Granny stayed on the seat beside Julia. Bobby crawled on her lap and snuggled contentedly in her arms. When at last Pastor Brown opened his Bible and prayed, Julia looked surreptitiously at her watch. The meeting had already lasted more than an hour. She smothered a sigh and squirmed on the hard, wooden bench, trying to find a comfortable position.

Julia hadn't had a preconceived notion of what she would find in Mistletoe, but in her wildest imaginings, she had never expected any of this! In the past two days she'd been stranded in the middle of a muddy creek and rescued by a handsome mountaineer, who had stirred her emotions as no man ever had. Then the man she'd traveled hundred of miles to see had threatened to kill her. She'd been accepted like family by a mountain woman and her son, and she'd been confronted with local customs that were fifty years behind the outside world's. She felt as far removed from her normal lifestyle as if she'd suddenly landed on the moon. What else might happen to her before she left Mistletoe?

Julia stopped woolgathering and turned her attention to Pastor Brown's message. "Friends," he began in the slow, nasally vernacular common to most of the natives, "I wrestled with the Lord most of the night about today's sermon. When I went to bed, I was easy in my mind that I'd be preachin' on the Shepherd Psalm. Soon after midnight, the Lord woke me up and changed my mind. After tossin' and turnin' for over an hour, I got up and started searchin' the Scripture for a new message."

He put on his spectacles and lifted his Bible. "Today's text is from the writings of the Old Testament prophet Joel, chapter three, verse fourteen. 'Multitudes, multitudes in the valley of decision: for the day of the Lord is near in the valley of decision.'"

He cleared his throat and spoke in a loud yet compassionate voice. "These words describe what's goin' on in our country today. All durin' the war, everybody was busy, focused on winnin' the conflict. Now that peace has come, a lot of people are at a standstill. Men came home from war expectin' life to be like it was before they went away. It wasn't. Women, who'd always stayed home, worked at men's jobs while they were away fightin'. The menfolk expect their women to take up livin' the way they did before the war, and it's caused a lot of trouble." The pastor continued his sermon by citing incidents to bring out the truth of the message.

Although in other situations Julia would have expected his homespun delivery to bore her, she leaned forward, intent on every word he said.

"We might as well forget about 'the good ol' days,'" the preacher continued. "They're gone forever. Our country didn't come out of this war with the innocence it used to have. Even this little holler along Buffalo Crick has changed. A lot of our boys who went to war, and other people who moved to the big cities to work in defense plants, didn't come back to Mistletoe. They'd found an easier side of life, and they weren't willing to give it up."

Julia could readily understand why former residents of the hollow, once they'd become accustomed to modern conveniences, would prefer to live elsewhere.

"But we've still got a lot to give. We're God-fearin' people, and it's up to us to proclaim the Word of God up and down this holler. Too many people have come back from the war wonderin' if God is alive. Imagine! Wonderin' if the Almighty is still on the throne. I'm here to tell you that He is, and it's time for you to decide where you stand with Him today."

Pastor Brown motioned to his wife, who went to the piano bench and started playing softly. Because of her infrequent church attendance, Julia was surprised that she recognized the words of a song she'd heard when she was a child.

**"I'll go where You want me to go,
 dear Lord,
O'er mountain or plain or sea;
I'll say what You want me to say,
 dear Lord,
I'll be what You want me to be."**

Julia could identify with the song lyrics. She had been on plains in the West during her basic training for the WAC. She'd spent two years overseas, and now she was in the Appalachian Mountains. She didn't believe that she'd ever been what God wanted her to be, but at this moment, she desperately wanted to know His will for her life. She focused again on Pastor Brown as he called for commitment from the congregation, knowing in her heart that God had sent his message especially for her.

"Brothers and sisters, we're at a crossroads. Someone in this congregation—or maybe lots of people—needed this sermon today, or God wouldn't have laid it on my heart. People will make decisions in the next hour or the next week that are gonna change their lives forever. Maybe you're one of them. I don't know, but God knows. And *you* know.

"Maybe the crossroad you're facin' is to get right with God. Is your heart burdened down with a load of sin? Don't put off settin' your feet on the right road today. Be like the prodigal son, who left the worthless life he'd been livin' and came runnin' home to his father. Just like that earthly father, God stands with open arms waitin' for you."

Preacher Brown pulled a bandanna from his hip pocket and wiped his brow. "You may be standin' at a crossroads wonderin' what decision to make about a job. Or about gettin' a better education. Maybe you're all mixed up inside, not knowin' which road to take. The future lies before you. My friends," he implored, "which road are you gonna take?"

When the pastor asked for those who wanted to rededicate their lives to come forward and pray at the altar, Julia wasn't tempted to go. She had serious decisions to make, but she was a private person. If her future changed directions, it would come at a meeting between herself and God alone.

Chapter Seven

....

David carried Bobby as they walked home from the church service, and Granny congratulated the two-year-old on being a good boy at church.

"I good?"

"I'll say," David said. He tickled Bobby's ribs lightly, which elicited a delighted giggle. Bobby proceeded to dig his fingers in David's side.

David yelled, squirming, as if he felt the pressure of those tiny fingers. "Don't tickle me," he begged, holding Bobby so he couldn't move.

"I was surprised by how good he was,"

Julia said. "Mother and Dad take him to church every Sunday, but children under three stay in the nursery during the worship service. I thought Bobby would want to play like he does at home."

"No. Good boy," Bobby insisted.

"Yes, you were, and I'm proud of you." Julia bent to kiss his cheek.

David whispered, "I was good too. Don't I get one of those?"

Choosing to believe that he was joking, Julia lifted her eyebrows. "Not yet!"

At the house, Granny took off her hat and explained to Julia, "We have just a light dinner at noon on Sundays. I'll cook at suppertime." She stirred up the coals in the cookstove and filled the teakettle. While the water heated, she sliced a loaf of bread and placed it on the table with butter and strawberry preserves.

"David, bring apples from the cellar and some milk for the boy. Julia, if you'll put Bobby in the high chair, you can set the table. David and I will drink coffee. Do you want a cup too?"

"Yes, please."

"So how'd you like our preacher?" Granny asked after they started eating.

"He seemed very sincere in his beliefs," Julia answered truthfully. "He gave me a lot to think about."

Her comments must have pleased Granny, because she nodded. "He's a good man. He works long hours in the coal mines for a livin' but still finds time to visit the sick and help out where he can."

Julia and Granny washed the few dishes they'd used and cleaned the oilcloth table covering while David took Bobby to the front porch. Julia heard one of the rockers moving rhythmically, and it wasn't long before David brought the sleeping boy inside and laid him on Granny's bed.

"I'd like to take a walk while Bobby is napping," Julia said. "He usually sleeps two hours or more."

"A walk will be good for you," Granny agreed.

"I'll go along," David volunteered.

"If it's safe enough, I'd rather go by myself," Julia said, hoping that she wouldn't hurt his feelings. "I have decisions to make, and this may be the only time I'll have any privacy."

"It's safe enough anywhere," David assured her. "Nobody will bother you."

"I won't be gone long."

"Take all the time you need. If Bobby wakes up before you get back, I'll take care of him."

Julia went into the bedroom, took off the clothes she'd worn to church, and put on pants and walking shoes. David was on the porch reading a newspaper when she left the cabin. "I'm going up the hollow toward your house," Julia said, grinning. "Is it all right if I trespass on your property or sit on the porch?"

"Sure. Go inside if you want to. The door isn't locked."

"Thanks, but it's a beautiful day. I'll stay outside."

As she walked, Julia remembered Pastor Brown's message. She *was* at a crossroads. She was committed to write a book about her war experiences, but that wouldn't take more than six months. What then? Before she'd enlisted in the WAC, she'd attended two years of college majoring in journalism, but she was undecided about continuing her education.

Julia sat on the steps of David's cabin

and surveyed the narrow valley before her. Again she noticed the peace and quietness. She recalled the noises that had shattered her nerves in the army—especially the rumble of engines, which had always made her wonder if Allied or enemy planes were approaching. Many times she was close enough to the battlefront to hear the guns. She'd seldom had a moment alone and was constantly surrounded by the sound of other people—breathing, talking, and singing.

The sounds she heard now were peaceful. The little stream sighed contentedly as it approached a slight waterfall a few feet from where she sat. A male cardinal perched on a fence post before he swooped to the ground and grabbed a grain of corn from the pile that David had left for the wildlife when he'd shucked his corn crop. A slight breeze wafted down the hollow, spinning an ornamental windmill in the yard. She wished that her mind was as peaceful as this setting.

Julia hadn't expected her war experiences to impact her psyche, but apparently they had, for she couldn't get enthusiastic about anything. For as long as she could remember, she'd had a troubled relationship with her sister. She had determined that, when she came home, she would put forth an effort to establish rapport with Margaret. She had hoped that they could share an affection they'd never enjoyed. To come home without her sister being there was almost more than she could bear. She had felt completely alone and cheated of an opportunity to deal with the past.

Throughout the war, while her coworkers had one love affair after another, Julia wondered why she couldn't be interested in any of the fine young soldiers she'd met. It seemed inconceivable that when she'd been thrown together with some of the best men the country had to offer, she hadn't encountered anyone who piqued her interest. Now, after two mere days in this isolated Kentucky hollow, she was attracted to a man who was content to stay here for the rest of his life. No one could be more unsuitable for her. So what was different about David to stir her interest in him?

Before she could consider why David drew her like a magnet, she had more pressing concerns. Julia had come to the valley of decision, and she had no idea which way to go. Should she leave tomorrow and forget she'd ever heard of David Armstrong and Mistletoe? And what was she going to do after she finished the writing assignment? Something was missing in her life, and she knew what it was. She was miserable because she no longer looked to God for guidance as she had when she was a teenager.

Kneeling in the shade of a tall evergreen, Julia closed her eyes and opened her heart. "God," she prayed, "I don't know the right path to take. Please guide me in the way You want me to go. Help me to become the kind of follower I ought to be."

When she stood, peace flooded Julia's soul, and she recalled a Scripture she'd learned long ago in Bible School: "And the peace of God, which passeth all understanding, shall keep your hearts and minds through Christ Jesus." When she'd memorized that verse, she hadn't understand what it meant. She did now.

Looking at her watch, she stood and stepped off the porch. She walked toward the large log cabin David had pointed out to her yesterday, climbed the steps, and peered through the window. The interior of the house was dark, but it appeared that the cabin was still furnished. Julia walked toward the creek and retraced her route to Granny's home.

When Bobby wakened, she took him outside, played tag with him, and walked with him to the barn, where they watched David milk the cow and feed the chickens. It seemed easier to keep Bobby occupied now, and he was more relaxed with her. Or had *she* changed and was no longer intimidated by her nephew? Hoping it was the latter, she returned to the cabin in time for the light supper that Granny had prepared. After helping with the dishes, Julia went to the porch where David sat on the steps keeping his eye on Bobby, who seemed inclined to investigate every rock, bush, and flower in the front yard. Julia sat on the steps beside him.

After a while, he said quietly, "I'm sure you haven't noticed, and I don't want you to look now. Keep watching my face. Do you understand?"

Puzzled by his manner but aware it must be something important, Julia nodded.

"Someone is lurking in that thicket of elderberry bushes at the edge of the woods. I think it's Bobby's grandmother."

Startled, Julia stared at David. It required tremendous willpower not to look at the thicket he'd mentioned. "Really?"

"I'm pretty sure. I'm going to the barn, where I can get a better view. I'll pretend to check the horses so she won't know that I've seen her. Don't look her way."

"What do you think it means?"

"That Mrs. Walden is trying to see the boy and decide if he *is* Robert's son. Knowing that they have a grandson might be the best way to bring them out of their depression. If you stay in Mistletoe a little longer, they may ask to see him."

Julia grimaced.

"I don't mean to place a guilt trip on you, but I think there's a possibility that the Waldens will accept the boy if you give them more time."

Now that she was getting along better

with Bobby, Julia considered his suggestion. She was a person who always finished what she started, and she knew she'd never be completely satisfied if she didn't carry out Margaret's request. If she thought this would happen in a week or two, she might stay, but she'd seen enough to know that events moved slowly in this hollow. It could be months before the Waldens would acknowledge Bobby as their grandson—if they ever did. Recalling her renewed faith in God's guidance, she wondered what *He* wanted her to do.

"This raises a problem that's been in the back of my mind," Julia said. "What if the Waldens want to keep Bobby? My parents wouldn't be happy about that. He's been theirs for two years."

"If they're convinced he belongs to Robert, they *might* want him. I suppose it would take a court decision to determine who has prior claim to Bobby. Considering their present mental conditions, I doubt they could get custody of the boy."

"It wouldn't be good for Bobby to have his grandparents fighting over him." Julia shook her head. "They've had their chance, and I've done my best to fulfill Margaret's request." Suspecting that her determination to leave Mistletoe was caused by her mounting interest in David, Julia said firmly, "I'm going home."

Her decision left Julia with an indefinable feeling of emptiness. Judging from the resignation on David's face, she suspected he shared her feelings.

"Then *I'll* take you to Booneville tomorrow, so we can have a few more hours together. Tom leaves about seven o'clock, but there's no reason for you to go that early. I'll let him know that you won't ride with him."

He unlimbered his long frame from the steps and walked slowly toward the barn. When Bobby fell and started crying, Julia picked him up and took him inside the cabin. By the time she'd undressed Bobby he was almost asleep, but Julia lay beside him, hands crossed behind her neck, contemplating her future.

Chapter Eight

David's car, an eight-year-old dark blue Chevrolet, was parked in front of Granny's cabin when Julia got up after a restless night. She'd finished packing before she awakened Bobby. He started giggling as soon as he opened his eyes, which Julia took as a good sign. She didn't know what the day held for her, but having a happy baby was encouraging.

Fortified by a plate of Granny's cornmeal cakes, a slice of ham, and a cup of strong coffee, Julia thought she could face the week that was bound to be exhausting.

"Dade," Bobby called, holding out his hands when David walked into the cabin. David lifted Bobby from the chair and tossed him upward several times, Bobby squealing joyfully. When David put him on the floor, Bobby begged for more.

"Nope. I want another cup of coffee, and then we'll start to Booneville."

"Oonwill?" Bobby questioned.

David laughed. "Well, I guess that's close enough for a little shaver." After he drank the coffee Granny handed him, he turned to Julia. "Are you ready?"

"Yes," she replied in a dull voice.

He went into the bedroom for her luggage. "Granny, look for me when you see me coming. If Julia can't get a bus today, I'll stay the night in Booneville to keep them company."

Leaving Granny was more difficult than Julia had anticipated. It was uncanny that she'd become so fond of this woman in such a short time. Since childhood Julia had suppressed her emotions, but telling Granny good-bye caused a deep, unfamiliar pain in her heart.

"You've been very good to Bobby and me. I'll never forget you."

"My door is always open to you, my dear. Let us know how you and Bobby are gettin' along."

"Yes, I will."

Granny lifted Bobby into her arms, hugged and kissed him. Her eyes filled with tears, and Julia quickly took her nephew and left the cabin. She didn't look back as David drove away.

Julia watched closely as they passed the Walden house, but she couldn't tell if anyone was looking out the window.

David was unusually silent, and Julia wondered what he was thinking. When they came to the spot where she and Tom had been stranded three days ago, Julia said, "Thank goodness there isn't much water today."

"I didn't think there would be. It hasn't rained for several days."

Julia and David had always found plenty to talk about, but today the silence in the car was almost unbearable. Julia devoted most of her time to entertaining Bobby until he finally went to sleep. Then she counted the many clumps of mistletoe decorating the oak trees. Today her longtime fascination with mistletoe took second place to the sorrow of saying good-bye to David and Granny. She was sorry she wouldn't have the opportunity to celebrate Christmas in this area, the very name of which was reminiscent of the holiday, but she couldn't see that she had any choice except to return to Maryland.

* * * * *

When they were within a few miles of Booneville, David asked, "What do you want to do first?"

His voice must have disturbed Bobby, because the boy stirred and muttered. Julia patted his back comfortingly, and he didn't awaken.

"I guess the first thing is to find out when a bus leaves for Lexington. After that I'll call my parents to give them an idea of what day we'll get home."

"The station terminal is only open when buses are arriving or leaving, but you can make a call from Alex's gasoline station."

"I want to tell Alex good-bye anyway. He was very helpful when I arrived in Booneville." Awkwardly she cleared her throat. "It seems as if I've been here forever rather than three days."

David didn't answer. He didn't know what to say. Anguish seared his mind, and loneliness filled his heart. Julia was leaving, and he might never see her again.

She sighed deeply. "David, it isn't easy for me to leave, but be honest with me. Can you imagine me living in Mistletoe?"

David hesitated, not knowing how to answer. Could he tell her that he'd been awake most of the night remembering the hours they'd spent together? She had seemed to adjust readily to their habits, and he *had* envisioned her staying in Mistletoe and becoming a part of the community. At that point, however, thoughts of the past surfaced, and he knew it was better for both of them if she did leave. He had no future with Julia Mayfield, and his heart might as well accept it. He answered hesitantly, "That's for you to decide."

He took his eyes from the road long enough to glance at Julia. She was staring straight ahead, her jaw clenched, her eyes slightly narrowed. He tried to look at Mistletoe through her eyes, and he had to admit that a stranger could be daunted by the neighborhood. He couldn't imagine finding personal happiness in a *city*, so how could he expect Julia to accept this backwoods region?

"I've felt more at peace here than any other place I've been," Julia admitted slowly, and a small smile touched her lips. "I was worn out mentally and physically when I arrived. It was relaxing to enjoy a slower pace of life for a few days. Granny's serenity and strength soothed my fears and frustration about Bobby, but I have plans for my life that can't be realized in this environment." In a husky voice, she added, "That doesn't mean I'll *never* return to Mistletoe."

"I should hope not," he said, and somehow his heart seemed a little lighter. "I've been thinking that I might take a trip to Maryland some day."

Julia's eyebrows arched mischievously, and the secretive smile that touched her lips sent his pulse racing.

"Without being invited?" Her smile took the sting out of the words.

"I hoped I'd find the welcome mat waiting for me."

She placed her hand on his forearm. "You would, David."

His arm tingled where she touched him, and he took his right hand from the steering wheel and caressed her fingers. Since Julia had acknowledged that she would stay in touch, he felt better about her leaving. "I learned to be a good letter writer while I was in the army."

"Then I'll leave my address with you."

* * * * *

David parked beside the gas station and lifted a still-yawning Bobby into his arms while Julia stepped out on the uneven sidewalk.

"Leave your suitcases in the car until we see what you can do."

When they walked into the station, Alex was leaning over the engine of an auto, much as he had been when Julia had first seen him. She sneaked a grin toward David, wondering how much time Alex spent with his head under the hood of a car.

"Hi," Bobby shouted, wide awake now and squirming in David's arms.

Straightening, Alex said, "Well, sake's

alive, if it ain't Bobby and his pretty aunt. Howdy, miss," he shouted, adding, "You too, David. What can I do for you?"

"When does the next bus leave for Lexington?" Julia asked.

"Tomorrow at ten o'clock."

"Oh." Julia felt as deflated as a flat tire. "I'd hoped we could leave today."

"Sorry, ma'am. Today's bus left an hour ago."

With a resigned look toward David, she said, "Then may I use your phone? I need to make a collect call to my parents in Maryland."

Alex pointed to a little cubbyhole that passed for his office. "In there on the wall. Dial the operator to call long distance."

"I'll take care of Bobby," David said.

Papers were piled in wild abandon in the room Alex indicated. Even the chairs were covered with spare automobile parts and boxes, but that didn't bother Julia. Weary from the bumpy automobile ride, she didn't want to sit down. After she dialed, she waited at least ten minutes before she heard her mother's voice.

"Hello, Mother. This is Julia checking in."

"Oh, thank God you called," Rhoda Mayfield shouted wildly, and Julia gasped. What had caused her mother to be so distraught? She felt momentary panic, and a wave of apprehension swept through her.

"Is Dad all right?"

"Oh, yes, yes. We're both fine, but Grandmother Mayfield fell yesterday and broke her right hip. The first time in years that she's visited her sister in Noel, Missouri, and this had to happen! She'll be in the hospital two weeks or more, and I don't know how long it will be before we can bring her home. Your dad and I are leaving for Missouri this afternoon to take care of her. I was afraid we'd be gone before we heard from you and our grandbaby. It seemed as if you'd fallen off the face of the earth."

"Calm down, Mother. Both of us are all right. We're starting home tomorrow."

"We have a short time before we catch the train, so tell me about your trip. How's Bobby? What did the Waldens think of him?"

Julia decided that this wasn't the time to burden her mother with the way she'd been greeted by Bobby's grandparents, but she had to tell her *something*. "They refused to see him."

Rhoda gasped. "I've never heard the like. Why wouldn't they see the child?"

"After they received the news of Robert's death, the Waldens went into seclusion. They seldom leave the house, refuse to believe that their son is dead, and turn visitors away. Apparently, Robert hadn't told them he was married. None of the neighbors knew about it."

"Then where have you stayed?" her mother persisted. "Have you been in a hotel?"

Julia smiled to herself, imaging her mother's horror if she knew that there wasn't a hotel or any modern conveniences in Mistletoe. "No. We spent the weekend with a very nice woman, Elizabeth Armstrong. Everyone calls her Granny. Bobby took to her right away. Granny thinks that the Waldens might eventually accept Bobby as their grandson, but life moves slowly in this area. I can't wait around here forever."

"We hesitated about going to Missouri, but we think Mother Mayfield is our responsibility. We can't expect her sister's family to care for her. I don't know how long we'll be away, so if you come home now, you and Bobby will be alone. If you think the Waldens might change their mind, you could stay for another week or so." She stopped to catch her breath, adding, "Your daddy's reminding me that we have a train to catch. Tell me what you're going to do."

Julia wasn't surprised that her mother was more distressed about Grandma Mayfield than she was about her daughter. Anger at her parents flooded Julia's mind. She wanted to shout, "Bobby is your responsibility, not mine!" but they obviously hadn't given that any consideration.

She was bewildered by this sudden change in her plans. Finally she said, "Give me a telephone number where I can reach you in Missouri. I'll let you know soon whether I'm at home or still in Mistletoe." Julia scribbled the telephone number on a discarded envelope she found on Alex's littered desk. "I'll probably return to Maryland, but I need to think about it."

"If you don't go home, I should have a telephone number where I can reach you in Kentucky."

"There isn't any telephone service in Mistletoe. I'll have to call you when I come to Booneville."

"No phones!" Her mother thought for a moment, then added, "You wanted to find a quiet place to write your book. Maybe that's the place for you."

"A lot of writing I'd get done with a toddler to watch," Julia answered, so annoyed at this turn of events that she couldn't keep the sarcasm from her voice.

Julia heard her father's voice in the background.

"All right, Clarence, I'm coming!" her mother shouted, and Julia held the receiver away from her ear. "Are you still there, Julia?"

"Yes."

"Oh, I'm in such a dither I don't know what to do, but I can't keep Clarence waiting any longer. Take care of yourself, dear. Give Bobby a kiss from his grandma." Her mother rang off.

Julia stared at the phone receiver for a moment, unable to believe that her mother had terminated the conversation so abruptly. Not knowing whether the possibility of staying longer in Kentucky made her happy or angry, Julia went to look for David and her nephew.

Chapter Nine

David wondered what could have caused the bewildered expression on Julia's face when she walked slowly out of the office.

She kissed Bobby on the cheek. "That's from Grandma."

"Gama?" Bobby said, peering around Julia and apparently expecting to see his grandmother.

"She isn't here, baby. She sent the kiss over the telephone."

"I want Gama," the child insisted.

"Then you'll have to wait awhile." She sat on the rickety chair beside the door and took Bobby on her lap.

David hunkered down beside her. "Is anything wrong?"

Awkwardly she cleared her throat, her dark-lashed eyes remote and puzzled. "Not really."

Smiling, he said tenderly, "Then why don't you tell me what really *isn't* wrong?"

"I barely caught my parents before they boarded a train to go to Noel, Missouri, to take care of my grandmother. They don't know how long they'll be away." She quietly filled David in on what she'd learned from her mother. "This throws a hitch in my plans. I'd expected them to take care of Bobby when we got home."

"Then don't return to Maryland," David said, his pulse racing at this unexpected—probably unwise for *him*—turn of events that might keep Julia in Kentucky. "There isn't any reason you can't stay in Mistletoe now."

She shook her head. "I won't impose on Granny any longer."

He opened his mouth to protest, and she said, "Now, don't say she'd be glad to have us. I know that, but I can't stay here indefinitely. I have commitments at home.

When I left Maryland, I didn't expect to be gone more than a week. I'm dealing better with Bobby now, and I've learned to love him, but he isn't *my* responsibility."

David took Bobby. "You can't leave until tomorrow, so let's talk about it over lunch. I'm hungry. The hotel restaurant opens at eleven o'clock. Hey, Alex," he called, and the mechanic looked up. "Thanks for your help. We'll see you later."

Alex waved the wrench he held and continued his work. As they walked to his car, David prayed for wisdom to convince Julia to stay in Kentucky. Was it reasonable to pursue this undeniable magnetism building for someone as secretive about her past as Julia was? In the few days he'd known her, he'd learned more about Julia's parents, her sister, and Bobby than he knew about her. But his feelings for Julia had nothing to do with reason.

He guessed that Julia was in her midtwenties, not far from his age of twenty-seven. She'd indicated that she'd been involved in the war effort, but unless it was classified work, why hadn't she said what she had done? Most veterans were eager to talk about their contribution to bring peace to the nation.

As they ate, David could tell that Julia's mind wasn't on her present surroundings. From what she'd said after she talked with her mother, he sensed her family took her for granted, and because of that, she'd developed an armor that kept *everyone* at arm's length.

Suspecting that Julia needed time to deal with this latest upset to her plans, David left her alone after the meal and took Bobby for a walk around the courthouse square. When they returned, Julia was sitting on a bench in front of the bus station.

He sat beside her, their shoulders touching, but didn't speak. Her hazel eyes mirrored loneliness and confusion. Julia's beautiful face was crestfallen, like a child who had just learned that there wasn't a Santa Claus. He was tempted to put his arm around her, but instinctively David knew the gesture wouldn't be welcomed.

"David," Julia said tentatively, a slight tremor in her velvet-edged voice. "Just suppose, and I'm only mentioning this as a possibility, that I decide to stay in

Mistletoe for a couple of months. Is there any place for me to live?"

"You can stay in my house. I'll move in with Granny," he answered without hesitation.

"Do you think I'd actually take your home?"

"Why not? I lived with Granny after my folks died when I was a boy. I'd be welcome to stay there."

She dismissed the idea with a wave of her hand. "I will *not* move into your home. But I have been wondering about that house across the creek from yours—the one that belongs to a man in Louisville. Do you think I could rent it?"

David hit his forehead with the palm of the hand. "Why, of course. I should have thought of that right away. It's furnished, and there's running water and a bathroom, which you won't find in any other house in Mistletoe. I can call the owner before we leave Booneville to see if he's interested in leasing it." He smiled confidently, happily. "I believe that's the solution to your problem."

"Part of the solution," Julia said. "I have some work to do, which I can't complete when I have to look after Bobby twenty-four hours a day. Is there anyone I can hire to take care of him while I'm busy?"

David stifled his curiosity about what kind of work she could do at Mistletoe and answered, "Nellie would jump at the chance to work for you. She's trying to save money to go to college, but Millard won't let her leave home to find a job."

"She seems like a capable girl, and Granny said she helped take care of her younger siblings."

"Sure. Kids learn to take responsibility early on in these mountains."

"Let me sleep on it, and I'll tell you in the morning whether I'm going home or staying in Kentucky for the summer. I can think of advantages either way."

"I may be out of line to even ask you, but what kind of work will you be doing? I won't be offended if you tell me it isn't any of my business."

She hesitated with a pensive expression in her eyes for so long that David muttered, "Forget I asked. Sorry."

"No, it's all right." She took a deep breath and spoke in low, composed tones. "I was a member of the Women's Army Corps for over three years. About half of that time I spent stateside, but I was sent overseas in 1943. I worked with the office force of General Patton. Soon after D-Day, I was sent to France. I returned to the States last year, but I wasn't discharged from service until a couple of months ago."

David stared at her in amazement. "Why, we must have been in Europe at the same time. I was among the first squadron of paratroopers dropped behind the German lines in Europe. We'll have to compare notes and see if we might have brushed shoulders, never knowing that someday we'd meet in Kentucky." He thought for a moment. "The WAC made a noteworthy contribution to the war. Why should you hesitate to talk about it?"

"Because of the bad reputation servicewomen have gotten, especially now that the war is over," she said bitterly. "Some Congressmen and reporters are portraying women soldiers as prostitutes. Even people I've known for years look at me as if they wonder what *I've* done."

Frowning slightly, David said, "Pardon me for saying so, but I saw a few servicewomen who deserved that reputation."

Julia's hazel glittered dangerously. "A lot of soldiers didn't live like Boy Scouts either."

David held up his hands. "True enough. Please forget what I said. Women provided a great service to the war effort. But what does this have to do with your decision to stay in Mistletoe?"

"I studied journalism in college, and while I was in Europe, I wrote several articles about England and France that were published in the WAC magazine. The editor of *Nation at War* read them and asked me to write a book about my war experiences. The first draft is due by November."

"That sounds great."

"I am pleased with the assignment," she agreed. "I kept journals while I was in service, so I have plenty of information. I need a quiet place to work, and as soon as I took Bobby home to my parents, I intended to rent an apartment and start on the manuscript."

David grinned. "Mistletoe ought to be quiet enough."

She nodded in agreement. "I brought my journals with me, thinking I might have time on the long train trip to review them." With a wry smile she added, "That shows how much I knew about two-year-old boys."

David's pulse pounded when he considered having Julia living within sight of his house for several weeks, but he tried to conceal his eagerness. On the drive into Booneville, she'd given him a slight hope that he was more than a casual acquaintance to her, but that was when she intended to leave Mistletoe. *You're treading on dangerous ground, buddy,* his conscience prompted, but David pushed the thought into the background.

"Julia, I'll see to it that you find the time to write if you stay in Mistletoe. God has a purpose for everyone. You believe you came to Kentucky to fulfill your sister's dying request, but it may be that God has another purpose for you. Let's pray about it."

He reached for her hand, and she laced her fingers with his. "God, You have a purpose for Julia's life. Both of us need Your guidance. Help us make decisions based not on what we want but what You want. I believe I've found my purpose as a local teacher. Please confirm that as I continue my studies. As for Julia, guide her every decision this summer so that she won't harbor any doubts about Your will for her life. Amen."

David squeezed Julia's hand, and she smiled at him. "Thanks. My grandmother, the one who's in the hospital now, believes in 'putting out the fleece.' She often uses Gideon's example. If she wants to buy a new car, she might pray, 'God, I don't know whether I *need* a new car or if I want one because my next-door neighbor bought one. If it's all right for me to buy another car, let me find a black, two-door Chevrolet sedan. If there isn't one available in town, I'll know I should wait another year to make a trade.'"

Laughing, he said, "I understand that. 'Putting out the fleece' is a common practice among mountaineers. So what's your fleece going to be?"

"It's very simple. If I can rent your neighbor's house for two or three months,

I'll stay in Mistletoe for the time being. If not, I'll take the bus to Lexington tomorrow and return to Maryland."

Bobby was asleep by the time they settled into the Wilder Hotel for the night. Julia took him upstairs while David stopped in the lobby to place a call to Samuel Johnson. His housekeeper reported that Mr. Johnson was out of town and wouldn't return until nine o'clock in the evening.

Before he went to his room, David knocked on Julia's door.

"Yes, who is it?"

"It's David," he said. "Mr. Johnson isn't home now. I'll call later on, but if I can't reach him, I will tomorrow morning."

"Thanks, David. For everything. Sleep well."

"Yeah, you too," he answered softly.

Chapter Ten

Elated at the possibility of having a few more weeks with Julia, sleep eluded David until long after midnight. His emotions were topsy-turvy. More than anything, he wanted to see more of Julia Mayfield, but his common sense told him he was only asking for trouble.

Then, early in the morning, he awakened from a dream that left him trembling and as weak as a newborn puppy. Nightmares of his war years had haunted him repeatedly for several months after he was discharged, and they'd started again this summer.

Like a kaleidoscope, mental pictures of war experiences flashed through his mind. He remembered vividly the faces of enemies he'd shot in hand-to-hand combat. The defeated attitude of Europeans who'd lost everything in the Allied bombing. The fear displayed by some of his comrades before their first jump into enemy territory. The prayers he had offered for his own safety.

His worst nightmare was about the death of a comrade who had retreated from the enemy either by mistake or because he was running away. Several soldiers had shot at the approaching figure in the early dawn, but in the past few months, David often wondered if it was *his* bullet that had caused his comrade's death.

* * * * *

"Didn't you sleep well?" Julia asked the next morning when they met in the hotel lobby.

David's smile didn't erase the anguish in his eyes. "I slept most of the night." Smoothing back his dark hair, he joked, "I must look pretty bad."

Julia wasn't fooled by his nonchalance,

and she was aware that he'd evaded her question. This wasn't the same guy she'd known for the past few days.

"Hi, Bobby." David held out his arms and took the boy. "How're you this morning?"

"I hungry. I want brekfat."

"Then we'll see what we can do about that."

The middle-aged waitress brought a bib and high chair for Bobby. Julia and David ordered sausage, eggs, and biscuits, and Julia asked the waitress to bring cereal and juice for Bobby. While they waited for their food to be served, she asked, "Do you have any news for me?"

David seemed to have dealt with whatever was bothering him, for an easy smile lit his eyes. "I finally reached Mr. Johnson. He's willing to rent the house to you. For fifty dollars you can have it till the year's end. You're responsible for any destruction to the property. I assured him that he needn't worry about any damages."

Observing her nephew, who was squirming in the high chair and drumming on the table with a spoon, Julia said wryly, "I'm not too sure about that." She added, "I wonder if it might be best to commit for only one month at a time. I can't stay here for three more months. For one thing, I don't want to be stranded in the hollow by a snowstorm."

"We usually don't have deep snows until January. Regardless, Mr. Johnson is a reasonable man, and he wouldn't hold you to the lease if you have to leave before then. But I'll be pleased for you to stay. Everyone should spend at least one Christmas in Mistletoe."

Unwilling to make any long-term commitments, Julia didn't comment on his suggestion. "Do you think the price is reasonable?"

"It's a little high in my opinion, but you're getting a better house than any other property in the hollow. That price also gives you the privilege of using the car he has stashed in the barn. Or don't you drive?"

"I do. I got my driver's license when I was eighteen. I drove army vehicles during the war. What kind of car is it?"

"A '39 Ford."

"I've driven my father's Ford, so I'll use the car. Please notify Mr. Johnson that I'll take the house. And if you don't mind, please get his address so I can send a check to him while we're still in Booneville."

Julia realized that she was becoming more and more indebted to David, but he was enough like his grandmother that he would probably resent any effort on her part to try to repay him. "I'll have to figure out what I'll need to buy for an extended stay in Mistletoe. What time do you want to start home?"

"One o'clock will be all right. Granny knows I can take care of myself, but I figured I'd go home yesterday without you. She's bound to wonder where I am if I'm not home by tonight."

"I'll call the editor of the magazine and tell him where I am. When I contracted to have the manuscript ready for publication in November, I thought I could start writing before the month was out. I may have to ask for an extension."

Their breakfast was served, and they ate in silence for several minutes while Julia's thoughts rioted. Realizing that her hesitancy to leave David Armstrong had ruined her good judgment, she panicked.

"David," Julia finally said, and her voice

shook. "I don't know what I've been thinking. It's impossible for me to stay here. I'd have the responsibility of taking care of a house as well as a child. In Maryland, Bobby would be in his own home, playing with his own toys. If my parents don't return to Maryland soon, I'll pay someone to watch Bobby during the day while I work. I'll leave on the morning bus."

David's dark eyebrows slanted in a frown, and an inexplicable look of dismay crossed his face. He threw up his right hand. "Hey, hold on a minute," he said. "You're borrowing trouble. Excuse me for saying this, but you're apparently not short of money."

She was surprised at his frankness, but after all he'd done for her, Julia thought she owed him an explanation.

"I saved the majority of my pay while I was in the WAC, and I'll receive an advance payment on the book. I'll have to go to work eventually, but I figure I have enough money to provide for my needs until I complete the book."

He grinned sheepishly. "Excuse me for being nosy, but I suppose it's obvious that

I want you to stay. Can I make some suggestions to ease your mind about living here?"

She smiled. "Yes, of course."

"Mistletoe is a perfect place for you to concentrate on your book. Among other things, it's quiet; no phones ringing and no traffic. If your parents don't have to spend a long time with your grandmother, they might even stop in Kentucky on their return and take Bobby home with them. You'd just need help between now and then. As for that, Nellie will jump at the chance to help you. Although Millard won't let her leave home to get a job, he might not object if she works for you. She's helped raise her brother and sister, and I imagine she's a fair cook. She could also be your housekeeper, since Hattie would have taught her what to do. You could devote all day to writing and meet your deadline."

Feeling as if a load had been lifted from her shoulders, Julia reconsidered her options. "You make it sound possible." She deliberated awhile longer and then smiled. "Okay then, you've convinced me. I'll stay."

David grinned at her, and she grinned back for a few moments.

Then reality set in. "I'll have to buy groceries before I leave Booneville." Julia's mind spun again at the enormity of what she was undertaking. "Also, I'll need towels, sheets, pans, and other things to set up housekeeping."

He shook his head. "I don't think so. The house is completely furnished, but it's been vacant for so long that it would need a good cleaning before you could move in. You can stay at Granny's another day or two. Why not buy enough food to get along for a few days?"

"That sounds good. If I can drive Mr. Johnson's car, I'll come to town and shop after I determine what I should buy. It's frustrating to have to change my plans so quickly."

"Why don't I take Bobby on a walk around town," David suggested, "while you call your editor and make a list of things you need to buy?"

"Oh, would you? I'll hurry so we can reach Mistletoe before Granny starts to worry."

* * * * *

As they approached Mistletoe on their return trip, Julia said, "Granny is going to be surprised to see us again."

"Yes, but she'll be happy too. She took a liking to you."

"She's one of the finest women I've ever known."

"She is that," David agreed. "I sometimes think when the Good Lord made Granny, He threw the mold away."

As they drove by the church and the post office, Julia compared her present attitude to what it had been when she'd seen Mistletoe for the first time. She had been tired, troubled, and defeated. How could she have changed so much in three days that she was voluntarily returning to the area to stay for several weeks? Glancing at David's strong and rigid profile, his attractive male physique, and the unfathomable longing in his ebony eyes as he glanced toward her, Julia knew she wouldn't have to search far to find the answer.

Arms akimbo, Granny stood on the porch when David stopped the Chevrolet close to the steps. Julia stepped out of the car and lowered Bobby to the ground.

He scampered up the steps shouting, "Granny! Granny, I back."

Laughing, Granny lifted Bobby into her arms. "I see you are—you little scamp."

"Granny happy?"

Hugging him closely, Granny said. "I sure am." Looking at Julia, who followed Bobby up the steps, she added, "What happened?"

David and Julia took turns relating the turn of events that had extended her stay in Mistletoe for a few months.

"Now, ain't that great! I couldn't want no better gift than to have you spend the rest of the year in Mistletoe. Maybe by Christmas you'll like us so well that you won't leave a-tall." She glanced from David to Julia, a speculative gleam in her eye.

It wasn't difficult to know the turn Granny's thoughts were taking. Julia sensed that her face colored, but she shook her head and said, "That's not likely, but I'm pleased to know I'd be welcome."

"Will you watch Bobby while I take Julia to see the cabin?" David asked. "She'll have to stay here until we can get the place ready."

"Glad to do it. I'll have supper ready by the time you get back."

Julia and David drove the short distance to Mr. Johnson's cabin. Glancing toward the setting sun, David said, "The cabin will be dark, but I'll light a lamp so you can see what you've rented. I'll start the generator tomorrow so you can have power for lights and cooking. You'll have the most convenient home in Mistletoe."

"This is the first time I've lived alone. I stayed with my parents until I enlisted in the WAC."

Julia surveyed the outside of her new home with pleasure. The cabin faced west, and although the surrounding woodlands were shadowed, sunlight spotlighted the dwelling. She couldn't recall ever seeing a more beautiful sight, suddenly wishing she was an artist so she could paint the hollow as it now appeared to her.

"It's a sightly place," David said.

"Indeed it is," Julia said. "I was wishing I could put it on canvas so I could always remember it like this."

David parked the car in front of his cabin and went inside to get a key to the

Johnson house. Julia crossed the ravine and climbed the steps of her new home with satisfaction. She peered in a window, but she couldn't see anything until David joined her carrying a large flashlight. He unlocked the door, and standing back, he motioned for her to enter first.

She stepped into a large room that ran the width of the cabin. David pulled the curtain covering the double window. Although the sun had dipped behind the western horizon, enough daylight remained to illuminate the interior. The kitchen was separated from the living room by a four-foot wooden partition. Rustic furniture, grouped around a stone-faced fireplace, lent a homey atmosphere to the interior. The house needed airing and cleaning, but it pleased Julia.

"This cabin is about like mine," David explained as he struck a match and lit an Aladdin lamp on the library table. "There's a bedroom and bath downstairs."

He opened the door into a room dominated by a large wooden bed frame with a high backboard and a smaller footboard. A heavy comforter covered the bed. A dresser with a mirror and a low chest were arranged along one wall.

After examining the two sparsely furnished upstairs rooms, Julia sighed with satisfaction. "This is perfect for my needs. If Nellie will take care of Bobby, I can come upstairs and concentrate on writing."

"I'll ask Millard to help me move that desk in the living room up here," David offered.

"Oh, wonderful. Thank you. Is there any place I can buy a typewriter in Booneville?"

"You might find one in Alex Barrett's store. He carries about everything, and I believe he bought some office supplies from a factory that closed after the war ended. In fact, when Bobby and I were taking a walk, I noticed that he already has some Christmas gifts for sale. Just in case you're still here for the holiday."

Julia chose to ignore David's hint. "All right, then. I'll go to town in a few days and see if I can buy some office supplies. Then it looks like all I need to do is clean the place and move in!"

Chapter Eleven

Two days later, Julia and Bobby settled into their new home. Julia had expected that Granny and David would help her clean the house, but several of the local women also arrived at the cabin early Thursday morning. David had been up since dawn working on the generator, and he had a supply of water ready for the neighbors who brought cleaning supplies and willing hands and hearts.

Nellie and her brother, Addison, took charge of Bobby and kept him out of the way. Although Julia felt like a fifth wheel in a room full of industrious women who worked rapidly and effectively as a team, she insisted that she would clean the kitchen furniture and wash the dishes and pans. A sense of camaraderie existed among the women, and they talked and laughed as they worked. They used colloquial words and phrases that meant nothing to Julia, and she struggled to follow the gist of their conversation.

They were a bit distant with her, and she sensed that they didn't approve of her stylish clothes, her short hair, or her independent spirit. She could imagine their reaction when she started driving Mr. Johnson's car. In spite of their disapproval, they were doing what they would do for any newcomer. The neighbors also brought gifts, and when they finished at the end of the second day, Julia's kitchen cupboards were full of home-canned foods that would last for the duration of her stay in Kentucky.

David and Millard cut the grass and weeds in the yard and around the outbuildings. Tom Morriston, a good mechanic, put Mr. Johnson's car in operating condition. Having a vehicle of her own gave Julia a sense of freedom she wouldn't have otherwise enjoyed.

At the end of the first day, Millard and his wife stayed at Granny's for supper, which provided Julia with an opportunity to talk to Nellie about watching Bobby. She broached the subject while they were still sitting at the supper table. She didn't need to explain why she was staying in Mistletoe, because Granny had already spread the news about her parents' trip to Noel, Missouri.

"Now that I have a place to live," she said, "I have another problem. I've committed to do some work that didn't include taking care of a little boy." Briefly she explained about the years she'd served in the WAC and the book contract. The Armstrongs listened with rapt attention, and Nellie's eyes sparkled with excitement.

"Oh, I wish I'd been old enough to go to war," she said.

"Which I wouldn't have allowed, young lady," Millard said, giving Julia the impression that he didn't approve of women doing men's work. She glanced obliquely toward David, who sat at the head of the table. All eyes were turned toward her, and he mouthed, "Go ahead."

"I need someone to work for me during the day, not only to look after Bobby, but also to do light housekeeping. Hattie, you may need her at home, so don't hesitate to say no, but I wanted to ask Nellie before I approached anyone else."

It was obvious that Hattie wasn't the one to make the decision, for Nellie's eyes darted to her father. "Will you let me, Pa? Please."

Millard cupped his chin in his hand and deliberated. Except for Bobby's pounding on the high chair and his happy chortling, silence filled the room.

After a few moments that seemed like an hour to Julia, Millard spoke to Hattie. "What do you think, Ma?"

"Hit's all right with me," Hattie said. "I can handle the work at home."

"Granny?" Millard asked, and Julia decided that he wasn't the dictator he seemed to be.

"Hit'll be a good chance for Nellie to make some money. Besides, Julia needs help." Turning to Julia, she continued, "Hattie has taught Nellie how to cook, keep house, and take care of young'uns. You couldn't find nobody else who would do a better job."

Nellie's blue eyes beamed toward her grandmother with gratitude.

"Will ten dollars a week be enough for her wages?" Julia asked.

"That's more'n what people are paid for housework," Millard said.

"Since Nellie will be watching Bobby as well as cooking and cleaning, I thought it was fair."

"Then it's okay, Pa?" Nellie seemed to be holding her breath.

Millard inclined his head in agreement. "When do you want her to start?"

"If it's convenient, she can start right away. It looks as if Bobby and I can stay in our home tomorrow night. Tom says the Johnson car is ready, so I'll go to Booneville the next day to buy a typewriter and a few other things. Nellie can go with me and watch Bobby while I shop."

"You drive a car?" Millard asked, disbelief in his eyes.

"Yes, sir. I started driving my father's car when I was eighteen."

Millard shook his head, and Julia wondered if he thought she would be a bad influence on Nellie.

"I'd like to go to Booneville with her, Pa."

Eyeing Julia skeptically, he said, "I hope you're a careful driver."

"No accidents to my record," Julia said, "and I drove an army vehicle in France."

Julia was aware that David stifled a laugh when Millard stared at her and shook his head in disbelief.

* * * * *

Not long after they left Mistletoe two days later, Julia decided that driving a vehicle over Kentucky roads wasn't unlike driving on some of the roads she'd navigated in France and Germany. She stared straight ahead in order to dodge the potholes and to steer a straight course through the creek crossings. She was thankful that Millard had allowed Nellie to come with her, for the girl kept Bobby occupied, allowing Julia to concentrate on driving a strange vehicle.

"I sure am glad you offered me a job," Nellie said. "I want to earn all the money I can. I think I'll be admitted to Berea College next year, and I'll need money for new clothes and other extras. A college degree is my one-way ticket out of Mistletoe."

Julia smothered a smile. "You don't intend to come back here after you finish college?"

"Come back to what?" Nellie asked, seemingly surprised at the question. "There's nothin' to do here. I can't figure David out. With his brains and his war experiences, he could have found a good job anywhere. But what does he do? Builds a log cabin and intends to spend the rest of his life in Owsley County. Not me!"

"David has a dream that the neighborhood will develop into a place where people will *want* to live."

Nellie flipped her long honey-blond hair over her shoulder. "Well, good luck to him, but it's not for me. Livin' here reminds me of things I want to forget."

Julia considered this a strange comment from a girl as young as Nellie, but an indefinable expression of withdrawal spread across the girl's face. Julia didn't question her further.

"Just between the two of us," Julia

commented, "one of the main problems I have with this community is how women are treated as second-class citizens."

Nodding her head like a sage, Nellie agreed. "That's caused a lot of family trouble too. Women worked in plants during the war and earned the livin' while men were in the army. Some of the men came home expectin' their women to knuckle under like they always had, and that hasn't happened. When one of the local women left her husband and sued for divorce, I thought she'd be tarred and feathered." Laughing, Nellie shifted Bobby on her lap and continued. "Women like Ma and Granny don't have trouble with it. They let the men *think* they're the boss, but they do what they want to."

Considering this a subject she shouldn't pursue, Julia called attention to the clumps of mistletoe in many of the trees they passed. She told Nellie about her first experience with mistletoe and how she'd been intrigued by the plant since that time.

Nellie shrugged her shoulders. "People around here don't think much of it. It's a parasite that sometimes kills the trees it latches on to."

"Money can be made from the sale of mistletoe, though. My aunt, who runs a gift shop in Maryland, always orders a supply of mistletoe for Christmas. Let's stop so I can take a closer look."

While they kept watch over Bobby, who contented himself by picking up rocks from the road and tossing them toward the creek, Nellie pointed upward. "There's a big clump in that tall oak tree. You can't tell from here, but the leaves are grouped in horseshoe pairs. Soon they'll have little white berries. I've heard that the berries are poisonous."

"Yes, I think they are," Julia agreed.

"Wonder why people started kissing under mistletoe?" Nellie asked.

"I've read several explanations, but the first records of kissing under the mistletoe were in Celtic rituals and Norse mythology. Does anybody here sell mistletoe?"

Nellie shrugged. "Not that I know of."

"That might be a good way for you to make money for college. The plants could be harvested the first of December and shipped to eastern cities. But how could it be removed from these tall trees?"

"When visitors want to take some mistletoe home as a souvenir," Nellie said, "the men shoot it out of the trees."

It was Julia's opinion that a fall from the top of a tree would damage the plant and the berries, but she couldn't think of any easier way to harvest the plant.

"If you're interested, I'll contact my aunt Sarah and ask if she would let you send some mistletoe balls to sell in her gift shop. I'll help you make them."

Nellie didn't seem overly enthusiastic about the idea, but she agreed to Julia's suggestion to try and find a lucrative use for the local mistletoe. "Hundreds of people send their Christmas cards to Mistletoe to have them postmarked," she said.

"That's a great idea. I'll contact my relatives in Maryland and ask them to send their cards. It sounds like fun."

"It's hard work, not fun! I've helped the postmaster put on the special postmark, which has two young people kissing under the mistletoe. Every letter has to be stamped by hand, and it's slow going. If you're still here at Christmastime, maybe you can help us. It's interesting to see the different names and where the cards are sent."

Chapter Twelve

The next two months passed quickly for Julia as she settled into her log-cabin existence. After the tense years in the WAC, it was wonderful to work in her quiet upstairs office until mid-afternoon. Sometimes she walked through the woods behind the house, marveling each day at the slight change in the foliage as the trees slowly put on their colorful autumn coats. Nellie was excellent help. She not only had good rapport with Bobby, but she cleaned the house and prepared an evening meal before she returned to her home.

Bobby seemed content in their new quarters, but the stairs fascinated him. If Nellie wasn't watching him every minute, he'd crawl to the top step and then throw a tantrum until someone helped him down. This was a nuisance to Julia when she was trying to concentrate on her writing.

When she complained to David about it, however, he said, "I'll take care of that." The next evening he brought a gate and installed it at the foot of the stairs. Julia could easily unlatch the gate when she went up or down the steps, but Bobby couldn't reach the latch on the inside of the gate.

She always took afternoons off to help when the local women gathered to make Christmas items for the old folks' homes. She learned how to make comforters by placing a wool lining and a top layer of quilted blocks together and tying knots with colorful yarn to bind them together. In this close fellowship, she began to feel accepted by the Mistletoe community.

Julia's parents were still in Missouri, and they had never apologized for shifting their responsibility to her. Although Julia was irritated about this, she didn't resent Bobby. She devoted her evenings to him, and their relationship gradually cemented. They felt comfortable with each other. When the weather was pleasant, she'd sit on the porch while Bobby played contentedly in the yard. Both David and Nellie were convinced that Mrs. Walden often stood in the nearby trees and watched the child at play.

Julia started watching. When she spotted Mrs. Walden one day, she called and invited her to come to the cabin. The woman didn't answer, and when she knew she'd been detected, she skedaddled out of sight. As it became obvious that Mrs. Walden wouldn't leave the woods, Julia pretended she didn't see her and let the woman observe her grandson in her secretive way.

David attended the university the first two days of the week, but when he was at home, he spent each evening with her and Bobby, occasionally eating with them. Sometimes he carried Bobby to the crest of the mountain, where they had a bird's-eye view of the creek valley. Julia had seen a lot of the world, but she'd never seen scenery more superb than sunset in the Appalachian Mountains.

Julia enjoyed a rapport with Nellie—the kind of relationship she wished she'd had with her own sister. As she became closer to Nellie, however, she sensed that the girl was unhappy. Although she was cheerful and bubbling with enthusiasm most of the time, there was a hidden side of her that Julia couldn't reach. Occasionally Nellie would sit with hands folded, seemingly lost in memories. At those times, she seemed much more mature than a girl of her age should be.

One day a thought struck Julia. It seemed that *most* of the people she met in Mistletoe had a secret side to their lives. Even David. He had shared many stories about his boyhood in the hollow and some of his war experiences, but she sometimes detected an attitude of defeat and discouragement in his eyes. Having personal secrets of her own, Julia didn't pry.

* * * * *

When he opened the lid on the mailbox, David didn't have a care in the world. He'd enjoyed several enjoyable hours with Julia the night before and had dared to give her a brotherly kiss on the cheek before he went home. Their relationship was progressing beyond friendship, and he knew he had to tighten the reins soon. Try as he might, he couldn't think of any way to have a future with this woman who was the epitome of all he wanted in a wife.

When he lifted the small packet of mail from the box and saw the envelope, reality hit like he'd been sucker punched. *Why won't the guy give up? What does he hope to gain by this continued harassment?* David knew he should destroy the message without opening it, but morbid curiosity willed otherwise. He thrust the envelope into his pocket and walked up the hollow. He waved at Nellie, who was playing tag with Bobby, and hurried up the steps into his home. His legs felt like cooked spaghetti, and he slumped in the upholstered chair in front of the fireplace. The envelope bore no return address, but he knew who it was from.

David broke the seal on the envelope, but still he hesitated. A cold knot formed in his stomach, and he drew a deep breath and removed a single sheet of paper. He looked at a crude drawing of a veterans' cemetery with two tombstones prominently displayed in the foreground.

The stone on the right bore the name, ADRIAN TOLLIVER—1944.

The other stone was inscribed, DAVID ARMSTRONG—DATE TO BE DETERMINED.

He had received four similar messages in the past year, but there was a significant difference in this one. At the bottom of this paper was an additional message. "Prepare to meet God—SOON!"

David had never doubted his bravery until he started receiving these messages. How could he fight an unseen enemy? Instead of destroying this letter as he had the others, he put it in the Bible he kept locked in the small safe that contained the things he valued most. Only Granny had the safe's combination. If he was killed, at least the authorities would have some clue to his murderer.

David had nightmares about the tragedy that prompted these letters, but he seldom recalled the situation during daylight hours. As he slumped in his chair, however, he recollected vividly the night when he was in an airplane with several other paratroopers crossing the English Channel. He had been scared, dreading what would happen when they were dropped behind enemy lines. The soldiers had been well aware that their chances of surviving this mission were doubtful. All of them had been frightened, but none as obviously as the paratrooper beside him who was visibly shaking.

"Brace up, Tolliver," David had told the young soldier. "You've trained for this. It's the waiting that's the worst. As soon as we land and start doing our job, you'll be fine."

"But what if I mess up?" Adrian Tolliver had replied. "I've got a little brother at home, and I'm his hero." A touch of humor lightened his words. "He thinks I'm winning the war all by myself. I don't want to disappoint him."

The command "Prepare for landing" sounded from the cockpit, and David gripped Tolliver's shoulder. "You won't," he encouraged.

The next time David saw Adrian Tolliver, the young soldier was lying at his feet and nearly dead. In the misty darkness before dawn, the American paratroopers had seen a man approaching them. They'd been taught to shoot first and then ask questions, and that's exactly what they did. That morning, they fired dozens of shots at their comrade, mistaking him for an enemy soldier.

Adrian had been running away from the enemy rather than into Nazi-held territory as he was supposed to do. Considering the fear Adrian had exhibited prior to landing, it was generally believed by the officers who investigated his death that he had panicked in the face of danger. David had often thought about the little brother who considered Adrian a hero, and he prayed that the boy would never find out the truth.

When David's squadron discovered Tolliver, he was still alive, and David lifted him in his arms. The young man soon died, but not before he muttered, "Armstrong—why? I thought you were my friend."

David had been distressed, not only by Tolliver's death, but because the young man died thinking David had killed him.

He'd always considered Tolliver a friend, and he'd never forgotten the pain of that accusation.

Due to the many Allied casualties suffered during the D-Day advance, the nature of Tolliver's death had never become common knowledge. David couldn't imagine why the young man's family was blaming him for the death. Or was Tolliver's family even responsible for the threats? Perhaps another soldier who had been Tolliver's friend was sending the messages.

Considering the tone of the letter received today, David had a feeling that before too many weeks, he would have an answer to all of these questions.

* * * * *

Julia knew that David, and not her writing assignment, was keeping her in Mistletoe. She had tried to convince herself that it was only friendship she felt for him, but she knew that her interest surpassed friendship. His nearness kindled feelings of expectation, and when he put his arm around her as they sat on the sofa each evening, she felt a sense of happiness she'd never known.

She often encountered inscrutable glances from his dark eyes when she turned quickly and caught him looking at her. Still, David hadn't once given any verbal indication that he considered her more than a friend. That changed in mid-November when Julia received a letter from her mother. Puzzled that her parents had stayed in Missouri for so long, Julia had written asking the date for their return to Maryland. She was pleased at her mother's quick response until she read the short note.

Dear Julia,

Hadn't I told you? We're going to California before we come back to Maryland. You're getting along so well with Bobby. I'm sure you won't mind taking care of him for another month or two? Grandmother's hip is healed now, and we thought this trip would be good for her. Since the Waldens won't claim Bobby, no doubt you'll be returning to Maryland soon. We'll send future letters there.

Mother

Julia tore the letter to shreds, conscious of the inquisitive look that Nellie cast in her direction.

"What is it? Bad news?"

Julia clenched her fists and exerted all of her willpower to avoid being harsh with Nellie. "No one has died or is sick—nothing like that. I'm sorry, but I can't talk about it. Please look after Bobby until I come back."

Julia stuffed the letter fragments in her pocket and took a sweater off the hook by the door.

"Where are you going?" A frightened expression clouded Nellie's blue eyes.

"For a walk. I don't know when I'll get back."

"But Julia—"

"Don't worry about me." Julia forced a smile. "I just have to be alone for a few minutes."

Chapter Thirteen

David was chopping wood in Granny's barnyard when he saw Nellie running toward him. She was pulling a wagon with Bobby jolting up and down in the narrow bed, laughing as he enjoyed the fast ride. David anchored the axe in a chopping block and ran to meet her, his mind flooded with horrible scenarios of what might have happened to Julia. When Nellie saw him coming, she stopped and was still gasping for breath when he reached her.

"What's wrong?"

She shook her head. "I don't know.

Julia got a letter, and while she was reading it, she got madder and madder. Her face went white at first and then turned red as fire. She tore up the letter and left. Said she needed to be alone. I've never seen Julia lose her temper. It was scary!"

"Where is she now?"

"I watched until I saw her climbing the mountain in back of your cabin. I didn't know what to do."

He patted her on the shoulder. "You did the right thing. I'll find her. Take Bobby to Granny's and stay until I get back."

David broke into a run, but when he was halfway up the mountain, he slowed to a fast walk. He'd always sensed that something from Julia's past bothered her, but surely nothing so bad that she would take her own life—right?

When he reached the crest of the mountain, he stopped to get his breath. "God," he whispered, "You're in charge—I don't know what to do."

Sustained by the sense of God's presence, he quickened his steps until he came to a crossroads. Halting briefly, he turned to the right. "Julia," he called, "where are you?"

Every few feet, he stopped and called Julia's name. After his third call, he thought he heard an answer. He ran forward, still calling to her. He finally saw her leaning against an oak tree, looking down into a deep hollow. His breath caught in his throat.

"Julia," he called again. "Come to me."

She hesitated briefly before she started running in his direction. He hurried to meet her, arms outstretched. She flung herself into his embrace. "Are you all right?" he whispered.

She didn't answer but shook her head. He felt her body trembling against his chest, and he looked around for a place to sit down. He remembered a small cave nearby where he often rested when he was in the woods.

"Come with me," he said. "Then you can tell me all about it."

"How did you find me?" she asked in a choked voice.

"Nellie knew you were upset and came to tell me." He kept one arm around her as she stumbled along with her eyes closed. Her facial muscles were tight with strain, and he talked normally, trying to ease the tension he sensed in her rigid body.

"There's a cool breeze today, but we'll be comfortable in this little cave. Legend has it that Daniel Boone camped here."

Not receiving a comment from her, David said brightly, "Here we are. Look at the little bench nature carved out for us."

She lifted her head and looked around. Her eyes were filled with misery, and David knew this wasn't the time for small talk. He sat on the bench and gently pulled her down beside him, still keeping his arm around her waist. With his other hand he smoothed her hair, marveling at the silky texture of the auburn tresses. They had grown several inches since she'd arrived in Mistletoe.

"Nellie said you received a letter that made you upset." Recalling the messages he'd received from the man who was threatening his life, he thought Julia might be experiencing something similar. "Is somebody intimidating you?"

A bitter smile twisted her face. "No. The letter was from Mother."

"Is your grandmother worse?"

Julia shook her head. Tears flooded her eyes and spread over her face like a waterfall. David stared, realizing that this was the first time he'd seen Julia shed a tear. He pulled her into a tight embrace. "Oh, my dear! What can I do to help?"

Julia shook her head against his shoulder and between sobs muttered, "Nothing! It's a hurt I've carried since I was a child."

"Tell me about it."

As she talked, the trembling and tears gradually stopped until she spoke in a resigned monotone. "I was eleven months old when Margaret was born. Because of her frequent illnesses, she received special attention. I felt ignored. More than that, I was expected to do anything Margaret wanted me to do. I didn't mind that she was favored, truly I didn't, but I still don't understand why my parents couldn't love me too. I did everything I could to win their favor. I made good grades. I played on the basketball team because my father loved sports, but he never came to watch me play since the school games coincided with his bowling nights or lodge commitments." She sighed. "When I was crowned Mistletoe Queen in a fourth-grade pageant, neither of them attended the program because Margaret was sick. It seemed to me that she was 'conveniently' sick whenever my parents should have given me some attention."

After she gained control of her emotions, Julia continued to talk matter-of-factly about how her parents centered all their attention on Margaret. "I had clothing and food, and they sent me to college. We had a comfortable home, so I suppose I shouldn't have expected love too."

David ground his teeth in frustration. As she'd talked, he'd been able to look beyond her words and see an eager child always waiting for her parents' affection and never receiving it. Recalling the love he'd received from his parents and Granny, he realized what a void that must have left in Julia's heart.

"That's the main reason I enlisted in the WAC. I was still trying to do something to make them proud of me, but when I notified them about my promotions, they didn't seem impressed."

"What was in the letter today that upset you so much?"

"Grandmother is better, so Mother and Dad are taking her on a trip to California. Mother said that she was sure I wouldn't mind looking after Bobby for a few more weeks. She told me I could stay at Mistletoe or go back to Maryland. In other words, it still doesn't make any difference to them what *I* do."

Although sensitive to Julia's problem, David wondered momentarily about Bobby's future. If her parents didn't want the responsibility of Bobby either, what would happen to the child? His paternal grandparents wouldn't accept him, so he would grow up feeling the same way Julia did.

"You can stay here," he assured her. "We'll help you take care of Bobby."

Julia moved out of his embrace, and he wiped her tears with his handkerchief.

"No, I won't stay. Nellie has told me that the roads are sometimes impassable for weeks during the winter. It would drive me crazy to be penned up in this hollow. I've learned to love Bobby, and I won't neglect him. Soon after Christmas I'll take him back to Maryland and give him the kind of love I've always wanted."

David's heart swelled at her selflessness, her kindness. He took a deep breath. "I shouldn't tell you this, but I want you to know that *I* love you, Julia. I've loved you from the first moment I took you in my arms in Buffalo Creek and carried you to safety. My love has only grown stronger the more I've gotten to know you. So whether you're in Maryland or in Mistletoe, you can always know that *someone* loves you—even if it is a poor schoolteacher in the mountains of Kentucky. I can't promise you anything more than that, but I do love you."

David was amazed by the change in Julia. Joy spread across her face, and in one quick motion, she was in his arms again. His grip tightened around her.

"Oh, David!" Her voice was muffled against his shoulder. "Thank you." She pulled back to look at him. "Thank you for telling me. It's wonderful to know no matter where I am or what trouble I'm having, *someone* cares about me.

I can't change the past, but with God's help—and your love—I can face the future."

Softly she touched her lips to his. He knew instinctively that he shouldn't respond to her, but David's love overcame his common sense. His lips brushed her brow and her eyes, which had closed when he pulled her into a tight embrace. He kissed the tip of her nose, and then their lips met in a hungry kiss that lingered until Julia pulled away and buried her head on his chest. Although he knew he couldn't have a future with Julia, David had sealed his love for time and eternity.

* * * * *

Leaving David's arms was like moving from a warm fire into a frigid climate. His breath was warm against her face, causing her heart to race. She'd enjoyed a quick glimpse into Paradise, but she was as close as she would ever be. David's life was in Mistletoe, a place where she could never live. *Not even for David's love?* her heart questioned.

Julia reached out her right hand and

laced his fingers with her own. "Please forgive me for acting like a baby," she said.

"How long has it been since you've cried?"

Julia chuckled bitterly. "Not since the day I came home and told my parents I'd been chosen as valedictorian of my high school class and Mother said, 'That's wonderful, dear, but don't talk about it in front of Margaret. She would make good grades too if she wasn't sickly.' I knew then that they would always love my sister best and there wasn't anything I could do to change it."

David's black eyes resembled turbulent thunderclouds. "How *could* they treat you that way?"

Julia felt comforted by his anger. "To be fair, they have no idea how they've hurt me. I should have talked it out with them, but instead I've kept my frustrations bottled up inside." A sense of calm settled over her heart. "After I heard Pastor Brown's first sermon, I rededicated my life to God. I knew I couldn't be the kind of follower I should be with resentment in my heart. I've forgiven them, but God forgive me, when I received that letter today, the past swept back like the ocean tide and I lost control."

He kept his arm around her as they stood and walked along the trail. When it narrowed to a steep, downhill path, he asked, "What are you going to do now?"

Julia shrugged her shoulders. "Do what they ask of me, as I've always done. I've paid my rent through December, so I'll stay that long. I just hope I don't get snowed in before then."

A companionable silence settled over them. As they walked, Julia began to feel unnerved by her response to David's caresses and admission of love. She'd been drawn to him from the very first, but she had chosen to believe that he was no more than a good friend. During her war years she had avoided emotional ties with every GI she met. Whenever a serviceman made an overture beyond friendliness, she had a pat answer ready.

"I enlisted in the WAC to help win the war, not to start a romance or find a husband. If you want to be friends, fine; otherwise, look for another girl."

Considering the causalities of D-Day

and the number of soldiers she'd known who were killed during the invasion and its aftermath, she knew she'd made the right decision.

Her reaction to David was different. When he indicated that he loved her but had no intentions beyond that, she wondered if she had foolishly fallen in love with someone who was destined to break her heart. Did she *really* love David, or was it gratitude she felt toward him—gratitude that *someone* loved her?

Chapter Fourteen

Julia learned the answer to that question the last week in November, a week that would be forever etched into her memory. She had finished her manuscript and mailed it to the publisher. She had no other reason to stay in Mistletoe, but still she delayed going home. She excused her postponed departure by saying that she needed to finish the comforter and lap robe she was making as Christmas gifts for the area's elderly.

David had returned from his classes at the university the night before, but she hadn't talked to him yet. Asking Nellie to keep Bobby in the front yard where she could see them, she went to David's cabin. They sat, shoulders touching, on the front step while he talked about his studies and she enjoyed the scenery. The trees had turned varied shades of yellow, orange, and red in October, and the view that she'd always enjoyed had been more picturesque than ever. Now that many of the leaves had fallen, the forest floor resembled a multi-colored carpet. The evergreens were more visible, and the mistletoe plants made dark green patches on the limbs of numerous oak trees.

She saw a stranger striding purposefully up the hollow, and she felt David tense beside her.

"Do you know him?" Julia asked.

"I haven't seen him before."

Something in David's voice startled her, and she glanced at him sharply. The man came closer. He was young, probably still in his teens, and Julia marveled at the antagonism and hatred mirrored in his dark brown eyes.

David stood slowly. There was no fear on his face; rather, his eyes held a resigned look as he leaned against the porch post.

"Julia, you'd better go home."

She sensed danger and stood up quickly, but she didn't consider leaving David. A chill, dark silence surrounded them. As the stranger crossed the creek and approached the house, he didn't take his eyes off David. His expression was thunderous. Alarm rippled along Julia's spine.

She glanced toward her cabin, thankful that Bobby and Nellie were still playing. Her heart pounded and she started praying, sensing that tragedy threatened.

The stranger stopped at the foot of the steps. "Are you David Armstrong?"

"I am."

"Do you know me?"

"How could I? This is the first time I've seen you."

"Does the name Tolliver mean anything to you?"

David shrugged his shoulders, and his lack of fear seemed to anger the stranger. Julia gasped when the boy pulled a pistol from his pocket and waved it menacingly.

Swearing, he yelled, "I'm Lance Tolliver, and I'm going to kill you—you yellow-bellied murderer."

Julia gasped. David was an even-tempered man, but she didn't think he would overlook such an insult. His face flushed, and although he spoke calmly, his tone became thin and hollow.

"I don't know what you've been told—or who told you—but I've never murdered anyone. Deaths occur during a battle, but they aren't murder. My squadron of paratroopers was advancing in early dawn when your brother came running toward us. We thought he was an enemy. He must have become disoriented and turned in the wrong direction."

"He wasn't running from the enemy, if that's what you're hinting," the youth shouted. "He wasn't afraid of anything."

"Then he must have been the only paratrooper who wasn't afraid." David's voice was calm. "I shot, as did several other soldiers, and my bullet *may* have been the one that killed him. I don't know. We were trained to fire and ask questions afterward."

"Oh, yeah? One of our neighbors was in the same outfit, and he told me that with his dying breath, Adrian named *you* as his killer. Now I'm going to kill you."

"Tolliver, I knew your brother, and I liked him. I'm sorry about his death, but it's over and done with."

"Not for me! Our parents died before Adrian was drafted. He was all I had, and I don't want to live anymore. I'm going to kill you and then shoot myself."

Julia saw the desperate look in the boy's eyes. "David," she warned, and he waved her to silence. Then he turned his back and started inside the house. Tolliver lifted the gun.

"David, watch out!" Julia shouted. Tolliver's trembling finger tightened on the trigger, and in the split instant before he fired, Julia thrust out her arms and jumped in front of David. She heard the gunshot and felt a sharp pain in her arm before blackness engulfed her.

* * * * *

David hadn't thought the boy would shoot, but when Julia screamed, he turned quickly and caught her before she fell. Tolliver rushed up the steps and stared at Julia. With his left hand, David grabbed the gun out of the boy's hand and threw it toward the woods. He lowered Julia gently to the floor. Her pulse rate seemed faster than it should be, and blood was streaking her arm. He inspected her wound closely and thanked God that it looked superficial.

Lance Tolliver dropped to his knees on Julia's other side, and he was shaking like a willow tree in a hurricane. "I didn't intend to shoot her," he cried, tears streaking his face. "God forgive me. I didn't mean to kill a woman."

"Shut up, Tolliver," David said. "You didn't kill her. And it's a good thing you didn't."

David saw Nellie running toward them with Bobby in her arms. "Go get Granny," he shouted to her. "Julia is all right, but her arm needs to be bandaged. I'll watch Bobby." He took a clean handkerchief from his pocket and tried to stanch the blood running from her upper arm.

Nellie put Bobby on the porch, and he crawled toward Julia.

"Auntie sick?" he asked, his blue eyes puzzled.

"No," David said gently. "She's been hurt, just like you are when you fall down. Granny will fix her arm."

Bobby moved closer and patted Julia's arm. He lay beside her and cuddled against her body. She opened her eyes.

"What happened?"

"You got the bullet that was meant for me," David said, his voice shaking. During that split second when he thought she might have been killed, he had wondered if anything that had happened in the past was important enough to keep him from asking Julia to be his wife.

"It's just a flesh wound," he assured her, "but it's going to hurt, and you'll have a scar. I feel like shaking you. Why did you do such a foolish thing?"

She shook her head and closed her eyes, but he knew she was still conscious.

Tolliver slumped against one of the posts, his head in his hands. "I didn't know what it would be like to kill somebody. When she crumpled up, I almost turned the gun on myself."

Knowing the boy was on the edge of collapse, David attempted to distract him.

"Tolliver, go in the cabin and bring some towels from the kitchen cabinet. I'll try to stop the bleeding until Granny gets here." The boy stared at him. "Hurry."

Tolliver stood and on shaky legs tottered toward the cabin door.

* * * * *

Julia felt as if her arm was on fire, and she bit her lips to keep from sobbing. She didn't regret her action for a minute. She'd prevented terrible tragedy, and she thanked God that she'd moved as fast as she had. Her impulsive action had probably saved David's life. But she had to ask herself—why would she risk her life for his?

Her thoughts shifted to Jesus and why He had willingly died on the cross. He loved lost mankind so much that He'd submitted to the agony of a shameful death. On a lesser scale, when she took the bullet meant for David, didn't that prove beyond a doubt that she loved *him*? Why else would she have risked her life to save his? Was her love for David great enough that she would live in Mistletoe just to be near him?

Julia's eyes shifted to Granny. Although

Julia didn't believe that her regard for Granny could increase, the compassionate heart of the woman was never more apparent than in her treatment of Lance Tolliver. After she'd doctored and bandaged Julia's wounded arm and David had gently lifted Julia to the porch swing, Granny turned her attention to Lance. The boy was slumped against a porch post, his head on his knees.

"Now what's this all about?" Granny asked.

David explained about the death of Lance's brother and the threatening letters he'd been receiving from the boy. "He came to carry out his threats and probably would have killed me if Julia hadn't prevented it."

He flashed an indignant look in her direction, but Julia recognized the tenderness behind his displeasure.

"Where's the gun?" Granny asked.

"I threw it away."

"Find it and put it in your safe."

Granny sat beside the boy and tapped him on the shoulder. He lifted his head. "Go ahead and have me arrested," he said defiantly. "I don't care."

"Of course you care," Granny said. "What kind of upbringing did you have that you'd try to kill a man you'd never seen before?"

"I didn't have any upbringing," he said bitterly. "My folks died when I was a boy, and my older brother and I lived with our bachelor uncle. He hardly noticed us, but Adrian always looked after me. When he was killed, I didn't have anybody to care what I did."

"How old are you, son?" Granny asked.

"Seventeen."

"Unless Julia wants to press charges, we won't call the sheriff."

Julia shook her head.

"You look to me like somebody who needs a little lovin' care," Granny said. She reached out a hand and lifted Lance to his feet. "I'm takin' you home with me."

* * * * *

Using her injury as an excuse, Julia decided to stay in Mistletoe through the Christmas season. Granny had assured her that, while they often had a white Christmas, the heavy snows usually didn't start until January.

During the month of December, she

helped Nellie make mistletoe balls to
be sold in her aunt's variety store in
Maryland. They decided on an original
pattern. Julia bought all of the balls of
crochet thread to be found in Booneville
and ordered more through a Sears,
Roebuck and Co. catalog. Using straight
pins, they covered the balls of thread with
mistletoe and then sprayed them with
lacquer. When that dried, they attached
pinecones, vines, and berries to each
ball. To secure the items on the balls for
shipment, they covered them with strips
of nylon hosiery.

They mailed the first dozen balls to
Maryland, and when they received an
order for four dozen more, the entire
Armstrong family got into the spirit of the
project and helped them gather the
supplies they needed. David and Millard
shot numerous clumps of mistletoe from
trees. Nellie's brother and his friends
roamed the mountains and valleys
gathering pinecones, red berries, and
colorful vines.

They had one mistletoe ball left when
those orders were filled, so Julia sent it to
her cousin Annie Rose Walker in Noel,

Missouri, as a Christmas gift. After they'd mailed the last shipment of mistletoe balls, Julia and Nellie spent hours at the local post office helping the postmaster's family affix the special postmark on Christmas cards that were mailed to people throughout the United States and some foreign countries.

* * * * *

The change in Lance in the next few weeks was miraculous. He had gained weight, and he went with the family to church. He helped Granny look after Bobby while Julia and Nellie worked at the post office, and he even took over some of the chores so that David could devote more time to his studies.

One evening, Granny walked up the hollow and found David at Julia's house.

"I've been wantin' to talk to you about Lance. The boy ain't got any kin who want him. I've decided to give him a home."

David winked at Julia. "Don't you think you're getting a little too old to raise another kid?"

"No, I'm not. Not if the two of you will help me."

Tears misted Julia's eyes. "I don't know

how much longer I'll be here, but I'll help for as long as I can."

Granny nodded. "The boy hasn't graduated from high school, but he's sharp enough. If you and David will help him, he could get his diploma by mail. After that, he would be ready for Berea College."

David walked to his grandmother and placed an affectionate arm around her stooping shoulders. "God bless you, Granny. You know I'll help. I'll tutor him until he can pass the exams."

Julia felt that she was no longer grasping at straws for reasons to stay near David. In addition to helping Lance with his lessons, she became increasingly involved in the community's affairs. She went caroling with several of the church members and invited them to her house for cookies and hot chocolate afterward. She also drove her rented car to help Sadie Brown deliver gifts to the needy people in the area.

Julia couldn't envision a life without David, nor could she consider spending the rest of her life in Mistletoe. She felt lost in limbo until the day she went with

Granny to the family cemetery and became convinced that she must leave Mistletoe forever.

She had been curious about the cemetery but had never encountered it during her hikes through the woods with David. When she and Granny were walking home from church the first Sunday in December, Granny mentioned that she intended to visit the family cemetery the following day to prepare it for winter.

"I'd like to go with you," Julia said. "Where is it?"

"On yon side of the road." Granny gestured toward the hollow opposite her cabin site. "Lance will go, but we can use your help too. Take some heavy gloves with you."

As Julia dressed the next morning, she was thankful her aunt in Maryland had shipped Julia's winter clothes to her. She put on a pair of corduroy pants and a knee-length coat, wound a heavy scarf around her throat, and donned a brown toboggan she'd bought in Booneville.

When Julia arrived at Granny's cabin, she saw that Lance had filled a wheelbarrow with hoes, mattocks, and shovels. Granny handed her a sack of small wreaths to carry, which she'd made with pieces of fabric intertwined with pinecones and dried red berries.

"I kinda got the idea when I watched you and Nellie makin' the mistletoe balls. There won't be enough to decorate every grave," she said, "but these will brighten up the place."

Granny put a quart-sized jar of water and some sandwiches in a sack and carried it as they crossed the road and walked through a meadow for a half-mile before climbing a small hill. "Hit's a fur piece from the house," Granny said, "but when my man started the graveyard, he wanted to be sure it was high enough so's the graves wouldn't get flooded by Buffalo Crick. Hit's not easy to find enough level ground for buryin'."

Julia surveyed the burial ground, which was situated at the edge of the forest and surrounded by a rail fence. A few cedar trees grew within the cemetery, and she counted more than thirty headpieces. Granny set Lance to cutting weeds before she went to four small headstones in the center of the plot and bowed her head.

Julia stood beside Granny and read the crude inscriptions, JOSHUA, MARY, PAULINE, and JOSEPHINE. She assumed these were the graves of Granny's children who had died as infants. A nearby stone marked the final resting place of Elijah Armstrong, Granny's husband. David's parents were buried beside Elijah.

"He was a good man," Granny said of her husband. "David is more like him than any of my other kids or grandkids."

Granny took a mattock from the wheelbarrow, and Julia asked, "What shall I do?"

"Follow Lance and pull any weeds he can't get with the scythe. I'll dig up the roots of the big plants."

Wooden crosses marked most of the graves, but Julia eventually came to a small granite headstone that bore the inscription, ALICE ARMSTRONG AND INFANT SON, DAVEY. 1940.

"Davey? David?" Julia whispered. With a quickened pulse and a strange sense of apprehension, Julia called to Granny, "Who's Alice Armstrong?"

It was the first time Julia had known Granny to be jolted out of her calm serenity. "David ain't told you?" she stammered.

"Told me what?" Julia whispered, and the grim expression on Granny's face set alarm bells ringing in Julia's heart.

Granny drew a deep breath, and her arm encircled Julia's shoulders. "Alice was David's wife. He was only seventeen and Alice sixteen when they married. She died giving birth to a stillborn baby, and they were buried together." She shook her head sadly. "I'm sorry you had to find out this way. David should have told you."

Julia walked away from Granny and leaned against a cedar tree. She was trembling inwardly, whether from anger or sadness she didn't know. *Why hasn't David told me?* She couldn't say anything and didn't even look at Granny, just knelt by another grave and continued to pull weeds. Granny sighed deeply and whacked at the bushes with her mattock.

When they'd finished the work and started homeward, Granny walked alongside Julia. "There's somethin' else you ought to know. On her deathbed, Alice begged David to promise that he would never marry again."

Julia gasped and turned startled eyes toward Granny. "And he promised?" she whispered.

"He promised."

Julia's thoughts rioted as they walked the short distance, wishing she could leave Mistletoe before David returned from the university. She'd been here nearly four months, and the Waldens had made no move to claim Bobby as their grandson. She would leave for Maryland immediately if she hadn't promised the postmaster to help finish postmarking the Christmas cards.

Was there any way she could avoid David? She couldn't bear to talk to him now. He must know that she'd fallen in love with him. Why hadn't he told her about the vow he'd taken? David had proven by his actions and words that he loved her, but not once had he ever indicated that he wanted to marry her.

Chapter Fifteen

When David turned his Chevrolet into the
lane leading to his house, Granny stepped
out onto her porch and beckoned to him.
He parked the car and walked with long
strides toward her. His two days in
Lexington had seemed like a week, and
he was eager to see Julia. He was finding
it harder and harder to stay away from
her. He followed Granny into the cabin,
and the stern look on her face alerted him.

"What's wrong?"

"Why didn't you tell Julia about your
marriage?"

He slumped down onto the davenport.

"I assume that she *does* know now. Who told her?"

"I did. She went with Lance and me to clean the graveyard for winter. She pulled weeds around Alice's grave and asked who she was."

"How did she take it?"

"Poorly! I'm disappointed in you, David. You've always been forthright and honest. I don't know what's gone on between you and Julia, but a blind man could tell that you love each other. Why didn't you tell her?"

"I couldn't! She hadn't been here a day when I knew I loved her. I'm sure she loves me too. You don't know what an empty feeling that gave me—to know the only way I could have her was to break the deathbed vow I'd made to Alice. Tell me what I ought to do."

Granny sat beside him and put her hand on his shoulder. She could be very stern with her rebukes, but her voice was soft and warm when he needed comforting.

"My dear boy, I can't tell you what to do. In the first place, Alice was selfish to ask you to make such a promise, but we can excuse her because she was young and afraid of dyin'. I've studied the Good Book to see if you would be accountable to God if you didn't keep your vow to Alice. I haven't found any Scripture that deals with the promise you made. Best I can figure out, some vows *are* sacred. Any promise we make to God, we should keep. Wedding vows are sacred too. We promise to stay with the same man or woman till death parts us. I can't find anything in the Bible that has any bearin' on your vow."

"I made the promise willingly. What if Julia and I marry, and I always feel guilty? I suppose I'm like our ancestors who 'put out the fleece.' If God would give me some assurance that it's right for me to marry Julia, I'd propose instantly."

"I don't know what to tell you, but I can't see that anybody would be hurt if you didn't keep that promise you made to your dyin' wife. Continue to pray that God will show you what's right to do. Now, go to Julia—set things right between you."

David soon learned that was easier said than done. He went immediately to Julia's house. Nellie had gone for the day, and he thought it would be a good time to ask Julia's forgiveness. But one glance at her convinced him that she wouldn't listen to him.

"I see Granny intercepted you and told you what I learned today," she said in a tense, ominous voice that discouraged any discussion. "I can understand why you haven't wanted to talk to me about the situation. Now *I* don't want to discuss it. Please go home and don't bother me any more." She closed the door.

"Won't you at least let me ask for your forgiveness?" he asked through the door. Complete silence was her only answer, and his misery was like a steel weight in his heart. Bereft and desolate, David jumped off the porch and walked to his cabin.

* * * * *

Julia stood with her back against the door, wondering what she would do if David tried to force himself into the house. When he didn't, she knew it was all over between them. Bobby toddled toward her.

"Dade?" he questioned. She lifted him and carried him to a rocking chair, sat down and held him close. He hadn't had a nap, and he soon went to sleep. Julia continued to hold him while she considered her options.

It would be torture to live within sight of David's cabin and not even talk to him, but he had deceived her. He'd told her he loved her more than anyone else. What about his wife? If he'd been so distraught over her death that he'd fled Mistletoe and enlisted in the army, his love for Alice must have been great. Julia cringed at the thought that David might have said those loving words just because she'd acted like a baby and complained that no one loved her.

When Bobby finished his nap, she read to him for half an hour before she gave him a piece of chicken and some mashed potatoes that Nellie had prepared and put in the warming oven. She couldn't eat, but she drank a cup of coffee and listened to his chatter even though she had no idea what he was trying to say.

After Bobby was in his bed for the night, Julia lay on the couch and slept fitfully. When morning dawned, she had made her plans. She wouldn't return to

Maryland until she had finished her commitment to the postmaster.

"Hey, Julia," Nellie said when she arrived the next morning. "I stopped by the post office and picked up your mail. I think you heard from your publisher."

"Oh, I hope it's good news!" Julia snatched the envelope from Nellie, picked up a knife, and opened it. "Well, what do you know! Here's a check." She quickly scanned the letter.

> **Dear Miss Mayfield,**
> **We are very pleased with your manuscript, and we want to proceed with publication as soon as possible. Enclosed is a check for half of your royalty advance. After we return the manuscript to you for some minor edits and it's ready for the printer, we'll send the remainder of your advance. There's a great demand for war memoirs, and we intend to have the book in print by early next summer.**
> **I have another assignment for you, provided you are interested in taking it. Prior to the war, inhabitants of the Appalachian Mountains were**

somewhat isolated from the rest of the country. That changed when the war removed boundaries by involving everyone in the war effort. I would like for you to conduct a study on the mountaineers and their way of life as it is now, comparing it to the culture of the area prior to the beginning of the war. Now that you're acquainted with the people of Mistletoe, Kentucky, it seems that would be a good place for you to start. I'm eager to discuss this new project with you.

Julia felt like a deflated balloon. She had been resigned to leave Mistletoe, and now this new opportunity had been placed before her.

"God," she prayed mentally, "why has my whole world become topsy-turvy? I had fewer concerns when I was in the army!"

For the next two days she stayed inside the cabin, praying desperately to know God's will for her life. She hadn't yet written to her editor, either to acknowledge receipt of the royalty check or to accept or reject the new assignment.

She was cleaning Bobby's high chair on the third day when Nellie entered the cabin. "I'll take care of that," she said. "I'm sorry I'm a little late. The day is perfect, and I wanted to stay outside as long as I could."

"I'm just cleaning up the spills," Julia told her. "I do believe the child gets more food on the floor and chair than he does in his stomach."

"You've got to expect that from two-year-olds," Nellie said, as wise in the ways of children as her grandmother was. She hung her jacket on a wooden rack by the door. "I'm going to mop all the floors today, anyway."

"Then I'll go for a walk in the woods. I have to make a decision about that book the editor wants me to write. I'll put Bobby in the playpen to keep him out of your way."

Nellie chuckled. "I'll still have to watch him. He's climbed out of the pen a few times!"

To prevent David from seeing her, Julie entered the forest behind her cabin. After a brisk climb up the mountain, she walked by the cave where David had declared his love, remembering how happy she'd been that day. She'd thought her life had been complicated during the war years, but it was nothing compared to the frustration she'd endured during the past few months.

She wandered to a promontory, where she had a bird's-eye view of the church and Buffalo Creek valley. Julia sat on the wide ledge to get her breath and watched a few dried leaves drift lazily toward the ground.

What should I do? Indecision was driving her crazy. Until she'd met David Armstrong her life had been cut-and-dried, but since she'd come to Mistletoe, she had been on a merry-go-round. In her morning devotions, she'd read Psalm 27. The words of the fourteenth verse kept reverberating through her memory. *Wait on the LORD: be of good courage, and he shall strengthen thine heart: wait, I say, on the LORD.*

"But, Lord, I don't want to wait," she whispered. "I want to move on with my life." Why did the answers to her prayers leave her more unsettled than before she prayed?

Detecting a motion to her right, she looked up quickly. David leaned against a tree several feet away, peering at her intently. Her heartbeat pounded in her ears. The sun shone on his black hair, and he gave her an uneasy smile. Her eyes misted to know that she could never be a part of his life.

He walked toward her. "I'll leave if you say so, but I'd like to at least apologize."

She held out her hand. "I'm over my anger, hurt, frustration—whatever it was. I overreacted. But we can't be neighbors for the next few days and ignore each other."

He walked toward her, and she moved over to make room for him on the rock.

"I should have told you about my marriage," he said in a thin and hollow voice. "Alice's death was a terrible experience, and I don't like to talk about it. I thought Granny might have told you. Alice's family moved to Illinois soon after she died, so there are no reminders of her in Mistletoe, and I try to forget about the past. "

Julia laid her hand on his arm. "You don't have to tell me anything."

He covered her hand with his. "I *want* to talk now. It was the absolute truth when I told you that you're the only woman I've ever loved with my heart and soul. Alice and I were childhood sweethearts, and it was always sort of understood that we'd get married someday. There wasn't any great love between us. Still, she'd always been part of my life, and I blamed myself that she'd gotten pregnant. When I knew she was dying, I'd have done anything she asked. If she'd asked me to cut off my head, I might have done it. I made the promise willingly."

"David, it's okay."

He shook his head. "It isn't okay with me. I want to marry you, and hopefully you feel the same way about me. But I've been taught all my life to keep my word. What if we marry and I still feel guilty about breaking my promise? How would it affect our marriage?"

"It isn't an easy question to answer. Frankly, I don't believe you should be held to a promise you made under such stress, but I can't marry you anyway. Not even for *you* will I spend the rest of my life in this hollow."

He didn't answer, and with a long sigh she continued. "I've committed to stay here until after Christmas. I've contacted many of my acquaintances, inviting them to send their Christmas cards to be postmarked at Mistletoe. I'm not going to leave the postmaster with all the extra work. I'll plan to go back to Maryland between Christmas and New Year's. Let's at least be friends until then."

"It will be 'least' for me," David said. "But a half-loaf is better than none."

Julia slid off the rock. "I have to go and rescue Nellie from Bobby. I declare, I've had an education in childhood behavior in the past few months. That child changes from day to day—always something new."

David took her hand and pulled her into the circle of his arms. "We'll be 'just friends' in a few minutes." His large, tender hands slipped up her arms and clasped her body tightly to his. Having no desire to move out of his embrace, Julia buried her face against his chest. He kissed the soft hair that tumbled over her forehead.

"Look at me," he whispered. She leaned back slightly in his arms, and he kissed the tip of her nose. Soon his lips were warm and sweet on hers, and as she responded to his caresses, Julia wondered how she would ever find the courage to leave this man.

Sighing, he released her. "Thank you," he said softly. "I'll always have this moment to remember. When I'm lonely, I'll come here and think about you."

Chapter Sixteen

Once she decided to delay her departure, Julia made plans to celebrate Christmas in Mistletoe. She used part of her royalty check to buy presents for Millard's family as well as for Granny and David. Because she didn't want extra baggage for the homeward journey, Julia ordered only one toy for Bobby. His other gifts were new clothes. He'd outgrown many of his garments, and she bought a few outfits that would last him until they returned to Maryland. She intended to make the day a festive occasion. If this was her only Christmas with David, she wanted it to be one both of them would remember.

Julia had attended Christmas Eve services at home in Maryland for as long as she could remember. During the war years, chaplains had offered continuous communion on Christmas, and she'd attended those services too. But she had never anticipated any service more than she did the simple program planned by Reverend and Mrs. Brown in the Mistletoe church.

Snow flurries swirled around their heads as Julia walked with Granny, Lance, and David to the church. Astride David's shoulders, Bobby tried to catch the snowflakes in his tiny hands. Lance carried a lantern to light their way. The young man had adjusted quickly as a member of the family. Julia saw good qualities in him that would only improve under Granny's tutelage.

"I like a white Christmas," Julia said, "but I hope we don't have a big snow."

"Nothin' to worry about," Granny said. "We might have a dustin' by mornin', but the *Farmers' Almanac* predicts that snowfall will be light in the Southern Appalachians till early spring."

Her comment settled Julia's concern. Granny was always right!

Most of the benches were crowded when they arrived, but Pastor Brown motioned them to a seat near the front.

"Silent Night" had never been more meaningful to Julia than when she heard it played by David on his guitar, seconded by Millard on a fiddle. Several children presented recitations. David had persuaded Julia to sing "O Little Town of Bethlehem" with him. The applause was complimentary, and Julia herself thought their voices blended well. More and more it became apparent that their talents and interests made a good combination—an excellent basis for marriage. Resolutely, Julia shoved such thoughts out of her mind.

Mrs. Brown had just finished telling the story of the poor cobbler who had welcomed strangers to his home on Christmas Eve when a blast of cold air indicated that someone had opened the door. Julia turned to see a tall, gaunt stranger step inside. A stunned silence swept through the room, finally broken when Nellie shouted, "Robert!" and ran to the newcomer. He hugged her close before holding her at arm's length.

"So you've finally grown up," he said, leaning forward to kiss her.

Pandemonium swept through the church, and David hurried to the man and embraced him.

"Who is it?" Julia asked Granny, although she thought she already knew.

A peaceful, loving look shone from Granny's eyes. "It's Robert Walden, returned from the dead. Praise the Lord for a Christmas miracle!"

Julia eased down on the pew, because she didn't think her legs would hold her any longer. Her first thought was that her guardianship of Bobby had ended. *His father wasn't dead*. Her arms tightened about the sleeping child, and she suddenly realized how attached she'd become to Bobby. Could she hand him over to this stranger?

David's voice rose above the tumult of noise in the small building. "Hey, folks! We're all happy about Robert's return, and I know you want to greet him, but let's give him some air. Please take your seats so he can tell us what we want to know."

It must have been ten minutes before there was any semblance of order, but when the aisle was cleared and everyone seated, David and Robert walked to the platform. Robert sat in a chair facing the audience, and David said, "Tell us anything you want to. We don't aim to be nosy, but your parents got word that you'd been killed. It seems too good to be true that you're back among us, looking a little peaked, but otherwise alive and well."

"I've got a lot to say, but first, tell me about Mom and Dad," Robert said. "I came to Booneville on the afternoon bus and tried to hitch a ride to Mistletoe, but nobody was coming this way. I finally hired a taxi to bring me home, but the house looked vacant. I knocked and knocked on the door, and no one answered. Have my folks passed on?"

"No, buddy," David said, placing his hand on Robert's shoulder. "They're still alive. They took it hard when word came about your death, and they've never gotten over it. They won't let anybody come in the house. The mail carrier brings them groceries now and then, and once in a while your dad goes into Booneville to pay the taxes and take care of business. They couldn't cope with the world when they thought you were dead. You can spend the night with me, and when it's daylight, I'll go with you to see them. To know that you're alive will be the best Christmas gift they've ever had. But in the meantime, tell us where you've been. The war ended months ago."

"It'll take a long time to tell you all that's happened to me, but give me some water, and I'll give you the basic facts." He looked at Nellie, and a tender smile erased some of the tension on his face. "I don't intend to go far from Mistletoe for a long time, so we'll have plenty of time to catch up."

Granny came up the aisle, carrying a cup of coffee. "You need this more than water." She kissed his forehead. "Welcome home, Robert."

Tears filled his eyes, and he took a few swallows of the coffee before he could speak.

"I was captured by the Japanese

during the invasion of the Philippines. I escaped the Bataan Death March when the enemy took several of us to Japan to work in their coal mines. We were underground all of the time and had no news of what was going on. It was months after the war ended before the Americans found us. By that time, I weighed about eighty pounds and didn't know who I was. I suppose, to block out the horror of my mistreatment, I'd developed amnesia. I couldn't remember anything about my past. There weren't any records, and it took a long time to find the names of thousands of us who were reported missing in action."

While the audience waited in anticipation, he took another sip of coffee.

"It was a long time before I was physically strong enough for the doctors to deal with my amnesia. I finally remembered the name of a little girl named Nellie"—he flashed a fond smile toward her—"and a place called Mistletoe. Gradually I recalled events from my boyhood and my family life. By that time my service records had been found, and I learned I'd been married."

"But you don't remember anything about it?" David asked.

Robert shook his head. David motioned for Julia to come to him. She was trembling all over, and he took Bobby from her arms. "Then you don't know that you have a son. This is Robert Walden, Jr."

Robert's face blanched, and his blue eyes dulled with disbelief. Pastor Brown hurried to his side.

"And you're my wife?" Robert asked Julia incredulously.

The evening's activities had left her speechless. Julia shook her head.

"No, Robert," David said. "This is your sister-in-law, Julia Mayfield. Your wife, Margaret, died soon after the child was born, but she left a request for Julia to bring Bobby to meet his grandparents. She's been here several months, and they've refused to see him." He lifted Bobby's hands. "See, he has the mark of the Waldens."

Tears flowed from Robert's eyes, and Pastor Brown said, "Folks, I believe the kindest thing we can do is dismiss our services and go home. Tomorrow Robert can be reunited with his parents. This will be an emotional time for the Waldens, so let's remember them in prayer. We have much to be thankful for this Christmas season. God go with you."

The church seemed strangely quiet once most of the congregation had departed. It was obvious that Nellie didn't want to leave with her parents, and Julia asked Millard if Nellie could spend the night with her. He started to refuse, but Hattie intervened. "Yes, she can."

After they left Granny and Lance at her cabin, Robert turned to Julia. "I'm tired, but I won't rest until I learn something about my marriage. Can I talk to you before I go with David?"

"Julia and I are close neighbors," David said, laughing slightly. "If she doesn't mind, we can go to her cabin and talk."

She readily agreed. "I'd like that. I'm too excited to sleep."

When they entered the cabin, Julia took Bobby from David's arms, sat down in a chair, and rocked him until she was sure he was asleep. Nellie stirred up the coals in the stove and filled a pot with water and coffee. Robert watched her intently.

"Nellie, you're the first one I remembered, but I thought about you as a little girl. You've changed a heap since then."

She flashed a smile toward him. "I haven't changed in the things that matter."

"How old are you now?"

"Eighteen."

His eyes brightened. "Then you're old enough to make your own decisions."

"Yes, I am."

"Robert wanted to court Nellie," David explained to Julia," but Millard threw a fit, saying she was too young. Robert got mad and volunteered in the army."

"But why did you marry Margaret after such a brief acquaintance?" Julia asked.

Robert shook his head. "I may never know."

David took Bobby from Julia. "Robert, do you want to hold your son?" he asked.

"Yes," he said eagerly. "He looks like pictures of me when I was a baby." He sat on the couch, and David placed Bobby on his lap. When Bobby whined a little, Robert held him close and patted his back. "Tell me more about my time with your sister."

"I know practically nothing of your courtship and marriage to Margaret, because I was in Europe during the time. She had a part-time job in Washington, D.C., and met you there. You were married only three days before you were shipped overseas. My parents didn't meet you, but they knew that you were from Mistletoe, Kentucky."

David took up the explanation then. "Julia came to Kentucky to fulfill her sister's deathbed request that she bring Bobby to meet his paternal grandparents. She caught a ride with Tom Morriston, and I took her to your parents' house. Your father opened the door, but when she showed the baby to him, he went wild and threatened to kill her."

Robert's mouth dropped open. "That doesn't sound like Dad!"

"He's changed since they had news of your death. I need to warn you—they look terrible. I've only seen your mother a few times, but she's skinny as a rail, and your father's face is covered in a white beard. When it was warmer out, and Bobby would play outdoors, we're sure that your mother came into the woods and watched him. When we tried to encourage her to come closer, she ran away."

"This isn't the kind of homecoming I expected," Robert said. "But it's good to be home."

"I think your folks will snap out of their depression when they know you're alive," David said.

"Do you live here?" Robert asked Julia.

"No, my home is in Maryland. I've planned to leave Mistletoe a few times, but something has always prevented it. Now that you're here, I suppose I can go home knowing that I fulfilled my sister's request."

Robert's brows drew together in an agonized expression. "Oh, don't leave! I don't know anything about raising kids. And if Dad and Mom ain't up to par, what would I do with a little boy?"

Smiling, Julia said, "Nellie can help you more than I can. She took care of Bobby for me while I was working on a writing assignment. My parents haven't been at home, so I would have been alone in Maryland. I decided to stay here where I had some help. I didn't know anything about children either, but I've learned a lot." She smiled at Bobby's sleeping profile. "You will too."

When the coffee perked, Nellie brought cups to all of them.

"I feel pretty bad not to remember your sister," Robert said.

"Margaret tried to notify you about the baby. She had a few letters from you before your ship left San Francisco—nothing after that."

Nellie sat beside Robert, and Julia's heart was smitten. The three of them looked like such a happy family, and she was pleased for them. Yet she felt sorry for Margaret. The man she married had loved someone else.

"I have a photo album with a picture of you and Margaret on your wedding day. I'll show it to you. Perhaps that will help you remember."

"Let's wait until tomorrow for that," David said. "Robert, you look as if you've had enough stress for today. Let's go to my cabin, and we'll get up tomorrow and observe a Christmas Day that none of us will ever forget."

"Come over here for breakfast," Julia invited as the two men prepared to leave.

"Thanks," David accepted. "Granny is too busy preparing a big dinner to bother with us, and I don't have much to eat in the cabin."

"We'll wait until you come for Bobby to open his gifts. He was too young last year to enjoy opening packages, so I'm glad you're here to see it, Robert."

"I wish I had a gift for him."

"You gave him a father," Julia said. "He needed that gift more than any other."

* * * * *

Bobby was awake before Robert and David came the next morning, but Julia stayed in the bedroom and played with him until they arrived. Nellie had gotten up early to prepare scrambled eggs, fried potatoes, and ham. Biscuit ingredients were measured and the oven was hot, so she could finish breakfast as soon as the gifts were opened.

When Julia heard the men entering the cabin, she took Bobby from his playpen and let him walk into the living room. He ran toward David and held up his hands.

"Dade!" he screamed. "Play with me!"

David lifted him. "Here's somebody else to play with you now. This is your daddy."

"Daddee?" he asked, mastering the new word at once. Robert held out his arms, and Bobby drew back.

"Don't be afraid," David encouraged. "He's a nice guy. You'll like him."

With a little more coaxing, Bobby sat on his father's lap.

"I hope he can stay with you until I'm used to having a son," he said to Julia.

"I'd planned on returning to Maryland next week since I'd given up that your parents would accept Bobby." Thinking of the new offer from her publisher, she said, "Your return has changed that. I won't leave until you and Bobby get acquainted."

His eyes twinkling, David said, "You might get snowbound and have to stay all winter."

"I'll have to risk that. As soon as Bobby accepts his father and Robert has time to decide what to do with a two-year-old, I'll leave."

After they opened their gifts, Julia brought her photo album and showed

Robert the wedding picture of him and Margaret. The bewilderment on his face indicated plainly that he still didn't recall his wedding.

"It seems a little familiar, so I may remember eventually. My doctors said that there would be some things I'll never recall—for instance, the torture and abuse from my captors. I don't want to think of that, of course, but I feel bad that I can't remember my wife. If she's anything like you, she must have been a fine person."

"We weren't much alike," Julia said. She felt the envy for her sister and the hard feelings toward her parents disappear. Robert hadn't loved Margaret, but if she'd lived, she would have been troubled over his disappearance for years. His homecoming might have been a disappointment to her. And if he'd left her to marry Nellie, Margaret couldn't have dealt with that. She'd always had what she wanted. Finally, Julia was thankful that her parents had delayed her departure from Mistletoe; otherwise, she would never have learned to love Bobby—or David.

AN APPALACHIAN CHRISTMAS

Robert hugged Bobby to him and sighed. "I dread this, but I must go see Dad and Mom. Dave, you're a good friend to volunteer to go with me."

"I wouldn't have it any other way."

Chapter Seventeen

....

The snow wasn't accumulating, but snow
flurries were still drifting downward as
David and Robert walked down the
hollow. As they passed Granny's house,
she came out with a basket of goodies for
the Waldens, telling Robert she'd been
praying that the reunion with his parents
would be a happy one.

Looking upward to the trees as they
walked, Robert said, "Those are the first
mistletoe plants I've seen since I joined
the army. I thought about them and
Buffalo Creek hollow a lot during the early
years of the war."

When they approached the Walden home, Robert stopped and stared at the ramshackle house. "I can't believe it! It was dark when I walked up on the porch last night, so I didn't see how bad the place looks. It used to be the showplace of Buffalo Creek. How could the house get in such a terrible condition?"

"When they thought you were dead, your folks lost interest in everything."

"I don't know what to do except pound on the door and wait till someone opens it. If they don't, I'll force my way in."

David smiled. "I wouldn't advise that. Your dad keeps a loaded shotgun beside the front door, and he uses it often. He usually comes to the door when I stop here, and I have this basket from Granny. She sends them food every once in a while. Let me try to rouse him."

David stepped on the porch and pounded several times on the screen door. "Mr. Walden, it's David Armstrong. Granny sent you a Christmas basket."

Two or three minutes passed before David sensed that someone was peering through the window. Soon a key turned the lock and the door opened. Robert stood to one side, out of sight.

"Merry Christmas, Mr. Walden," David said. "Granny sent some goodies for you."

"Much obliged," Mr. Walden responded in a coarse voice, opening the door to take the basket. "And how is Mrs. Armstrong?"

"Right peart, as usual," David said.

Mr. Walden started to close the door. "Just a minute. I've also brought you something else." David moved aside and Robert stepped into view.

Mr. Walden uttered an anguished cry and stepped backward. David prayed that Robert's surprise homecoming wouldn't be too much for his parents.

"Who is it?" he croaked.

"It's me, Dad," Robert said in a low, tremulous voice.

"My boy! My boy!" Mr. Walden shouted. He turned toward the rear of the house. "Ma! Come quick. Our boy's come home."

Robert stepped inside the house and into his father's arms.

Tears streamed from David's eyes as he hurriedly left the porch and returned to

Julia's cabin. He stirred the coals in the fireplace, sat on the sofa in the living room, and drew a deep breath. What a day! Robert's reunion with his family. The big feast at Granny's. And finally, time alone with Julia. She was in the bedroom reading a bedtime story to Bobby after having convinced him that his gifts would still be there the next morning.

He picked up the photo album lying on the table and looked closely at the picture of Robert and Margaret. Knowing that Julia had always had to take a backseat to her sister, he tried to determine what kind of wife Margaret would have made Robert. He doubted that she had any of the independence Julia possessed. Margaret would have never adjusted to the rigors of Mistletoe, and it was apparent that Robert intended to spend the rest of his life here.

Half asleep, he idly turned the album's pages until he came to a photo that caused him to sit erect, staring in confusion. With shaking hands, he reached into his billfold and took out the "dream woman" photo he'd carried for years. Whoever had taken the picture had been closer to the woman than he'd been on the troop train, but there wasn't any doubt that the photos had been taken at the same time.

"Julia!" he shouted. "Come here."

"Quiet," she cautioned as she appeared beside him. "Bobby just went to sleep."

He grabbed her and pulled her beside him on the couch. He rained kisses on her hair, her face, and her hands. Startled, she leaned back in his embrace. "David, what's come over you?"

"Look here!" He showed her the picture from his wallet and pointed to the photo in the album. "It's a sign."

"I don't understand."

"Is that you in the photo?"

"Yes. A friend and I were picnicking along the Potomac a few days before we started to England. I didn't know she'd taken my picture until she had the film developed. Where did you get a copy?"

"It isn't a copy. *I* took this picture," he shouted, waving the photo in the air. "I was on a train. It slowed for a crossing. I raised the window and took your picture. I was on my way to the battlefields, and I didn't have any special person waiting for me when the war was over. I thought you were probably the wife or girlfriend of some soldier who was already overseas and you were thinking about him. I wondered how it would seem to have *you* waiting for me when I came home. I got the film developed before we sailed, and I've carried this picture in my billfold ever since. I had it in place of a pin-up girl beside my bunk throughout the war. You'll never know how many times I've looked at your picture."

Tears misted his eyes, and Julia looked at him questioningly.

"Don't you see? This is the sign I needed. I put out the fleece. If I received a sign that God didn't expect me to keep a vow unless it was made to Him, I'd know it was right for me to marry again. This isn't just a coincidence, Julia! It's God's way of bringing us together. Never in a million years would such a thing happen by chance. Will you marry me?"

Julia hesitated, and he sensed that she was counting the cost of becoming his wife. Suddenly she smiled and leaned more closely into his embrace. "Yes, David Armstrong. I'll marry you."

* * * * *

A week later, on New Year's Eve, David stood before the altar with Robert beside him. Mistletoe church had never looked so festive. Dim candlelight disguised the cracks in the wallpaper, the scarred furniture, and the peeling paint. Every seat was full, and several people stood along the walls. The homes on Buffalo Creek had emptied to attend an occasion that had never happened before. A double wedding, with two members of the Armstrong family getting married at the same time. And Robert Walden, a man who'd been given up for dead, was one of the grooms.

It also seemed like a miracle that Oscar and Mamie Walden were seated on the front pew of the church. Clothed and in their right minds, they had come to witness the marriage of their son, who "was lost, and is found."

David didn't know how they'd managed it in such a short time, but Julia and Nellie wore identical white dresses as they waited on the back row of the church for the service to begin. Their veils were held in place by crowns of mistletoe, and they carried small bouquets of the plant.

He wondered if Julia would have liked a more elaborate ceremony, but once they'd agreed to marry, neither of them had wanted to wait. She hadn't tried to notify her parents. They were still on vacation, and she didn't have any way to contact them. Knowing how disillusioned she was from the lack of love she'd received from them, David was determined that she would never again doubt that she was loved.

"The Armstrongs are my family now," she'd said.

They'd moved all of Julia's possessions to his cabin, leaving the rental cabin for Robert and Nellie. With the back pay he'd received for the time he was missing in action, Robert could afford the rent until he found a steady job. Fortunately Bobby was fond of Nellie and he would remain in the cabin with his father and new mother.

The service started when Mrs. Brown played softly on the piano and sang

"Love's Old Sweet Song," a traditional song for weddings in the area.

> **"Just a song at twilight, when the lights are low;**
> **And the flick'ring shadows softly come and go.**
> **Tho' the heart be weary, sad the day and long,**
> **Still to us at twilight comes love's old song,**
> **Comes love's old sweet song."**

Julia and Nellie walked slowly up the aisle to the altar, where the men joined them. Granny set Bobby on the floor and admonished him to hold tightly to the white box that held wedding rings for the brides. He toddled up the aisle and gave the box to Reverend Brown. Then Robert took his son in his arms.

The short wedding service followed, and after they'd each taken their vows, "till death do us part," the four of them repeated, in unison, words from the book of Ruth: "Intreat me not to leave thee, or to return from following after thee: for whither thou goest, I will go; and where thou lodgest, I will lodge: thy people shall be my people, and thy God my God: where thou diest, will I die, and there will I be buried: the LORD do so to me, and more also, if ought but death part thee and me."

* * * * *

Julia awakened the next morning in David's arms. She still didn't know how she would cope with living the rest of her life in Buffalo Holler, as the residents called it. Regardless, she'd chosen David's people for her own and Mistletoe as her home. Resigned to take one day at a time, she didn't try to envision what might cross their paths before she was buried by his side in the family cemetery. She hadn't taken her vows lightly—whatever it took to be David's wife, she was ready to do it.

After the night they'd spent together, she fully understood what God had meant when He said to Adam, "And they shall be one flesh." Perhaps the day would come when they would leave the mountains, but if not, she would stay in Mistletoe without complaint, make a good home for David, and bear his children.

She hadn't realized that he was awake until David pulled her close and kissed her. "How does it feel to be the wife of a mountaineer?"

David was struck dumb when her answer mimicked the mountain vernacular. "You're my man. Hit's my business, accordin' to the Scripter, to obey e'er word you say. I've put on my heavy yoke of wifehood, and I aim to toe the mark, no matter whar I'm livin'."

He erupted into laughter, and Julia joined him. Then he swept her into his arms, and after a pleasant interlude, she concluded that the yoke of wifehood wouldn't be so heavy after all.

About the Author

In a writing career spanning three decades, Irene Brand has won numerous awards and published nearly fifty books that have sold more than two million copies. Irene primarily writes inspirational romances, but she has also published nonfiction books, devotional materials, and magazine articles. Before she became a full-time writer, Irene taught for 23 years in public schools. Her other passions include traveling (she has visited all fifty states and thirty-five foreign countries) and history (she holds a Master's Degree in the subject). Her published titles include *Love Finds You in Valentine, Nebraska*, *Where Morning Dawns*, *Listen to Your Heart*, and the Kentucky Brides collection. Irene is an

ABOUT THE AUTHOR

active member of her church and is affiliated with several writing organizations. She is a lifelong resident of West Virginia, where she lives with her husband, Rod.

www.irenebrand.com

Love Finds You Under the Mistletoe:
Once Upon a Christmas Eve

BY ANITA HIGMAN

Nothing in the world is single;
All things by a law divine
In one spirit meet and mingle.
Why not I with thine?

Percy Bysshe Shelley

Prologue

....

One Christmas Eve a baby girl was left on the front step of The Little Bethlehem Shoppe in the village of Noel. The young mother watched from a distance, waiting until the owner of the shop found the wicker basket with the sleeping child inside. Then the young mother, a stranger to the town, disappeared into the night and was never seen again.

The shopkeeper, a kindly gentleman named Albert Goodnight, adopted the baby and named her Holly Rose. She became the greatest treasure in his life . . .

Chapter One

The people of Noel always said Holly
Goodnight was like a rock tumbler—that
she had a gift for smoothing out the
edges of other people's lives. Holly
grinned at the thought. *I probably have
more in common with a rock hammer.*

With a smile and a wave Holly breezed
out of the post office and then darted
across Main Street, just in time to grab
Miss Flora's arm as she stumbled on the
curb.

"Thanks, dearie." The older woman
patted Holly's cheek.

"No problem." Once Miss Flora got her

bearings, Holly kicked a ball back to a youngster before it rolled out into the street. The kid, little Perry somebody, didn't thank her. He never did. *The little knave.* Holly rolled her eyes at him and headed toward The Little Bethlehem Shoppe on Main.

A male tourist, a tolerably handsome one, ambled out of one of the shops, yanked out his earbuds, and stared at Holly as if she were wearing her reindeer antlers. "Hi."

"Hello." Holly felt one of those mysterious life moments coming on, when the casual gaze between two strangers takes a crucial turn. It goes like this: somewhere in the heavenlies an angel flips a switch, bathing the couple in a halo, suspending time while the two assess each other. For dating potential, love, marriage, children. Retirement. Term life insurance.

Get hold of yourself, Holly. The sweet alchemy between them, which may have been only in her imagination, vanished like a whirl of snow.

The stranger bowed slightly. "Good day, mademoiselle." He winked.

The man, who had appeared to be around her own age of thirty and who really was more than sufficiently handsome in a Hugh Grant sort of way, traipsed off, leaving Holly on the sidewalk gazing after him.

An early autumn breeze, chillier than usual, sent a shiver right through her, making her snuggle inside her red cape. It was just as well that the ogling incident hadn't turned into a coffee date. He was wearing loafers, after all. That couldn't have been a good sign. And tweed and tortoiseshell glasses and a skinny tie no less. So *passé*. Worst of all, he smelled like antibacterial soap.

She shook off her discombobulation and stepped inside the little red brick Christmas shop where all things were bright and beautiful. "Dad, I'm baaack."

Her father came from the storage room, embracing a pumpkin pie as if it were a long lost friend.

"You look flushed, Dad. You okay?"

"I'm merely famished from hunting down all the sweets you keep hiding from me." He took a forkful of filling from the middle of the pie and ate it without even the slightest expression of guilt. "Where are the red roses for the counter?"

Holly shrugged and replaced her cape with a velvet bibbed apron.

"So, you didn't make it back with the pot of flowers again?"

"Well, I ran into Vincent Hagerdey. He looked so sad about his wife that I—"

"You gave the roses to Vince to cheer up his wife." He grinned.

"She never leaves the house anymore with those inoperable bunions, so—"

"Bunions, my eye. The woman never leaves the house because she's addicted to the soaps."

"Well, that too. But I told Vincent to tell his wife that the roses would thrive if she just planted them outside. Maybe it'll get her working in her garden again." Holly opened her satchel. "Look, I bought you a present."

He wiggled his bushy eyebrows. "Did you get me any of those tea cakes full of white frosting?"

"You mean full of heart attack–inducing cholesterol? I bought you something useful." Holly pulled out a blood pressure machine she'd found at the pharmacy.

Her father mouthed the word, "Boring."

"Look, it's got all sorts of digital features. It even detects an irregular heartbeat. Isn't that awesome?"

"Well, *irksome* might be the preferred word." Her dad placed the pie on the counter. "Okay, Cricket." He gave Holly a bear hug. "I know the present really says I—"

"I want you around for a lot more Christmases to come."

Their foreheads dipped toward each other, touching. Always a nice fit. Even though her dad wasn't her biological father, God had cut them out of the same material. They had the same shiny dark hair and chocolatey elfin-shaped eyes, and they were both soft around the fringes, enough to make a hug feel like home.

Her father released her and then walked away with a grin full of mischief.

What was he up to? "So, did anything interesting happen while I was gone?"

"Lily showed up, and her pet mouse, Dracula, got out again. Sharp teeth, you know. There was a lot of screaming among the customers until we got him back in his cage, but other than that all was quiet." He disappeared into the back room.

Holly picked up her favorite snow globe and gave it a shake. The tempest of white encircled the castle and its tiny folk with enchantment. If only she could make life as safe for everyone she loved as the world encased inside that snow globe.

Her father came back into the main room with his hands behind his back, obviously hiding something.

"What is it?"

He had a twinkle in his eye. "Our store was just voted the number one Christmas store in America. This just came in the mail." Her father pulled out a plaque from behind his back and handed it to her.

"Really?" Holly studied the shiny gold lettering engraved on the wood, which stated those very words about their shop. Then she remembered their customers sending in a marathon of letters to a contest through one of the independent business associations. She'd never given it another thought. "So, it was all those notes people sent in. We have such good customers."

"Yes, and it'll only improve our business. We can add this award to all our promotion materials . . . put it on our Web site. And I'll call the newspapers."

"Good thinking."

"What a day. What a day. I think I'll celebrate with a nap." Her dad headed toward the back room again, doing a circling Hobbit jig all the way. It was great to see him so happy. Holly mulled over every angle of the news, located the perfect place on the wall for their award, and then busied herself dusting ornaments and singing "Ring, Christmas Bells."

After a few minutes of work Holly paused as she did every day to take in the wonder of the place—the old-world atmosphere, the golden warmth of thousands of twinkly lights, the angels suspended in the rafters. It was a bit like heaven come down to earth. God had certainly chosen a lovely place for her to grow up.

She stepped on a small ladder and gave a swish of the duster to the Christmas ball, a glass orb that held the cherished cluster of mistletoe that had been passed down from her grandmother to her father and now to her.

Holly gazed inside the ball, listening for whispers of the past. Not much left of the bouquet of mistletoe and berries and pinecones, but it represented a sweet story nonetheless. In 1946, as the tale went, a young woman named Annie Rose Walker received a package from her cousin Julia Mayfield in Mistletoe, Kentucky. The package contained a mistletoe ball, and when Annie held it up, the young man standing next to her—a stranger passing through town—swept her into his arms and kissed her. One day later he proposed, and Annie said yes. That was the history of Holly's grandparents! She knew stories got embellished over the years, but she liked to imagine all of it was true.

The shop bell jingled, and Owen Quigly—Holly's dearest friend since diapers—burst through the front door, smirking all over the place as usual. "Hey, Holl."

"Hey, Quig." Holly stepped down from the ladder. "What's up?"

"I heard the news about the shop."

She smiled. "Dad's right. News *does* travel faster in Noel than it actually happens."

Owen walked over to Holly and gave her the infamous elbow-rub, shoulder-bump greeting they'd been giving each other since the second grade. He wore his usual ensemble—jeans and a flannel shirt, which he claimed was the ultimate utilitarian attire for work, play, church, and in a pinch, bed. He pointed to the pie. "Pumpkin." He scooped out a hunk from the middle and stuffed it in his mouth. "Mmm. Your dad's getting better . . . no globs of eggs this time."

When the bell jingled again they both looked toward the door. A stranger stood in the entry as if he'd just burst through the saloon doors in Dodge City. On closer inspection she saw that it was the antiseptic loafer guy she'd encountered on the sidewalk earlier.

The man's face lit up when he saw her. "It's you."

"Yes, it's me."

"So you are . . . *the* Holly Rose Goodnight?"

"I am."

He pushed on the bridge of his glasses, making a production out of it.

"How may I help you?" Holly tried not to start her romantic assessments again. He was probably seeking her out on some business-related matter. Perhaps it had to do with winning the contest.

"Well, I, uh—" The stranger cleared his throat. "I'm Van Keaton." He announced his name as if there should be a trumpet flourish.

Holly walked over to him and shook his hand. "I'm glad to meet you."

"I guess you don't know who I am."

"No, I'm sorry. Should I?"

Van Keaton glanced over at Owen and then back at her. "Well, I was wondering if I could talk to you about something—in private."

Holly straightened. "Whatever you have to say may be said in front of Owen. He's like part of the family."

"Okay, then. I have a rather delicate question for you." Van Keaton stepped closer to her. "I'm just going to say it."

"I wish you would." To busy her hands, Holly picked up a snow globe and gave it a swish with her duster.

Van paused, catching her gaze. "Is it true that when you were a baby, your mother abandoned you on the doorstep of this shop on the night before Christmas?"

Holly's fingers lost their hold on the snow globe. She let out a gasp as the glass ball—with its tiny perfect world inside—crashed to the floor.

"Oh. I'm so sorry." Van reached downward, gaping at the mess.

Owen stared at Van. "I think you'd better explain why this is any business of yours."

Numb, Holly looked down at the shattered snow globe, the broken castle, and the pool of sparkly water. In one brief query, the man named Van Keaton had performed quite a magic trick by conjuring up a subject the town had been silent on her whole life—until now.

Chapter Two

....

"I'll pay for the snow globe." Van Keaton set a wad of cash on a display table. "And I'm sorry I came off so blunt. Well, blunt*ly* is correct. Hate poor grammar." He laced his fingers together. "But I really do need to talk to you *alone*."

"Being *alone* won't matter." Owen handed Van a broom and a dustpan as well as a trash bin. "This isn't a topic people talk about here. Especially strangers."

Holly crossed her arms. "All of what you said is true, Mr. Keaton, but I'd like to know who gave you the information. Are you a reporter?"

Van swept up the pieces into the dustpan. "It was an anonymous tip. I have no idea who—"

"This subject is painful to Miss Goodnight." Owen put his hands on his hips. "And so—"

"I'm not a reporter." Van pulled a handkerchief out of his pocket, knelt down, and began daubing at the water.

"Then who are you?" Holly tried to keep the edge out of her voice.

"I'm a novelist." Van wrung out his handkerchief into the plastic waste bin. "When I heard about your story, I thought it might make a great novel."

"A great novel." Holly pondered his words. "I thought writers were supposed to come up with their own stories."

"Yes, but some of the best books are based on true stories." Van kept using his hanky method of cleanup. "You know, creative nonfiction."

His efforts were so pathetic that Holly nearly chuckled. "I doubt I'd be interested." Really, though, she already knew what her answer would have to be.

She wouldn't put her father through such an ordeal.

Owen showed up with a wad of paper towels and started to sop up the water.

Van backed away and scrubbed his hands on a sanitizing wipe, which he'd just whipped out of his pocket. Then he pulled out a little card as well. "I'll leave my business card on this table. Let me know your decision as soon as you can. I'm only in Noel for a couple of days."

"Actually, just so you'll know, the name of our town is pronounced like the name Joel, not like the song, 'The First *Nowell.*'"

"But isn't this called the 'Christmas City of the Ozarks'?"

"Yes."

"Guess I'll have to do some more research about it online." Van scribbled something onto a notepad. "Nice to meet you both." And then the stranger walked out the door without another word.

"Odd sort of guy." Owen put the wet paper towels in the trash and looked over at Holly. "I know that must have been hard to hear—after all this time. Are you all right?"

"I'm okay." Holly grimaced. "I guess I

just never expected to hear my past described like that by a stranger." People in town had always known her history, and yet to hear the words spoken out loud had taken her by surprise. Unfortunately, Van's question still hung in the air like rotten mackerel, so Holly lit a few spiced candles. At least her father hadn't been in the room at the time. It would have made the scene much more complicated.

After everything was put away from the cleanup, Holly tried to put Mr. Keaton and his strange proposal out of her mind.

Owen lowered himself under one of the new Christmas trees. "I noticed you have some limbs dangling funny here."

"Hey, weren't you supposed to be at an investors' conference in St. Louis?"

"Postponed."

"You know, if I ever started paying you for all your work around here, I think I'd owe you about ten thousand dollars by now."

"I don't need the money."

"True." Holly stepped over Owen's long legs. He was such an incredible guy—all things kind and fun as well as handsome in his own boyish way. And even though he was wealthy, he never flaunted it. She couldn't believe some woman hadn't snatched him up. In fact, she could hardly believe someone hadn't snatched *her* up too.

"Hey, wanna go to a movie sometime?"

"Wish I could, but I've got too much to do with Christmas season coming." Holly opened a new box of ornaments and one by one placed them on the same tree Owen was working on. "Why don't you ask Marlene? She's always fluffing her feathers around you."

Owen huffed. "Yeah, and I know why. She just thinks my money will make a nice soft lining for her birdhouse."

"Oh." Holly opened up the branches of the tree, poked her head inside, and looked down at Owen. When he grinned, his dark eyes glistened at her. "Wow, do you know who you remind me of when I look at you upside down?"

"I look like Spiderman, right?" He cleared his throat. "You know, in that cool upside-down kissing scene."

"No, I was thinking you looked more like Gollum from *Lord of the Rings*."

"You are so cruel." Owen placed his hand over his heart. "Do you know that?"

Holly chuckled. "*You* were my mentor."

An all-out war of words commenced, and then they dissolved into a laughing, heaving mess.

When they recovered and Owen had scooted himself out from under the tree, he took on a most curious expression. It was a look Holly couldn't place, but then it disappeared as quickly as it had come.

"Hey, I've got a great new tree theme."

Holly gave Owen's curly red hair a flick with her duster to remove the dust bunnies. "Oh yeah? What is it?"

"For the ladies, a Jane Austen tree. It could be covered with faux candles, miniature horse-drawn carriages, tea pots, and antique books." He held up his finger. "And—"

"And tiny ball gowns, satin bows, and lace hankies shaped like fans." Holly pretended to fan herself and then gave Owen an affectionate shove. "Great idea, Quig. Let's do it for a summer promotion."

The front door jingled, and in rushed the four Westin boys—Jake, Jude, Jerald, and Jeremy—full of bluster and sticky fingers. Fortunately, their mom followed closely behind them.

"Hey, Sandra."

"Do you have any of those miniature Christmas trees?" Sandra asked. "Jake needs some for a school project. Oh, and I need five more boxes of those blue Christmas lights and three of those miniature music boxes I saw in the window."

"All right." Holly gathered up all the merchandise as Jake reached into her apron pocket for some candy.

"Better ask your mom first."

"Mom?"

Sandra nodded.

"Thanks." Jake lifted four pieces of sugar-free taffy out of her pocket as stealthily as a thief, popped one into his mouth, and gave one to each of his brothers. "Got a sorry grade in math." He waved a sheet of paper like a white flag, wadded it up, and tossed it in a nearby trash bin.

Holly retrieved the paper and smoothed out the wrinkles. "And did you see what went wrong?"

"Yeah, Mom and I finally figured it out,"

Jake managed to say around the taffy in his mouth.

"Cool." Holly folded the paper while Jake was talking and while the rest of the family shopped. When she'd finished her tucks and creases, she handed back Jake's math paper in the shape of an origami lion. "You were brave to face all that red ink on your paper." She ruffled the boy's hair. "Good job."

Jake pulled away, pretending not to like the attention, but his smile gave him away. "Sure."

When the purchases were made, Sandra walked to the door with her boys. "Thanks."

"You're welcome." Holly signed the words "See you later" to Jeremy, who was hard of hearing, and then waved good-bye to all of them as they exited the shop.

As soon as they were gone, Owen started gathering up gold plastic eggs from here and there around the shop. Apparently, while Jake schmoozed her for taffy, his three brothers were snatching up what the six geese were "a-laying" from a display and were "a-hiding" them like Easter eggs. *Very clever, boys.*

Owen looked at her with a quizzical expression. "Hey, Holl? I was just wondering . . . is your dad still retiring soon?"

"Maybe at the end of the year. Why?"

"I know you're always worried whether he'll have enough to retire on. So, I was thinking about that novelist, what was his name? Van something. Maybe it wouldn't be such a terrible thing to have him write your story. It could bring a lot of attention to the store. Might be good for business. You know, add to your dad's nest egg." Owen juggled several of the gold eggs and then let them land next to the six geese.

"Sure, Quig. I'll give it some thought."

"Holl?"

"Yeah?"

"I can tell you're blowing me off. I know what your mother did to you is hard for you to talk about, but sometimes letting things out is good. Telling this guy your story might not only be lucrative for the store, but freeing for *you*."

Holly paused and looked him over, surprised at his sudden assertiveness on the subject, and then nodded. "Okay. I really *will* think about it."

"For real?"

"For real."

"By the way, since we're on topics we don't discuss, I have something to tell you. Something important." He tapped his knuckles together.

There wasn't much Owen could tell her that would shock her, but she was curious about his earnest tone. "So, what astonishing thing do you have to tell me? Please don't say you're going to buy a pickup truck."

"No." Owen grinned. "I've decided to get married."

Chapter Three

....

"What do you mean you've decided to get married? To whom? You haven't even been dating anyone. Have you? I mean, I would have known if—"

"Holl."

"Yes?"

Instead of answering her, Owen walked toward the back of the store. Being his usual tall self, his head almost grazed the bottom of the beloved Christmas ball. How funny. Over the years Owen must have passed under the mistletoe a hundred times, and yet she hadn't noticed before how close he came to touching the heirloom.

Owen sat down on the loveseat, which was situated in the little space reserved for the children's story hour. "Come sit." He patted the seat next to him.

Sensing the seriousness of his request, Holly complied. "What is going on?"

"I haven't proposed to anyone yet. I haven't even been dating anyone. But all these years when I didn't seem too interested in getting married—well, I am now. I'm going to actively pursue *it*." He scrubbed his hands along his jeans.

"You say *it* like you're hunting skunks."

Owen laughed. "I hope it turns out to be more pleasant than skunk hunting."

"Depends on the woman I guess."

"Holly Goodnight, are you trying to discourage me in my quest?" Owen sounded hopeful for some reason.

She gave him a nudge. "Not in a thousand, trillion years would I do that. I want you to be happy. It's just, well, this news—it's so *huge*." Holly stroked her earlobe to help her think. "So, what in the world brought on this epiphany?"

"I guess it's been a lot of little

things . . . over the years. And as I grow older I think more about having a family."

"Wow, a family? Well, you *would* make a great dad. It's just going to take some getting used to." Holly tapped her shoes on the rope rug. "This is just *so* huge."

"You said that already."

"Because it is." She loosened her velvet apron, since the ties suddenly felt too constricting. "So, how are you going to find a woman to marry?"

"I thought I'd just put up a mesh trap during tourist season. See what it brings in."

"Come on, now. Seriously."

"I don't know yet. But if I can figure out how to make money in the stock market during a bad economy then I can figure out how to marry the woman of my dreams."

"I think the latter might be a tad harder. Falling in love with the right woman can't be easy. And then, of course, you've got to make sure she falls in love with you too. That could be a real problem." Holly took a piece of taffy out of her pocket and stuffed it into her mouth.

"You're right." Owen shrugged with mock surrender. "Sounds impossible."

"Not impossible, no. But love is as fickle as the weather. No, much worse." Holly had come close to falling in love a couple of times. "Do you ever think about destiny?" She handed him a piece of taffy.

"Not much." He took the candy but only toyed with it, twisting the wrapper until it tore.

"I mean, it's all so scary if destiny is real." Holly leaned down with her palms resting on her knees. "What if you pass someone on the sidewalk and that person is *the one*, but you just don't know it? What if you don't follow the trail of crumbs to your own destiny? Will that person come back and give you one more chance, or will you lose your one chance forever? Or if you lost your one chance, maybe it wasn't meant to be after all. But what you end up with, no matter how terrible, is really your real destiny." She looked back at him. "What do you think?"

Owen blinked. "I have no idea what you just said."

Holly rolled her eyes at him, snatched the candy out of his hand, and crammed it into her mouth.

"You sure you don't have dating confused with Russian roulette?"

Holly grinned and then pressed the tips of her fingers on her temples.

"Getting a headache?"

"Maybe." She chomped on the large wad of taffy in her mouth like a cow chewing cud. The peppermint candy made her jaws ache and her head pound even more, but she couldn't seem to stop herself.

"Here, turn around."

Holly did as he said, and Owen kneaded her shoulders.

"All right. That does feel better." She took in a deep breath and let it out slowly. "So, this decision you've made about getting married. I guess you've officially added this to your life list then?"

"You could say that. Right alongside setting a world record in a fruitcake-eating contest."

Holly leaned back on Owen, chuckling.

"Hold still now."

She straightened.

"What about you?" Owen massaged her neck and back. "I know you always talked about getting married."

"I'm not sure what went wrong over the years. It just never happened. I never fell in love. Not really." She swallowed a wad of candy and then packed another piece in her mouth. Perhaps the shop had consumed all her younger years, but it felt wrong to say those words out loud.

Owen stopped his massage and just held her by the shoulders. "We sound like a sad pair, you and I."

"We do." She relaxed and leaned into his touch.

"Holl, is there something else wrong?"

"No, why?"

"Because you're eating taffy like you actually like the stuff."

* * * * *

Holly closed the shop at five o'clock, which was a treat, since soon they would need to stay open later for the Christmas season. She sank onto the office chair and let her arms go limp. Her father had left early, and Owen had gone home only after she'd assured him there was nothing left to do. Holly filed a pile of paperwork, and then she checked out Van Keaton online to see if he was indeed who he said he was. The man had nine novels to his credit. Not bad.

Within moments, though, the rocking of the chair lulled her into a dreamy land of gnomes, and her eyelids weighed as heavily as her father's pumpkin pie.

Some minutes later she heard herself murmur the word "mother." The dark stage of her nightmare opened its curtain to her conscious mind, and she awakened with a start. Her dreams were almost always the same—she was a child again, peering through a keyhole, forever searching for her mother in a room full of strangers. She would catch a glimpse of her hair, her arm, and a trace of her perfume, but just before she saw her mother's face, she would awaken.

Here she was, thirty, and still unable to shake off the nightmares. Some part of her was still waiting for her mom—and probably always would be. Where did she go, and why didn't she come back? Holly had always envisioned her mother rushing up to the front step of the shop, out of breath and desperate to find her daughter. *God, I'm still waiting and wondering.* Holly looked upward. *Are You listening, God? If You are, now is a good time for a sign. You know, to let me know You've got it under control.*

She slipped on her comfy headband, the one with the fuzzy reindeer antlers attached to it, and stared at her computer screen.

A new e-mail popped onto her screen. Not from anyone she knew, though. When she clicked on the message it mentioned *The St. Yves Show.* Holly had heard of it, since it was a popular local talk show, but why were they e-mailing her? Surely *that* wasn't a sign from God. Then she remembered the award. Hmm. She scanned through the rest of the e-mail, hoping it wasn't a request for an interview.

It was.

People from the network had heard about the award, and they wanted her on the show within a matter of weeks. *Oh, no. Oh, no. Oh, no.*

Visions of her utter failure in high school speech class came back in vivid detail—the time she tried giving a talk on the history of her grandmother's mistletoe ball and passed out in front of the whole class. She'd hit her head hard enough that her teacher had to take her to the emergency room. Her classmates had tormented her about the incident until she graduated, and the memory lingered in her psyche as potently as a steaming cow patty.

I'll just decline the interview. There, she'd made the decision. Ahh, life was easy again. Well, *easier.*

Just as she'd finished typing out a gracious and articulate reply, she remembered her father's upcoming retirement. Any free advertisement would mean more sales, and that would translate into extra money for him to live on. Holly sighed. She couldn't possibly say no. Her father would call the invitation a divine overture.

Holly deleted her response and began another one, this time stating how pleased she was to accept the interview on *The St. Yves. Show.* She hit the SEND button before she could change her mind. Angry rumblings rose in her gut. So not good. She got up from her chair, turned off the "Silent Night" CD, snapped off the lights, and trudged out the front door.

The artificial Christmas tree on the outside step had toppled over again. Even the smallest puff of wind easily knocked the thing over. *Just like me.* She shoved the tree into the entryway and locked the front door. Why was she Miss Clever when it came to helping other people, but such a wuss with her own problems? And then it hit her. There would never be a good time to talk about her mother, to work things through. It was just easier to press out the crinkles in other people's lives than to deal with her own. How cliché.

Her subconscious had tried to take care of the problem for her, tried to force the issue. But the nightmares about her mother had only increased over the years, and if she didn't deal with her past, perhaps her troubles would visit her in a more potent way. Who knew what form it might take next. Addictions? Obsessions? Paranoia? After all, when someone squeezes a balloon on one end, it only bulges out somewhere else.

Holly felt a buzz in her purse. Knowing it was probably a text from her father, she glanced at her phone. It was Owen texting her, and for some reason he wanted to meet her at the pizza shop. Hmm. She buttoned up her cape, tightened her wool scarf, and strode up the sidewalk with the pesky feeling she'd forgotten to do something back at the shop.

The sky was looking more Gothic by the minute, but Holly didn't mind, since it meant Christmas was coming—only three months away! Just the thought of it was enough to lighten her mood. It was the time of the year to reflect on holy things, decorate the church, dress up the store, buy loads of poinsettia plants, and sing about geese getting too fat for their feathers. Holly let out a snort—a habit only Owen thought was endearing. Guess she'd better not release a chortle like that on live TV.

Anita Plumtree waved from across the street. She was always so friendly, but why was she pointing at her head? Holly remembered the reindeer headband and yanked it off. "Thanks, Anita!"

"I need one more postal volunteer to help stamp the 'Christmas City' postmark on all the Christmas cards coming through," Anita called out. "Can you help out this year?"

"Oh, I don't know. I'd love to, but we're always so busy during this season—"

"Honey, we're expecting over forty thousand cards and letters this year. Hope I can count on you in November."

Holly always found it impossible to say no to the woman. "All right, all right, count me in." She waved back at Anita and then opened the door to the pizza parlor. The scent of rising dough and simmering toppings filled her nostrils. Mmm. A hug for the senses. *Such pleasant memories in this cozy place.* She had just raised her hand to wave to Owen, who was sitting in their usual booth, when she noticed he wasn't alone.

Uh-oh.

Van Keaton, the novelist, sat across from him. So, Quig and Keaton had set up an ambush.

Chapter Four

Owen shot Holly the peace sign as he tried to read her expression. She didn't look pleased to see Van. *And she's not too pleased to see me either.* He reached for another napkin since he'd already torn the first one into bits.

Holly ordered a hot chocolate—a double—and strode over to the table. "I've changed my mind."

Van brightened. "Really? You've changed your mind about the interview?"

"No." She leaned on the table. "That I won't give Owen a good thrashing for inviting you here."

Owen's chuckle came out more jittery than he'd intended.

Van joined in the laughter, but he had a microcosm of terror in his eyes.

Owen pulled out a chair for his dearest friend. "Sit . . . please."

Holly slapped her antlers on the table and sat down.

With a bit of flair Owen pushed a fresh-out-of-the-oven, deep dish, everything-on-it pizza in front of her. It was what she always ordered.

Holly's eyes narrowed into a half-lidded glint as she looked back and forth at them both. "So, is this a bribe?"

Van winced. "Is it working?"

"We'll see. I think I deserve to hear your most convincing spiel." She reached for a large, gooey slice of pizza, slid it onto a plate, and dug in.

Owen thought Holly enjoyed their squirming a bit too much. "It's pretty simple, I think," he said before Van had a chance to reply. "As I said earlier, it really might be a healthy thing for you to talk about your mother and what happened. And this might be a good way for you to let it out. And it might help other people who've experienced . . . something similar."

Genie, the waitress, came over with a huge mug of hot chocolate.

"Thanks, Genie. Put it on *their* tab." Holly grinned.

"Be happy to." Genie picked up the ticket and sashayed away.

Holly dabbed her mouth with a napkin. "I realize it was only a matter of time before someone brought this up."

"I wanted to say—" Van folded and unfolded his hands. "I wanted to say how sorry I am for the way I approached you earlier. Totally botched it."

"Yes, you did botch it." She stared into her cup. "Apology accepted." Holly took a sip of her beverage. "When I was a kid, I would sometimes ask questions about my mother, but every time I did, I could see the pain in my father's eyes. He knew nothing about her really, so it was an impossible situation. So I let it go. Now he's older, and I'm afraid that if I wallow in the topic too much, or if I try to search for my mother, it might be too much for his heart."

Owen touched her hand. "But not

talking about the past—not facing the anger and confusion you must feel over what your mother did—may cause *you* health problems someday. And I know your father wouldn't want that."

Holly cringed. "Who said anything about anger?"

Owen looked down at her fingers as she squashed her pizza into a wad.

She stared at her hands. "Okay, maybe I'm a little angry." She sighed. "I *might* consider this proposition—if my father approved."

"He does approve," Van said.

"Oh yeah? How could you possibly know that?"

Van winced. "Because I saw your father on Main Street earlier and asked him."

She dropped her pizza onto the plate. "What—what would make you do such a thing?"

"Stupidity." Van smiled.

"I have to agree with you there." Holly pursed her lips. "What did my father say . . . exactly?"

Van took a deep breath. "He said he'd always wanted you to settle things in your mind about your mother, and so this book might be a godsend for you."

"A godsend. My father said that?" Holly ran her finger along the edge of the table.

Van nodded. "Your father said he'd wanted to talk to you about the subject, but it always seemed to upset you."

"Upset *me*? I can hardly believe it." Holly sank back in her chair. "And here I never broached the topic because I feared it would worsen his health." She mumbled as if speaking to no one. "What a terrible miscommunication we've had all these years."

Owen had guessed at Holly's reasons for not talking about her abandonment, but he'd never imagined that Mr. Goodnight had buried the past for the same reasons—only in reverse. *What an unfortunate misunderstanding.* He reached out to Holly and squeezed her hand. He could barely stand to see her shoulders sag from the weight of the news. He would have taken her into his arms to comfort her if Van weren't inches away.

"I guess sometimes it takes a stranger to shake things up," Holly said to Van, "to make us see what has become totally obscured." She pushed her hair away from her face. "Before I give you my answer about the book, I have some questions for you."

"Anything at all."

"Why would an author of your caliber need my story?" Holly picked up another large piece of pizza. "I looked you up online, and you have lots of books out. None of those novels were true stories—were they?"

"Not one of them." Van organized the condiments like he was lining up an army of defenses.

Holly placed her hands over his, which stopped his fidgeting. "You obviously know how to tell a good story without me. Why take my personal tale of woe when your head is full of them?"

Van pulled free from her grasp. "Good question. I guess it's because I want to do things differently now. People like stories that are based on something true. It makes them invest their hearts more . . . deeply."

Owen wasn't buying his answer.

Holly seemed to study Van. "This is

just a feeling, but I think you're holding something back."

That a girl, Holl.

"Okay, you're not going to let me get by with anything. That's a good start." Van grinned. "You see, I have my own tale of woe." He downed the last of his water.

Van was stalling for some reason. Owen cleared his throat.

"Okay." Van looked at them both. "You saw my Web site, but what you didn't see were my book sales. They have been declining significantly—with my last two books especially. My publicist is concerned. Jerry, my agent, is concerned. *I'm* concerned. My publisher has been gracious, but even *I* wouldn't trust me again. So, you're my only hope, Holly." He put his hands up. "No pressure, of course."

"Your whole failing career is in my hands, and there's no pressure?" Holly chewed on her lip.

"Let me word it more tastefully," Van said. "I think one of my problems is that lately I've had no passion for my stories, my characters. And readers are intuitive. They can sense these things. So when I heard about your story I thought this could be . . . well, destiny."

Holly's face was suddenly awash with solemnity as she pressed her hand over her mouth.

Bingo. Van hit the jackpot with his word choice. Owen wasn't quite sure why women got so enamored with the word *destiny.* It was definitely overrated.

Holly took hold of Van's sleeves so he couldn't move his arms. "If we do this, I can't promise you my story will sell more books for you."

Van straightened. "And *I* can't promise that talking through your past will help you move on."

"Okay, fair enough." Holly released him. "But one more thing . . . I don't really think my life has enough story. I mean, I was left there on the doorstep of the Christmas shop, and we have no more information than that."

"When a book is based on a true story, writers are usually given some leeway. Poetic license."

"In other words, you're going to fill in the gaps of my life like smearing putty in a crack."

"Yes—some putty will have to be added here and there." Van poured some water onto a napkin and daubed at his mouth.

Owen hoped Holly would be fine with all the sudden attention. Opening up a delicate subject that had been closed for so long might be more painful for her than he'd first imagined. And he hadn't given much thought to the actual interviews or the final manuscript. "What if Holly doesn't like the putty you use?"

Holly took a deep breath. "Good question, Quig."

"All right," Van said. "I won't be writing anything that would be contrary to your beliefs—nothing that would tarnish the integrity of your life."

"Okay, good reply. But there's no grand finale to my story. No happy ending. Will you need to manufacture that too?" Holly asked.

"I don't think so," Van replied. "You seem like a well-adjusted woman who is loved by her adoptive father and who helps run a Christmas shop that has just won a national award for excellence. I think there's a happy ending already there. Don't you?"

"I do." Holly smiled.

"Good." Van picked up his water glass, circled it away from his pizza around the outside of the table, and then lifted it to his mouth.

Holly chuckled. "That's an odd way to drink water. Sort of the long way around."

Van laughed. "Well, I'm kind of a germ freak. I didn't want to drip any condensation from the bottom of my water glass onto my pizza."

Owen stared at Van. *Excuse me?* "Yeah, but your water glass is clean."

"True." Van pointed to the bottom of his glass. "But the underside of my water glass has been sitting on this table, which might or might not be clean." He raised his eyebrows. "You know, direct contact."

Owen didn't quite know what to make of Van's bizarre confession, but his mind was flashing the word *loon*. "This table may not be sterile enough for open-heart surgery, but it's plenty—"

"Hey, don't get the wrong idea," Van said. "I'm not crazy. I'm just a writer. All writers have your basic phobias, obsessions, and compulsive disorders. It's all pretty standard stuff. Comes with the territory. You know, like birds trying to fly into a pane of glass."

Owen wasn't sure how the examples paralleled, but he let it go.

"I guess I've heard of that." Holly pulled the last piece of pizza off the platter. "I suppose those kinds of issues don't matter as long as they don't interfere with your life too much."

Van smiled at her as if she'd handed him a brick of gold bullion. "Thanks for saying what you just said." He sniffed the air as if it were scented with posies. "It's sort of liberating to hear those words out loud."

Owen refrained from rolling his eyes, which was the reaction he'd expected from Holly. But she merely seemed pensive.

"Hope *this* makes you feel better too." The waitress handed Van the bill.

Owen leaned against the brick wall and gave Van another study. Guess he seemed harmless enough, but Owen certainly wasn't going to invite the man to his house. He'd probably want to alphabetize his frozen entrees or sanitize his laptop.

"There's one more thing I need to

mention," Van said to Holly. "Your life story will be an open book now—not only to me but to tens of thousands of readers. I'm hoping that'll be something you can live with."

"Tens of thousands?" Holly stopped mid-bite and looked at Owen.

Was he encouraging her to do something she would forever regret? Owen paused for a moment. Was he dealing with fate or feeble-mindedness? Hard to know. He gave her a nod. *God, forgive me if I'm wrong.*

Van leaned forward in his chair. "Well, what is your final answer, Miss Goodnight?"

Chapter Five

While staring at her trembling fingers, Holly suddenly remembered Julia Mayfield, her grandmother's cousin—the one who'd sent the amazing mistletoe ball. Julia had also been an author. Was it a sign? She doubted it. Too much of a stretch. And yet? She slowly nodded her head at Van, hoping she was making the right decision. Maybe sharing her story really would help other women who'd known abandonment. "My answer is yes." She reached out to Van and gave his hand a good shake. It felt a little like latching onto a giant gummy worm, but his expression seemed warm and genuine.

"Since we're in agreement, I'll stay in the area for a couple of weeks. If it's convenient, I'd like for us to get started right away." Van whipped out his credit card.

"I'm getting ready for the tourists, but—"

"Tourists?"

"We're gearing up for the Christmas season. I guess you could ask me some questions in the evenings." Holly wondered what kind of time commitment Van was talking about.

"Maybe you could take me to some of your local haunts."

Owen nodded. "Why don't you take Van out to Short Bottom?"

"Do I even want to know what that is?" Van steepled his fingers up and down like a spider on a mirror.

Holly frowned. What was Owen thinking, giving away their secret place—their little refuge ever since they were kids? "Short Bottom is just this tiny wild cave, you know, *way* outside of town. It's not a show cave or anything. Actually, there're thousands of wild caves in Missouri, so it's—"

"Short Bottom sounds intriguing." Van perked up. "But wouldn't we be trespassing?"

"A friend of ours owns the land, so we've always had permission to be there." Owen grinned.

What was Owen up to? "But there's always the coffee shop. It's a great place to meet. It's quiet, easy to get to, and I'll buy the coffee."

Loud voices erupted at a nearby table. Two men were apparently disagreeing about the railroad explosion of '69, a topic that still made the rounds in Noel.

When the discussion calmed, Van turned back to them. "This wild cave, Short Bottom, will give the book some local color. Just like everything else that's so quaint about this town. Like the winding roads. The signs that read, 'Noel, Where the River Runs.' And the American flags everywhere. This is great. Very Mayberry-ish."

Holly couldn't have agreed more, but Short Bottom was off-limits. "The cave isn't very bright. I'm sure you won't be able to take notes." She stared at Van over her cup of chocolate, still hopeful to turn things around. "And wild caves are notorious for being *dirty*."

Van shook his finger at her. "But it's nature's dirt. Totally different thing. I'm pretty cool with that. And I have a digital voice recorder, so I don't have to write down my notes."

"Holly, why don't you want Van to see Short Bottom Cave?" Owen appeared deep-fried in bafflement. "And why are you kicking me under the table?"

Holly rolled her eyes. There were times when men were so clueless, she wondered how they ever navigated spoons to their mouths at mealtimes.

Van beamed like a kid who'd just gotten an adult joke.

Her insides shriveled. "Okay. Short Bottom Cave it is." She retrieved a hair clip from her purse, twirled her long bob up on her head, and fastened it in place. "But we'll have to hurry before it gets dark."

* * * * *

Van folded himself up in the passenger seat of Holly's Smart Car, and together they rode past the sign welcoming people to Noel, Missouri, past her favorite bluff, and past rolling hills dotted with cattle. Van took in the view with only occasional comments and dictations into his voice recorder, but Holly was reminded once again why she'd never moved away from Noel. *It would be such a great place to raise kids.* She sighed, not knowing how long the wait would be. "Okay, Van, here we are."

"So, is the cave in that cliff over there?"

"Yep. We'll have to walk now. I think your loafers might get muddy."

"I can handle it."

"Okay, your call." Holly retrieved two flashlights from the back of her car, and they started their hike through a grassy field. Once they were near the cliff, Holly lifted a few tree limbs out of their way. They waded through underbrush for a while until they came to the mouth of the cave, which appeared like a black-eyed ogre on the hillside.

Van stayed just behind her. "This really is hidden from the road, isn't it?"

"Almost no one knows about this cave,

and it's hard to keep a secret in Noel."
Holly stepped along a rocky path and into
the grotto.

Van held back for a moment and then
followed her into the cave. "Any bats in
here?" His voice had a slight echo.

"You scared of bats?"

Van chuckled. "If I came across a bat,
I'd get anaphylactic and probably go into
cardiac arrest. Nothing major."

Holly shook her head at him. "How do
you live?"

"I manage. But I happen to think there's
a lot to be scared about in this life."

"True enough." Holly turned on the
flashlights, handed one to Van, and then
sat down on a boulder in the middle of
the cave.

Van shined the beam around the
space, studying each nook and cranny as
if he were Sherlock Holmes looking for
clues. "I understand the name of the
cavern now. Not very deep."

"It's just a name Owen and I came up
with when we were kids. And it stuck."

"Kind of damp and musty in here, but
it's at least warmer than that cold wind
outside." Van leaned against the back

wall and shined his light through a fissure in the rock. "I see a crack here. And I hear the sound of dripping water. Has anyone ever tried to get through this opening?"

"Even when we were skinny kids we couldn't squeeze through."

"I'm surprised no one has tried to break through the rock to see what's beyond this room. I mean, the largest cave in the world might be just beyond this wall."

Holly grinned. "I've dreamed of it too, but the owner isn't interested in checking it out, so for now, it's just Short Bottom Cave. Maybe that's why Owen and I made this our place. There's mystery in not knowing what lies beyond that wall. And there's such quiet here."

"'Far from the madding crowd'?" Van took out a handkerchief, dusted off the boulder, and eased down next to her.

"Not many crowds in Noel unless it's a tourist season. But yes, I do like this place."

Van took off his glasses and slipped them into a pocket. "Do you come here by yourself sometimes?"

"Yes." She looked over at Van.

"Sometimes." Without his glasses on she could tell he had gray eyes with bits of green, like a pretty stone found in a pool of water.

"Aren't you afraid to be alone way out here?"

"Afraid of what?" What did he mean? Holly rose and strolled to the north wall of the cave. The heebie-jeebies ran through her as she realized that while Van seemed like a decent man, he was still a stranger. She searched his eyes for any serial killer qualities, but what she saw didn't seem scary. She saw a writer with some benign neuroses and a ghastly sense of fashion. Amusing combo, but probably not too dangerous.

"Sorry, that's a city boy talking. I guess small towns really are a sanctuary from all things fast-paced and fearsome." He rested back on his hands, and for the first time, she saw glimmers of serenity in him. He wore it well.

Holly also mellowed as her gaze drifted around the room. Rays of light from the sunset filtered in through the foliage and fell on the far wall, enhancing the yellow hues of the limestone. The cave took on

a warm golden glow—like a topaz.
Beautiful. But unfortunately it was just
enough sunlight to illuminate the thing
dangling just above Van's head. A small
leathery creature.

A bat.

Chapter Six

Holly took in a slow breath to control her emotions. Should she tell Van? Would he freak out? Yes. Van would wind himself up so tightly he'd spin right off the planet. It was a tiny bat, and almost cute, but she was pretty sure he wouldn't see it that way. What if he never looked up? What if he never knew about the bat? After a few frantic moments spent weighing pros and cons, Holly allowed ignorance to reign in Short Bottom. But her decision still couldn't keep sweat from breaking out all over her body.

Van reached into the inside pocket of

his coat and pulled out a musical instrument, which looked like some sort of bamboo flute. He raised it to his lips and started to play.

Now that was about the last thing Holly had expected Van to do—pull a flute out of his pocket like some pied piper. The sweet but woebegone melody echoed through the hollow cave. Lovely and lonely and irresistible. The kind of music that summoned fairies. Holly just hoped it wasn't the kind of music that summoned bats.

When the tune came to a close, Holly applauded while keeping an ever-present eye on the creature. It apparently wasn't moved by the music. *Thank You, God.* "That sounded enchanting. What was the tune?"

"Something I wrote a long time ago. I've never played it for anyone until now. Guess I was waiting for the right ears to hear it." He looked at her. "I've waited a long time."

Holly felt as if she'd burrowed her face into a warm load of clothes straight out of the dryer. "Do you often whip out your flute while wild caving?"

"Only when the spirit moves me—as it does now, Holly Rose."

The man did have a nice smile. "Oh?"

"I'm not always moved, but I'm always observing." Van slid the bamboo flute back into the inner pocket of his coat and looked at her. Really looked at her. "I think of myself as a historian of sorts—a recorder of life. Sometimes this calling of mine is a great burden to me, and at other times it's such an intoxicating pleasure that human terms can't define it suitably."

Holly didn't miss the lush quality of his voice or that smoking-jacket gaze he gave her. "And what are you recording right now, Mr. Keaton?"

"Well, if you were a character out of my imagination, I would place you within the fairy archetype, which is a very good place to be. You have a mystical quality, and people are a little bewitched while they're around you. Even now, you have an angelic glow about you."

Holly tossed her head back, chuckling. *Yeah, that glow is really perspiration because of the bat suspended over your head!*

"There's more." He raised his hands.

"You think you're simply Holly, but you're much more than that. You have gifts of the heart you don't even recognize. You have the ability to change a person's life in an instant. You give of yourself, but you're holding something back. Maybe something you've tried to hide even from yourself."

"But everyone is holding something back. Even you."

"Even me." His answer came more as an echo of her words than a confirmation.

Holly put her hands behind her and leaned against the cave wall. "You've made me curious about something." Or maybe she just wanted to change the subject.

"I love curiosity. It's the fuel that propels my life."

"I was wondering how writers see the world. Do you see it differently than the average person? Let's say we were strolling in a rose garden. What would you see beyond the flowers and the sun and the honeybees?"

Van picked up a flashlight and pointed it around the cave, making eerie shadows on the wall but continually missing the bat with his beam of light. "Garden. I might see the drooping head of a rosebud and think—how tragic that the flower never had a chance to bloom."

"Hmm." Were all writers so teeming with innuendo? "Well, that's insightful, but why does everything have to come out so melancholy?"

"Writers should experience life as if they had no skin on, so the world and its inhabitants can be portrayed more vividly, with more feeling. Then, hopefully, the reader can walk into our stories and live them with us."

Holly couldn't figure out if she were captivated by his words or merely dodging the interview. "I think I understand."

He grinned. "Do you mind if I ask *you* some questions now?" He pulled the tiny voice recorder from yet another pocket in his coat.

"Oh, I get it. You've been romancing me so I'll talk into that little device?"

"Did it work?"

"Maybe, but before you begin, I have one more question."

"More?" Van dropped his head to his chest. "Fire away."

"What are you most afraid of in the whole world?" *Besides bats.*

Van crossed his arms. "Why do you want to know?"

"I'm about to reveal some pretty intimate details of my life, and so it would help if you showed me some vulnerability first."

He chuckled. "Couldn't you just ask me about my favorite color? It would be so much faster and easier."

"Sorry."

"Okay, okay. I don't mind really . . . he said with building apprehension."

Holly laughed.

"Sorry." He put up his hands. "I'm used to a lot of emotional bloodletting through my characters." Van shifted his weight on the rock. "My darkest fear is failure."

"More than dying?"

"I've made my peace with the Lord, so eternity is settled. But it's the earth-bound trials that cause me grief. Failure feels like this faceless creature pursuing me. The only thing is—the faster I run from it, the more I'm chased."

"What happens if the beast catches up with you?" Holly reached into her pocket, pulled out "her stone," and rolled it around in her palm. She'd handled the same stone for so many years, all the edges had been worn smooth.

"Failure and the fear of it has mauled me a few times, but I keep getting up."

Holly saw sadness in his eyes. What was it like to be Van Keaton? Did people send him hate mail? Worship him? Stalk him? Trash him with bad reviews? She had more questions than ever, but she wasn't the one conducting the interview. "Thank you for sharing a piece of yourself."

"You're welcome." Van smiled as he fingered the recorder. "I know this will be hard on you—my writing your story. But I promise you this, Holly. I'll try to make it as easy as possible. And who knows, maybe it'll cure you of your nightmares."

Holly dropped the stone. "How did you know about my nightmares?"

"Just a feeling."

She hugged her middle. "I'm sorry I haven't read any of your novels."

"That's okay. I'll give you a few, and I'll donate some to the local library." Van shrugged. "But don't worry if you're not familiar with my work. Even my parents haven't read my novels."

"Why not?"

"They're just not interested. Never have been. They're too busy traveling around Europe."

"I'm sorry, Van."

"Guess I gave you more vulnerability than you needed."

"No, not at all." Holly made another quick assessment of the bat, and since the creature wasn't fluttering its wings, she continued to let sleeping bats hang.

"I suppose it is getting late. We'd better get started."

Holly sat down on the boulder next to Van.

He switched on the voice recorder and then asked, "Why do you think your mother left you on the doorstep that Christmas Eve?"

Holly pondered his question while she stared at her hands. "To have done something like that to her own child . . . I think she must have been desperate. To leave her baby on Christmas Eve. You know—a time when parents are gathering around the tree with their most precious ones, laughing and loving and being thankful. So I think something dreadful must have happened to make her do what she did."

"I'm sure you're right." Van cleared his throat. "But in your little narrative just now, you referred to yourself only in the third person. If you don't mind my saying so, you seem detached from the baby who was left behind, even though that baby was you."

"I thought you were going to make this pleasant for me . . . she said with a hint of irritation."

"Cute comeback." He grinned. "But don't you want me to be honest too?"

"Of course." Holly massaged her hands. "There've been so many times I've awakened in a cold sweat, dreaming of her. But in my dreams she remains at a distance. I can't see her face. I suppose that's because I've felt severed from her all these years. I've never understood the *why* of it. I mean, I was inside her, sharing everything. We were laced together for nine months with such intimacy, not like anything else on earth.

We were both given life from the hand of God. Such a holy thing."

Holly touched her abdomen with reverence. "If it had been me with the child, I would have made that baby my life. I could never leave such a treasure on a stranger's doorstep." She shook her head. "I just need to know why. It would help anyway. When my father found me that evening, I was dressed warmly for the cold night, and I was well fed. So, maybe my mother did love me. At least she had taken care of me. But perhaps she was ill, or dying, or just too young to understand what she was giving away."

"And would knowing the truth about her make everything all right?"

"No, but it would help me understand her, and understanding is the beginning of healing."

"But what if your mother's reasoning wasn't noble? What if she had been frivolous or selfish? What would you feel then?"

Holly looked at him. "I don't know. I've thought of that before. Those scenarios. If one of them were true, I might not want to know. It might be better not to know."

"But it would only reflect poorly on your mother, not you."

"When it comes to family, though, sometimes we lack reason." She slapped the flashlight in her palm. "The irrational mind runs amok."

He sighed. "Yeah, it runs amok in my family too."

"You have to understand something. Talking about the past feels like complaining. And I was so fortunate, really, to be placed in the hands of such a fine man. God ordained that Albert Goodnight should find me. He took me in as his daughter. I never wanted to say or do anything to upset our lives together. But we both need to talk about what happened. Perhaps it will help us take the sting out of the past, give us some kind of closure, and, well, help other people in the process. Women who are on this same journey."

Van set his voice recorder on the rock and laced his fingers together. "You know, it's not wrong to want to know the answers, Holly. It's not whining. I would want to know too."

"You would?"

"Of course." Van nodded. "Do you ever wonder what would happen if you could alter your story in some way? Like a writer deleting a scene and then starting again?"

"What do you mean?"

"Well, what if you made an effort to find your mother? Would it make a difference? Change your life in some profound way?"

"It's crossed my mind—a few thousand times. But if my mother wanted to see me, to find me, she could. I'm still in the same place where she left me all those years ago." Tears stung Holly's eyes, but she pressed her nose with the side of her finger—something she always did to keep her emotions in check. Owen's suggestion about the cave had been a good one after all. It was easier talking in a cocoon than in a bustling coffee shop.

Van reached over and shut off the recorder. "That's enough for now. I don't want to dim those inner lights of yours with too many questions."

"Inner lights?"

"I'm not kidding. You really do have some serious wattage going on. Since you're a fairy and all, you're sort of lit from the inside."

Holly rolled her eyes. "Now you're just being silly."

"How so?"

"We've known each other for only a few hours. I'm not sure how you can—"

"I know my stuff. I'm telling you—you could walk into a dark room and light it up. Just as you're doing right now."

"Hmm. Inner lights." She cupped her chin in her palm. "I don't believe a word of it, but you're more than welcome to go on."

Van laughed. "You're funny too."

"Are you sure those aren't lines you're practicing for one of your novels?"

"I would *never* do that. Well, maybe I've done it once or twice." His expression became somber. "But not now—not with you." His hand inched closer to hers.

When Holly looked up, Van was gazing at her, and he seemed to be taking some serious notes with his eyes.

"Holly," he murmured, "you have cave dust on your face."

She chuckled. "Now *that* was a line." Holly fastened her cape all the way up to her chin, and in the process loosened her hair clip. It dropped onto the rock, which made her hair tumble down around her face.

Van touched her cheek. His grin melted into one of those serious "looks"—like in a chick flick when the guy is about to kiss the girl.

"Are you flirting with me?"

His hand lingered on her face. "Depends on what definition we use. Have I teased you? Maybe a little. Am I toying with you? Merely amusing myself with you? No."

Holly marveled at the way things had gone from descriptive to dreamy in a moment. She didn't move, but she knew she'd have to back away. They'd just met, after all. They weren't on a real date. Kissing was not allowed. There were whole guidebooks written on the subject, stored in a celestial vault somewhere.

Van lifted her chin. "I think you're adorable."

Holly's breath caught in her throat. "It's twilight outside. Maybe we'd better—"

"Some call twilight the blue hour," Van said in a voice as other-worldly as his flute. "It's that precarious time right after the sun has kissed the world good night and disappeared under the earth's covers."

"Oh?" Her voice jumped an octave. "What a fascinating bit of trivia."

Van chuckled and leaned closer to her. "Your comments are adorable, Holly Rose."

Repeat: you will not let your eyes drift shut. "Actually, I've been known to be quite the curmudgeon."

"Curmudgeon is such an adorable word."

"But it has the word 'mud' in it." Holly opened her eyes wide and then hiccupped.

The spell broke.

Van lowered his hand. "You're right." He eased away. "I did get carried away, didn't I?"

"You did." *Carried away did feel lovely, though.*

"I'm sorry. I don't know what came over me. Must be the altitude."

Holly stifled a snorting laugh, but the faux pas wouldn't have mattered, since the romantic interlude had hit a snowdrift. The air between them now was uncomfortable but necessary. Like wearing galoshes.

Holly sensed movement out of the corner of her eye and looked toward the opening of the cave.

Owen stood there, looking like a monster in the fading light. "Hey, you guys okay? It's starting to get dark." He stepped inside.

Holly felt like she'd been caught doing something naughty and jumped up from the rock. "Sure. We're good. Fine."

"Now there's something you don't see in here very often." Owen pointed to the rock just above Van's head.

"What's that?" Van asked.

Owen grinned. "There's a bat hanging right above your head."

Chapter Seven

....

Owen covered his ears as Van let out a
holler so egregious, so full-throttled it
must have sent up a sonar vibration to
the poor bat, which retreated to a safer
part of the cave. Van fled outside and
made an aerial leap into a brambly bush,
which had thorns nearly the size of his
aunt's crocheting needles.

What drama. Actually, Owen felt sorry
for the bat. But Van came in a close
second, since his expression was
particularly pitiable. Owen stepped out of
the cave and reached down toward the
novelist. "Hey, I'm sorry. You okay?"

Van looked around. "Well, amazingly, I'm still alive."

Owen helped Van up and then flicked a few dead leaves off his coat. "I had no idea you were afraid of bats."

"Isn't everybody?" Van asked.

The man had such an expression of incredulous horror on his face, Owen laughed.

Holly shot him a look like she was miffed. Mightily.

Owen shrugged. What had he done wrong, really, except to point out one of God's furry creatures?

Van lifted a thorn out of his jeans. "If you guys don't mind getting the flashlights and voice recorder, I'm heading back to the car. I think I need some quiet time."

"Sure. We'll be along in a minute." Holly went back inside the cave, scooped up the gear, and came back out wearing an expression Owen couldn't read.

When Van was well out of earshot, Holly's face eased into a grin. "Okay, that was kind of funny, Quig." She put up her hand. "But." Her expression went stern. "It wasn't excessively funny, mind you, since

Van could have gotten hurt, leaping like that."

Owen took the equipment from Holly. "I came out here because I got worried about you. I don't know what possessed me to encourage you to escort a stranger off to an isolated place like this. Especially when it's getting dark."

"Oh, that." Holly waved him off. "Van's an okay guy. You didn't have anything to worry about."

"More of a bumbler than an outlaw, I gather."

"I thought you liked Van."

"Sure, but everybody knows writers are as stable as the Dow Jones."

Holly chuckled. "We'd better go. There really isn't much light left." She headed down the path.

Owen followed her. "So, did he interview you for his book?"

"He did."

"How did it go?"

"It's going to be good, I think."

Owen gave her shoulders a squeeze. He thought of their childhood. Their youth. All those years they'd been together. Best friends. And then he remembered, once again, a solemn promise they'd made concerning marriage when they were kids. Right inside Short Bottom Cave. He chuckled, thinking of the scene.

"Okay, what's so funny now?" Holly glanced back at Owen.

"Do you remember the promise we made to each other when we were twelve years old?"

"Hmm. A promise. I vaguely remember something. What was it?" She slapped her hands together. "Oh, I do. I remember now. We made a vow that if we weren't married by age thirty, we'd marry each other."

"That's right." Owen opened a small gate, and after they passed through, he locked it back up.

"I remember something else. It was supposed to be a blood pact between us, but when we tried to prick each other's fingers, you passed out."

Owen halted on the trail. *Guess I'm as lily-livered as Van.* "I remember that when I opened my eyes, you slugged me and told me never to scare you like that again."

Holly laughed. "Sounds like me." She stopped on the trail.

Owen's gaze followed Holly's down the path toward their cars. Van's silhouette could be seen running from a herd of cattle, but the beasts were so occupied with searching for grass that they hadn't even bothered to send him an inquisitive glance. "Guess our novelist isn't used to small-town life, being from Houston and all."

"Guess not." Holly released a moan. "What is Van swatting at?"

"Who knows? Some vicious blood-sucking gnats, no doubt."

Holly grinned. "Yeah, except it's too late in the season for gnats."

Owen grinned back at her. "Hey, how about going camping one of these weekends?"

"Sorry. Can't."

"Fossil hunting?"

Holly chuckled. "One of these days we'll do something fun. I promise. My mind is focused on the Christmas season right now—all the tourists. You know that."

"Yeah, I know that." He arched an

eyebrow. Or was she thinking about one tourist in particular?

"And now I'll have to take off extra time for Van's interviews."

Which was totally my doing, Owen reminded himself. "Listen, I know you're working to build up your dad's retirement fund. I wish you'd let me help—"

"No. He would think of it as charity—which it isn't, I know. But he wouldn't accept it." Holly circled her arm through Owen's as they walked. "You have the most generous heart of anyone I know, but I hope you can understand—"

"I've already put the money in a separate account. I want to do this for you both."

Holly tugged on his sleeve, which meant she didn't want to discuss the matter further.

"All right. I'll stop. For now."

"By the way, because of the national award, there's a TV station in Springfield that wants to interview me. I'm sure it'll help business. And Van's book won't hurt either. All of this might turn out to be a financial blessing for Dad."

Owen patted her arm. "I'm glad about

the interview. You'll do great. I'll go with you if you want me to."

"Thanks." Holly rested her head on his arm for a second. "Just so you know—I think I like Van. Enough to go out with him if he asks me. He's got some germ issues, but he's also fun and sweet-tempered."

Owen smirked. "Are you sure you're not talking about a beagle?"

"Very funny. I'm still going out with him." Holly gazed up at the sky. "Look. There's a light snow coming down. How unexpected."

Indeed.

They stopped for a moment to enjoy the bits of swirling fluff and then walked on.

"So why don't *you* ask Van out if you like him so much?" Owen was aiming for nonchalance, but he needed to know what Holly really felt for Van. At the same time he hated himself for his kamikaze fact-finding mission.

"Me? Ask *him* out?" Holly blew the bangs off her forehead. "I couldn't possibly do that."

"You used to ask *me* out when we were in high school."

Holly snuggled a little closer to Owen. "But that situation was sooo different. We were just friends, and I knew you'd fill in if I didn't have a date."

"All right. I'll tell Van to ask you out." Owen shrugged but watched every nuance of her expression.

She jiggled his arm. "Don't you dare tell Van to ask me out."

"Okay. Well, you'll see him a lot while he interviews you. Maybe you could just pretend those are dates." *Good grief, man. Talk about reckless.* He warned himself that if he dug for information too deeply he might just bury himself.

Holly winced. "Talk about pathetic. To *pretend* I'm on a date."

"It's easier than you think." *And a lot closer than you can imagine.* It was what Owen himself had done when they were teenagers, always pretending he was on a date with Holly—until he finally wised up and realized she just wanted to be friends. He'd made "friends only" his mantra since then, and it had been a comfortable and livable fib for a very long time. But lately the friendship route was getting littered with emotional debris. He cared for Holly beyond friendship, and someday soon he'd have to own up to it.

She looked at Owen with a curious air. "I know you're joking. In fact, that's one of the many things I love about you, Quig. You don't have a fake bone in your body."

Chapter Eight

Some weeks later, Holly found herself at one of the TV stations in Springfield, sitting in a fake living room, hooked up to a mike, and feeling woozier by the minute. *Okay, they said not to look into the camera. Oh, wow. How many cameras are there? Concentrate on the host. Don't look nervous. Keep my legs together.* She smoothed her red suit once again. Was red bad for TV? Maybe she should clasp her hands together to keep them from shaking. *Repeat: do not pass out. Do not throw up.* Holly wished she had taken

Owen up on his offer to be there for support.

The host glided down in her comfy swivel chair like a swan folding its wings. She set her coffee mug down and reached out her hand. "Hi. I'm Savanna Cummings."

"Nice to know, well, meet you. I'm happy to be . . ." Holly forgot the greeting she'd practiced. Oh, great. Here came the meltdown, and she hadn't even made it on TV yet.

"We'll be on in a few seconds. Are you ready?" Savanna smiled, and the shine off her white teeth lit the studio.

"Sure. Kind of. Maybe not. No." Holly meant to relieve some of the tension with a chuckle, but it came out as a burping hiccup. "I'm *so* sorry."

"Relax. It'll be fun." Savanna shuffled through some papers on her lap.

Holly stared at her mug of water on the coffee table. Even though her mouth had gone dry, she didn't want to pick up anything that contained fluids. Her shaky hands might slosh the water right out of it.

People in the studio got quiet, and then

someone started counting downwards as if they were going to launch the space shuttle.

Suddenly Savanna came to life. "Welcome back. As promised, we have Holly Goodnight with us, the young woman who co-owns The Little Bethlehem Shoppe in Noel, Missouri, which was just voted the best Christmas shop in America." Savanna turned toward her. "Congratulations, Holly."

"You're welcome." Holly tried to smile, but the expression wilted when she realized she'd flubbed her first reply. *God, help me!*

"So I hear you won this honor because your customers sent in stacks of letters, praising your store and your service. Is that right?"

"Yes." *Okay, I'm on a roll.* Holly latched onto the arms of the leather chair.

"Well, I know you and your father must be excited about this award. But what I think is even more interesting," Savanna went on to say, "is the amazing history surrounding your shop—that when you were a baby, you were left on its doorstep on Christmas Eve. And the owner,

Mr. Goodnight, found you there and eventually adopted you. Is this true?"

Holly opened her mouth, but nothing came out. *Breathe, Holly.* "I—uh—that is private information." Was that too confrontational for live television? But how could they ask her such a personal question without warning?

"Well, we found the story in a very public forum, on the blog of popular novelist Van Keaton. In fact, we learned that Mr. Keaton will base his upcoming book on *your* story."

Holly's face reddened to match her suit. She could either get up and leave or tell the truth. "Yes, what you've said is true. My mother *did* leave me on the doorstep of Mr. Goodnight's shop on Christmas Eve."

Savanna tapped her fingers together. "And you've never seen your mother since?"

"Not that I know of."

"What do you mean, Holly?"

"I supposed my mother could have come through town to check on me. But if she did try to seek me out while I was growing up, I never knew about it."

Savanna leaned toward her. "And how does that make you feel?"

Was she on TV or a psychiatrist's couch? "Do you have a mother, Ms. Cummings?"

Savanna raised a manicured brow. "Yes. Everyone does."

"Well, how would you feel if your mother abandoned you?" Holly took a sip of her water while Savanna mulled over the question.

"I'd feel anger and fear, I suppose."

"Yes, anybody would. But the real story here is the divine intervention that took place that night. My father—Mr. Goodnight—was working late at the shop, and as he was locking up he found me in a little basket. He'd never married, but he'd always dreamed of having a family. He considered my appearance on the doorstep a miracle. A Christmas gift. He adopted me, and he's been the best father any girl could have. So on that Christmas Eve I may have been abandoned, but I was also greatly blessed."

Tears welled up in Savanna's eyes. "I love a story with a happy ending. But what about your mother? Would you still like to meet her?"

Holly panicked. Was it a trick? Had they gotten her on the show to spring her long-lost mother on her? Equal amounts of excitement and terror coursed through her. "Yes, I would."

Savanna turned to the camera. "If you are Holly Goodnight's mother, she has a message for you. Your daughter has grown up, forgiven you, and she'd love to meet you. There'll be no problem finding Holly since she's still working at the same shop where you left her thirty years ago."

* * * * *

After the absolute worst seven minutes of Holly's life, she drove home to Noel. Then she drove straight to her father's house, cut the engine, and glanced up at the old stone frontage with the green shutters—a place she still loved to call home.

Her father opened the door and waited for her on the porch.

She ran up the sidewalk and fell into her father's arms.

"You did great, Cricket. A real pro. Owen thought so too."

"Thanks." She rested her head on his

shoulder, and then they settled in the living room on her favorite overstuffed couch. She wondered who was watching the shop. *Must be Owen—dear, sweet Owen.*

Her father's pet parakeets, Nicholas and Kringle, argued like an old married couple in the next room, and the scent drifting from the kitchen meant cookies had just come out of the oven. *Home.*

Holly wasn't sure where to begin. "About the woman who interviewed me—"

"Savanna Cummings?"

"Yeah."

"Boy, that woman. Don't get me started. You were being vulnerable, and she brought out a stick to beat you with it. And that novelist, Keaton. He should have gotten your permission to blog about your life. He should have honored the fact that you needed to take things slowly, that maybe you weren't ready for the world to know everything all at once—on live television, no less."

Holly picked at one of the throw pillows on the couch. "I thought maybe they'd found my mother, and they were going to bring her out in the studio right then.

When I realized it was just a request, I felt let down." Holly looked at him. "I'm sorry, Dad." She tossed the pillow on the floor.

"Every girl longs to have a mother. It's only natural. I told that Keaton fellow I wanted you to talk about the past. Get it out. Always wanted you to do that. But I never wanted to stir the pot if you didn't want it stirred. We should have talked more, though. I regret it now."

Holly took hold of her father's hand. His skin felt cooler than usual, and the veins were more prominent than they used to be. It bothered her to see it. She hated to see her father age. "I was always afraid that if I talked about my mother or tried to look for her, it might be too upsetting for you."

"I won't lie, Holly, and say it would have been a piece of cake if you'd taken a sudden interest in finding your mother. I mean, you might have reconciled with her and left Noel. Left me. You might have grown to love her more than—well, these things had entered my mind. And yet I always knew it was selfish to think that way."

Holly gave her father's hand a

squeeze. "I could never have cared for her more than I do you. Because of you, I never became an orphan. I wasn't moved from one foster home to another. Instead, I had a home and love and meaning in my life. We have history, you and me. We're family, and we have a bond that no one can break."

Tears fell from her father's eyes, staining his cheeks. "Thank you, Cricket. I wish my parents could have lived a bit longer, so they could have met you. I know they would have loved you as I do. Without grandparents, I'm afraid you've always been short on family. So if you ever want to search for your mother—or your father—you have my blessing."

"Well, as they said on live TV, my mother knows exactly where I am. If it's meant to be, she'll come back. And *you* are my father. Nothing can ever change that." She kissed his hand and then released him. "But I do wish I could have known my grandparents before they died."

He swiped at the wetness on his cheek, paused for a moment, and then turned his kind gaze on her. "You know,

Cricket, beyond all of this, you've seemed so unsettled lately. Is there anything else on your mind?"

"You know me so well." Holly gazed at a photo of them canoeing the Elk River together. Her father kept it near him, where he read every evening. "On my drive home I realized what I needed to do. Savanna Cummings said I'd forgiven my mother, but it wasn't true. So right now I make the choice to do that and say the words out loud. I forgive my mother." Holly took in a deep breath and released it.

"You've done a good thing. One more peel off the onion." Her father smiled and then said, "I've often wondered if the only reason you stayed at the shop and never moved away was because you were waiting for your mother to return."

Holly fingered her earring. "Some part of me was waiting, hoping she'd come back. But I love Noel, and I love you. I don't ever want to move from this place. It's home. The old saying is true—that no one ever leaves Noel. At least it's true for me."

"That goes down real good—like a fine

cup of cocoa." Her father laughed, sounding like Santa Claus. "Speaking of which, how about some hot chocolate and a plate of sugar cookies?"

"How about you hold onto your health?" Holly teased.

He slapped her with a throw pillow. "I know you're just trying to keep me alive, but I'd like to have some fun in my last years."

"I know you won't leave me like my mother did, but I don't want you dying before your time. I can't even stand to think about it." Holly crossed her arms, trying to hold onto a frown.

"All right. All right." Her father rose from the couch and picked up a cushion. "How about I whip us up some tofu pumpkin pie then?"

"Ew." Holly picked up a throw pillow and pelted her father with it. "How about we have some cocoa and *one* whole wheat cookie?"

"Haven't you heard the latest? Whole wheat is the leading cause of heart disease and strokes." Laughing, her father hobbled along the back of the couch and launched a surprise attack on Holly with the cushion. After a rather spirited pillow fight, the two finally headed toward the kitchen, still chuckling. They finally decided on one cup of cocoa and two sugar cookies each.

Holly downed the last of her cup and wiped off her cocoa mustache. "So what do you think of Van Keaton now, Dad?"

"Well, for his behavior with that blog, I guess you can either shoot him—or marry him."

* * * * *

Van Keaton was sweating again. It was something he'd grown proficient at over the years as he tried to keep his career afloat. But this time his perspiration came from two new sources.

Van paced back and forth in his hotel room, fingering the stubble on his chin. First of all, he was in love. He'd spent enough time with Holly during his earlier visit to know how he felt. But he had no idea if his sentiments would be reciprocated. There was the rub. He'd even written out a proposal of marriage within the manuscript, hoping to surprise Holly. He picked up the pages that contained the proposal and rolled them up into a sweaty scroll. He didn't just want to make readers weep, he wanted to make Holly say yes. But when would he give it to her? Would he hand her the pages and say nothing? He was totally without a plan. Not good. It made him sweat even more.

He put dilemma number one on hold while he pondered predicament number two. Fortunately he'd already apologized for blogging about Holly's life. He could be so insensitive sometimes it scared him. But his exchange of e-mails a few minutes after her TV interview would make that blogging blunder look like a pencil scribble on a building marked for demolition. Holly might feed him to the sharks when she found out what he'd done to facilitate the delivery of even worse news.

Van made a quick mental note not to use mixed metaphors in his writing. Then he walked into the bathroom and began to shave the bristles off his face. Since he was used to being the mastermind behind his characters' lives, constantly raining down discord on their heads, he knew well it could happen in real life. Fiction reflected reality, after all, so no matter how precise or distorted a work of art, it usually rose from something within the human experience. He believed that. But the news Holly was about to receive went far beyond art.

Any minute now a stranger would walk into The Little Bethlehem Shoppe and tell Holly about her mother. It would be gritty, and it had the potential to alter the course of Holly's life.

He rested his hands on the edge of the sink and released a groan. Then he pulled out a bottle of disinfectant spray from his travel case and gave the bathroom a spritz.

He went through all of his grooming rituals, repeating some of them twice, because his obsessive-compulsive tendencies worsened with stress. Then he pulled on his author's uniform—slacks, crisp white shirt, knit tie, tweed jacket, and loafers. Van stared at himself in the mirror. Why hadn't he ever noticed he looked like a clown? No, a better description would be that he looked like a con artist—a man hiding behind a costume. He yanked off his clothes and dressed in jeans, a North Face coat, and Nikes. *Better.*

Van let the hotel door slam shut and then wiggled the handle three times to make certain he'd locked it. *Lovely. I'm a mess.* He strode down the hallway, wrestling with more questions. How would Holly feel when she found out his role in bringing news about her mother? She might love him for it, which is what he prayed for. On the other hand, she might hate him for participating in the dispensation of such bad tidings. It might even jeopardize the project.

From a purely professional standpoint, this sudden turn of events came at the perfect time. Just when he thought he might need to supplement Holly's story with imaginary events, a fresh plot twist had arrived. The newest development would give him a lot more literary clay to mold. *Pretty selfish, Keaton.*

Van slid into his pre-owned Lexus, unscrewed the lid from a bottle of Evian, and took a sip. Then he backed out of the hotel parking lot, maneuvered his way onto Highway 71, and sped toward Noel.

Amidst his anxiousness about the marriage proposal, he felt even more anxiety over what would happen when a woman named Beatrice Monroe showed up with the tragic news that Holly's mother was dead.

Chapter Nine

The bell over the front door jingled. Like curious little elves, all the customers looked up. Holly did too.

Van Keaton strolled through the door of The Little Bethlehem Shoppe.

"Hi, there," Holly called out to him. "Welcome back to Noel."

Van waved.

She didn't take her eyes off him as he walked toward her.

The customer at the counter gaped at Holly. "The bow goes on my gift box, not your hand." The woman noticed Van and then turned back around with a knowing look. "Oh, I see."

"Sorry." Holly taped the bow on the box and handed it to the woman. "Here you go. I hope you have a happy Thanksgiving. Oh, and merry Christmas too."

"Thank you." The woman grinned at them both and left the shop.

Holly offered Van her hand. "I'm so glad you're here."

"Now, now, we know each other much better than that." Van went behind the counter and pulled her into a hug.

It was true. They were indeed beyond handshake status. During Van's first visit to Noel, their interviews had very quickly turned into dates. After his return to Houston, they'd shared phone calls and e-mails daily. Their budding relationship was a surprise to her, but she received it with delight.

He rocked her gently in his arms. "You're irresistibly soft—like the gossamer caress of a butterfly's wing or the murmur of celestial beings."

"It's just the velvet apron, Van."

"No, it's your velvet nature."

Holly grinned at his hyperbole and yet melted a little too. This time he smelled of woods. Vast improvement over the antiseptic.

She was so grateful they'd hammered out the issue of his blog-tattling spree. All had been made right with an eloquent speech and a fervent apology. She grinned, thinking Van really could finesse the honey right out of a bear's mouth. "How's the writing going?" She eased out of his embrace, suddenly concerned that a customer might pop in and see them.

"I have almost half of a rough draft." Van glanced at his watch, and then his gaze darted around the shop.

Was he looking for someone? "You really are a prolific writer."

He focused on her again. "I can be productive when I'm inspired."

Holly felt a familiar flush creeping up to her face and began organizing all the froufrou Christmas wrappings on the counter. She certainly couldn't deny her feelings for Van, but she didn't want to get too moony. "Did you have a pleasant drive from Houston?" She noticed a sack of her father's buttermilk donuts on the counter and hid them in a drawer under a pile of papers.

"Well, things are pleasant now that I'm here with you."

There was that smile of his again, full of innuendo. What was she going to do with him? She had to admit his creative ways and beautiful words had won her affections. Even his phobias and loafers were somehow endearing. She glanced down at his feet and was surprised to see them clad in athletic shoes. In fact, his whole look was different. Were the changes for her? To impress her?

"I just wondered." Van coughed. "Have you had any special—visitors—today?"

"Visitors? Yes, we've had some Christmas shoppers come in. Quite a few, actually. Business is picking up." In spite of their sweet reunion, Van looked anxious about something. "Is everything all right?"

He pressed his hand over his heart. "I just thought—"

The door jingled open, and a woman wearing a gray coat and an even grayer countenance stepped inside the shop.

"Hold that thought." Holly grinned at

Van and then turned toward the woman. "May I help you?"

"My name is Beatrice Monroe, and I need to speak with Miss Holly Goodnight."

"I am she." Why was the woman so stern and pale? Holly walked over to her. "You look like you could use some hot spiced tea to warm up. Would you like some?"

"I'd better not, but it's kind of you to offer." Ms. Monroe straightened, but her shoulders still seemed to sag. "May I talk to you in private? Please."

"Of course." Holly glanced at Van, whose face had lost all its joy. He was such a kind and sensitive man to be concerned. Then she caught a glimpse of Owen and her father coming into the shop, but she didn't stop to wave at them. Instead she led Ms. Monroe into their small office area, shut the door, and offered the woman an armchair. "How may I help you?" Holly sat down behind her desk and inspected her visitor.

Ms. Monroe appeared to be a middle-aged woman with brown eyes and mousy hair. She sat twisting the handles on her purse until they looked as though they'd tear into pieces. Her gaze darted around room and then landed on Holly.

"I can see you have something unpleasant to tell me. Please feel free to just say it straight out." Holly rested back in her chair, hoping it would make the woman feel more at ease.

"I saw you on television," Ms. Monroe finally said.

"Oh, that. It didn't go so well, did it?"

"You did a fine job." She licked her lips. "But when I saw you I realized I hadn't kept a promise I'd made a couple of years ago. So I drove here as quickly as I could to make things right." Ms. Monroe touched a hanky to her nose. "You see, I knew your mother—briefly."

"My mother?" Holly leaned forward. "Where is she?"

"I'm sorry to give you the sad news that—that your mother is dead."

Holly covered her mouth with the back of her hand. "My mother? Dead? But how? When?" Her heart skipped a beat. "How do you know this?"

"I didn't really know your mother. I merely shared a hospital room with her.

This was two years ago. She made me promise that if she died I would tell you—that I would give you the news in person. I've had my own hardships, so I've been delayed in coming. I'm very sorry. But I'm glad I was able to be here now—to fulfill my promise."

"I see." Holly pressed her palm over her forehead. All the hopes she'd ever had of meeting her mother now vanished with the woman's revelation. Such terrible news. It was hard to breathe. *God, give me courage.*

"I'm afraid that beyond her name, I don't have much information."

Holly looked up. "What *was* her name?"

"Your mother's name was Lizzy Smith, and she died two years ago in a small hospital in Dallas. That's all I know."

Lizzy Smith. Had that really been her mother's name? Could she trust a stranger with such news? But what would Ms. Monroe have to gain by telling a lie? "Did she give you a message for me? Anything at all?"

Ms. Monroe lowered her gaze. "Only that I was to give you the news of her death."

Holly felt overwhelmed with questions. "Did she mention her job or a husband or other children?"

"No." The woman's eyes clouded over with mist. "I wish I knew more. I really do. I can see how important this is to you."

Holly had waited so long for news about her mother, it felt shocking that there was so little offered. So little to say good-bye to. She felt like a parched woman given only a drop of water. "My mother—did she seem like a kind woman?"

"We had very few words because we were both so ill, but she seemed kind in her spirit." Ms. Monroe nodded. "Yes, I would say so."

Holly hated badgering the poor woman, but desperation still ran through her. "Do you have any idea what she died of?"

"I'm not sure, but I believe I overheard the doctors say something about her liver. I—I think she may have had a drinking problem."

"I see." Holly looked down at her velvet apron, which she had twisted into a knot. "Thank you for telling me, for being honest."

"You're welcome."

"I've dreamed of my mother all my life. I didn't even get a chance to say good-bye."

Ms. Monroe closed her eyes for a moment as if in prayer. They sat in silence for a while, and then the woman spoke up. "I wish you the best with your life, Miss Goodnight. I will say this—from watching your interview and visiting with you now, I think your mother would have been proud of you. I know I would have been—if you had been my daughter."

"Thank you. That means a lot to me." Holly pressed her nose to stop the tears, which were now threatening to choke her. *Later. I will cry later.*

Ms. Monroe handed her a business card. "If you have any questions, you may call me. But I think I've told you all I know."

Holly accepted the card and then reached out to shake the woman's hand. "Thank you for coming."

"You're welcome." She rose and gave Holly's hand a vigorous shake.

"By the way . . ."

The woman stepped away from the chair and paused. "Yes?"

"What did my mother look like?"

Ms. Monroe lit up for the first time. "Ah,

that one is easy. She looked a lot like you."

Holly took in a deep breath and smiled. After a few more pleasantries she said good-bye to Beatrice Monroe at the front of the shop and shut the door.

There were no customers left, but Van and Owen and her father were standing in the middle of the store, all with beseeching expressions directed at her. Did they know what had just happened? She hated to leave them there, gaping at her, but she needed some air. "I'm going for a walk."

Holly did what she always did when life got complicated. She headed down to the Elk River to watch the clear blue water flow through her town. It was the place she sometimes met God—and sometimes wrestled with Him too.

She crossed the railroad tracks, walked along the sidewalk, and then hiked down to the river. The park looked empty. So much the better for a few minutes of tranquility. She buttoned up her cape, eased onto the ground next to the water, and waited for its calming effects to take over. Eventually the sounds of nature embraced her—the soft flow of cool air, the chants of birds, and the hypnotic movement of water ebbing beyond her world.

Holly looked up to the heavens. "This is not how I imagined things, Lord. Not at all. Death isn't the right way out of the maze. I'd hoped for real closure. The kind where I'd meet my mother and she'd tell me she loved me all along. There should be reconciliation. There should be joy." She picked up a twig and ran her hands along its rough surface.

Beatrice Monroe had said her mother's name was Lizzy Smith. *And she looked a lot like me.* Were those words a sweet comfort to her, or did they compound the sadness of never meeting her? Holly stared at her hands, the light olive skin, the shape and size. She'd often studied her features in the mirror, wondering which ones had come from her mother and which ones from her biological father. She'd been curious about so many things. Even though Beatrice had offered her very little news, she'd given her enough information to start a search of family records. Bit by bit she would be able to put her mother's life story together and perhaps even find her biological father. But would the striving for facts help with closure, or would it only lead to heartache? She tossed the twig into the water and watched it drift far from sight. *My father lives in Noel, and* he *is my family.*

Holly heard footsteps behind her and turned around. "Quig? How did you know I'd be here?"

"Are you kidding?"

"Right."

"Mind if I sit down?"

Holly gestured to a dry spot next to her.

He lowered himself to the ground. They didn't say anything for a while. That was the beauty of old and comfortable friendships—like a great cup of coffee that's tasty even without all the foam and sugar.

Finally Holly looked over at him. "I guess you guys figured things out?"

"Your father has a talent for eavesdropping."

"I've never heard that called a *talent*

before." She shook her head. "So, are you here to give me advice?"

"No."

"I guess I'm a little like Job in the ashes."

"Then I *really* shouldn't say anything. I'd hate for God to come back later and say I did a lousy job of advising you. Or comforting you."

Holly touched his arm. "You are a comfort to me—just being here. You're like an old shoe."

"I genuinely hope not."

She pulled her legs up, hugging her knees. "You are the kind of shoes people look forward to putting on when they get home from a hard day at work. The kind that hug your feet without pinching."

Owen chuckled. "Okay, I guess you've redeemed yourself." He reached into his pocket, pulled out a mysterious object, and held out his closed hand. "Do you want what's in my hand?"

"You've played that game with me since we were five. I've gotten everything from candy to a toad."

Owen's expression was somber yet playful. "Well, life is full of risk."

"That is more true than I want it to be. Okay, I think I might want what's in your hand. *Maybe.*"

"No, you need to be certain."

Holly rolled her eyes. "All right. I want what's in your hand."

Chapter Ten

....

Owen turned around to face her.

What was he up to? Holly placed her hand under his.

He unlocked his fingers, and a small brass compass fell into her palm.

"Oh, it's lovely—and so unique. But why are you carrying a compass around?"

"My grandfather gave it to me before he died. He said the compass was for the long journey ahead."

"Since your grandpa Josiah was a philosophy professor, I assume he meant life."

"He did." Owen closed Holly's fingers around the compass. "I want you to have it—for keeps."

"No. I can't possibly take this. It's a family heirloom, and—"

"But you've always been family to me. I have no brothers or sisters. And I have no wife." He smiled. "I know you have trouble accepting gifts, but I really want you to have this. Please."

Holly didn't feel right accepting such a treasure, and yet he'd been right about their being like family. Neither of them had any siblings. They'd been as close as two friends could be. "All right. But under one condition only—if you ever want it back, I insist you ask me straightaway."

"It's a deal."

She looked at the compass more carefully, at its delicate etchings and the dark golden hues that came from age. No matter which way she turned it, the mechanism would swivel back around, righting itself, offering perfect direction. "So the compass was meant to be a reminder of some kind for you?"

"Yes, but I'm going to tell you this only because you asked." He smiled.

"Grandpa Josiah told me I should never forget that the Almighty is the only true compass, and His guidance is only a prayer away."

"I like that." Holly leaned over and kissed Owen on the cheek. He leaned toward her, making the kiss last a second or two longer than she'd expected. His clothes were suffused with cinnamon from the shop, so she found herself lingering there by his side, enjoying the fragrance. "Thanks. I will always treasure this compass." *As I do you.* "Was this something you carried around with you often?"

"Never. But I slipped it into my pocket this morning. For some reason I had a strong urge to give it to you today."

She looked at him. "You couldn't have known Beatrice was coming to the shop today."

"No, I didn't know."

"Sounds providential."

"I believe you're right." Owen got up from the ground and stretched.

Holly lifted her hands up to him, and in one sweeping movement he lifted her off the ground.

A freight train, which had been making distant thunder, wound its way toward Noel and suddenly roared through the middle of town.

Owen looked at his watch. "Right on time."

Just like you. Holly gave Owen an affectionate pat on the back.

"So, what about Van Keaton?" He dusted himself off.

"You mean the book? I suppose I'll let him interview me about Beatrice and the news about my mother. I'm sure he'll want to add it to his book." Holly pushed her hair away from her face. "I guess it adds another dimension to all of this—to have this new information read by tens of thousands of people. I can hardly think of it without cringing. Yet I made a promise to Van, and I intend to keep my word."

"That wasn't my question about Van."

"What did you mean then?"

Owen shuffled his feet the way he did when he was a boy—usually when he was guilty of something. "I mean the way he looks at you."

Holly gazed at the compass one more

time and then slipped it into her pocket. "So you noticed that Van has a look."

Owen tilted his head and smirked. "Everyone in town can see it."

"Oh." Holly fiddled with her earring. "Well, to be honest, I didn't expect to like Van so much. And I do like him—a lot. Is that going to be all right with you?"

"Oh, sure." Owen huffed. "Great guy. I'm mean, he's totally deranged, of course, but otherwise he's a good choice."

Holly laughed. "You are too much, Quig. You build bridges just to tear them down. Don't you see it?" She put her hands on her hips. "Van may have some issues, but he's also a good man."

Owen cringed.

"I'm sorry. But surely you understand what I mean. You're a good man and my dearest friend, but not someone I'm considering for a husband."

This time Owen turned away from her.

"Quig?" Holly touched his sleeve. "What's wrong?"

"Van has fallen in love with you."

Was Owen kidding? *Van loves me?*

The wind charged through the park in a snit, thrashing the trees and Holly's scarf. When the wind calmed its temper she said, "I don't think Van could have fallen in love with me so quickly."

"It takes some people a lifetime and some people fifteen minutes."

Holly slapped the dust off her slacks. "What you're saying is improbable."

Owen frowned.

"And why are you frowning at me?"

"Because I think you've gotten it in your head you're unattractive and undesirable. That no one could fall in love with you."

"I've dated for decades, and no one has bothered to take enough interest in me to propose."

Owen sighed. Heavily.

"Well, isn't that true?"

"And did you want to marry any of those guys?"

Holly didn't have to think about that question very long. "No." It was an honest answer. "But that doesn't prove your point." She cocked her head at him.

"But it doesn't disprove it either." He narrowed his eyes and grinned.

Holly wished life were as easy as their banter, easy as the wind through the trees. "I guess we'd better get back to the shop." They walked up the incline, past the police station, and onto the street. "Do you mind staying at the shop a bit longer today?"

"I'm at your service."

As you have been my whole life. Holly circled her arm through his as they walked. She felt fortunate to know someone like Owen, a fun and kind friend to share life with. And to have him gifted at trading stocks was an added bonus for them all, since it gave Owen free time to hang around the shop and keep her dad company. And keep *her* company as well. What would she ever do if he got married and moved away? He did mention wanting to find a wife. At the moment, life felt so stretched with transitions she couldn't bear to think of one more.

Holly leaned nearer to Owen, but he didn't seem to mind. In fact, for a second he rested his head against hers. She assumed the recent events in her life had caused them to show their affections more readily, and she counted it as a blessing. Out of the blue she recalled something funny from their past. "Do you remember the code word we used to say sometimes on our double dates?"

"I do." He laughed. "If either of us said the words 'teddy bear,' it was a signal that we were in agony and needed to make a speedy end to the date."

"That was pretty terrible of us." Holly shook her head.

"*And* pretty vital."

Holly chuckled. Then she waved at Carl Rodriguez, who was stringing up Christmas lights on his storefront across the street. "Hey, how's your wife, Carl?"

"Much better," Carl hollered back. "She loved your beef stew. Thanks for bringing it by."

"Oh, you're welcome."

When Holly and Owen entered The Little Bethlehem Shoppe, Mr. Goodnight was standing in the entryway. "Do you mind a chat?" her father asked.

"Of course not. You okay? How's your heart?"

"It's still beating. Listen, Holly, you need

to know that I overheard Beatrice. I couldn't help but overhear."

"Well, it *is* easier when your ear is smashed against the door." Holly smiled.

"True." Her father put his arm around her. "But about your mom—I'm so sorry, Cricket."

Owen quietly busied himself at the back of the store.

She noticed a tremor in her father's hands. "I'll bet you could use a nap."

"Maybe. It feels like a long day, doesn't it?"

Holly could sense her father's grief, but she could tell there was something else bothering him. "I'll walk you over to my house. It's closer." She yoo-hooed to Owen, letting him know she'd be gone for a bit. Then she glanced over at Van, who'd been so quiet she'd almost forgotten he was there. She searched his eyes for any hint of Owen's prediction of undying love. She saw nothing but compassion. "I'll be back soon, Van."

"I'll be waiting right here for you."

How sweet was that?

Van smiled back at her as he stood just beneath the Christmas ball. She had an urge to kiss him right there under the mistletoe, but the timing was as off as a broken watch.

After Holly and her father left the shop they walked up Main Street. When they arrived at her house Holly gestured to the porch, and they sat down together on the swing.

They remained quiet for a while until her father blurted out, "I'm guilty."

Holly chuckled. "What could you possibly be guilty of, Dad?" She placed a pillow behind his back.

He buttoned his sweater—the one that made him look like Mister Rogers—and then rested back on the pillow.

Her father folded his hands in his lap. "I'm guilty of loving you too much. In fact, sometimes I've wondered if I don't love you more than God." He dipped his head. "In my younger days some of my male friends didn't want to give up their independence to marry and have a family. But *I* did. I just never met the right girl, never fell in love." He pointed toward the heavens. "And then there was that Christmas Eve when someone left a miracle on my porch step. Suddenly I was a father, and joy was mine." He took a handkerchief out of his shirt pocket.

Holly scooted closer to her father.

He wiped his eyes. "Even though I knew you were a gift from God, I didn't trust Him like I should have. I kept thinking your mother would return and demand I give you back. I feared that every day for a long time. Even after I'd adopted you, I knew she might come back, and I felt the law would probably be on her side. She would have taken you from me. And it would have whittled away at me until there would have been nothing left. . . ." His voice caught in his throat.

Holly sat quietly with her father while he recovered his emotions.

"The pain would have been unbearable, since I had fallen in love with you as an infant and then all those years growing up. And now as my friend." He ran his fingers along the metal links of the swing and then clasped his hand around them. "But even though I knew you loved me too, I feared—all this time—that your mother would come back and take you away. Until now, that is."

Holly tried to understand her father's

suffering. She could only imagine how acute it must have been. "I'm so sorry this caused you pain all these years. I wish you'd told me. It would have been good to talk about these things."

He nodded. "I guess I didn't mention it because I was embarrassed by my selfishness. And I must confess something else. When I heard Beatrice talk of your mother's death—instead of feeling sadness like I should, I felt only relief." He covered his face with his handkerchief and wept. "Forgive me."

"Of course I forgive you, but I doubt there's anything to forgive." Holly gently rubbed her father's back. Had there been flickers of dread in her father's eyes that she'd never noticed? Was she listening to people without really hearing them? "I'm so glad my mother didn't come to take me away. You've been the best of parents. I couldn't have asked for more.

He blew his nose into his hanky. "Thanks, Cricket."

The sun peeked out from behind the clouds like a child playing hide and seek, and the cheerful sounds of Tejano music floated in from someone's backyard.

Feeling warmer and lighter, they took turns pushing off on the swing. She remembered well the day she'd purchased her Victorian house. The first thing she did was to install an old-fashioned porch swing just like the one she'd grown up with. Didn't seem right to have a porch without swing. "So tell me, what do you want me to cook for Thanksgiving dinner this year?"

"Oh, the usual, I guess. Banana nut bread, apple pie, and those cinnamon spice cookies."

Holly grinned at her dad as a FedEx truck came to a squeaking halt in front of her house. A deliveryman slipped out of the vehicle, trotted up to the porch, and handed her a brown package. Before the man made it back to the sidewalk, Holly tore into the box.

Her father watched over her shoulder as she opened the lid. "What is it?"

Holly stared inside the box. The container was empty except for a sheet of floral notepaper. She held it up. "This is all there is."

"What does it say?"

"It's a note from Van." She looked at

the handwriting. Sort of swirly, but not feminine. "It says, 'Please join me at the entrance of Big Sugar Creek State Park for a hike this Saturday at 9:00 a.m.' And it's signed, 'Van Keaton.'"

"Sounds like a date."

"A *cheap* date." Holly laughed.

"It's *still* a date." He wiggled his eyebrows. "Go tomorrow. Have fun. It'll do you some good. I'll watch the shop."

"Thanks, Dad."

"What a day." He rested back on the swing. "Let's see, if you add in those earlier dates with Van before he left for Houston, you two should be up to about nine. Am I right?"

Holly pulled back, gaping at her father. "I can't believe you've been counting my dates."

"Well, it's my job. I do want grandkids, after all."

"Hey, no guarantees, Dad."

Her father grinned. "What may look like a cheap date on the outside may end up changing your life. I mean, what if you fall in love tomorrow?"

Chapter Eleven

Owen paced back and forth in front of the state park sign. He couldn't believe he'd allowed Van Keaton to talk him into a blind date—even worse, a double date with Van and Holly. Huge error on his part. Right up there with his mistake in not selling before the tech bubble burst.

Van had promised to introduce him to the perfect girl—Lindy, an author friend of his. But if she were perfect, why hadn't Van married her? Maybe authors didn't date other authors—too much competition. Owen had no idea how that system worked. He felt so out of his element that he'd broken out in a rash. But he knew the rash had little to do with his blind date and everything to do with Van's date—Holly Goodnight.

Owen kicked at a patch of grass but stubbed his toe on a rock instead. *Great.* Someone was coming up the road—Holly in her Smart Car. When she pulled up in the parking lot, he walked over to her.

Her window rolled down.

"Hey, Holl."

"Hey, Quig."

Owen opened her car door for her. "You feeling any better now—you know, about your mother?"

"A little." Holly nodded. "Thanks for asking."

"You're welcome."

"I didn't expect to see you here."

"Van didn't tell you?" Owen took hold of her hand and helped her out of the car.

"Tell me what?"

"That he set up a double date."

"No, he didn't mention it." Holly's expression wilted, which made Owen's heart constrict.

"Van's bringing an author friend of his

to meet me. Lindy somebody. He thought we'd hit it right off. Can't imagine that Keaton would know what kind of woman I want."

Holly laughed.

He stared at her for a moment, taking pleasure in her mirth. "I'd like to know what's so entertaining about that." He tried to scowl, but it came out as a one-sided grin.

They did their usual elbow-rub, shoulder-bump greeting. "And so what kind of woman *would* you want, Quig?"

Someone like you. A Lexus turned into the parking area, absorbing their attention. It was Van, and the passenger had to be Lindy, his blind date. Owen took in a deep breath and readied himself for change. New people always made an impression on one's life, even if it was only a small one. They fused themselves forever in one's memories, therefore altering that person's life. In other words, Owen wasn't big on Van tampering with his life. Or maybe he just didn't want Van tampering with *Holly's* life.

After Van got out of his car and knocked a few invisible specks off the hood, he gave them all a Charlie Chaplin stance with a twirl of an invisible cane.

What a goofball. Owen put on a happy face, but he really felt like kicking himself for encouraging Holly to spend time with Van. This had all been his doing. It had been such an innocent act of benevolence born of the desire to help Holly find healing about her past. And yet in the process he'd opened the henhouse so the fox could stroll right in! What was the old saying—no kind deed ever went unpunished. He was living proof.

Lindy eased out of the car, almost in slow motion, looking thirty-something and meadow fresh. She had Bambi eyes, and her skin was as creamy as whole milk. He reminded himself that he was lactose intolerant. But it was impossible not to notice that God had blessed her with an ample supply of femininity. All those soft curves were hidden not so successfully under a clingy pink sweater. He blinked and looked away, knowing he'd have to bear the burden of being a gentleman with his eyes. He'd never had a problem with this before, but a hundred victories suddenly threatened to dissolve like a bad investment. *Talk about distracting.*

"Hi." The un-introduced woman slipped on a coat and then walked right up to him and gasped. "Look at you. Just look at you."

Owen glanced around, wondering whom she was addressing.

Lindy laced her fingers around her throat. "Why, you must be Owen Quigly."

"Yup. That's the *who* of it." *What a moronic thing to say.* He shook Lindy's hand.

"I'm Lindy. Van's description of you was perfect." She tilted her chin. "You are dashing."

Owen nearly choked on his salvia. *Dashing?* Who was she kidding?

"Jeans and flannel always says outdoorsy and adventuresome." Lindy said the words with conviction, as though she expected no further argument.

Was she waiting for a compliment in return? "And you seem very pastel. Sort of mother-of-pearl . . . ish." He dropped his gaze. The breeze released a groan through the woods, as if nature, too, cringed at his ridiculous comment. Unfortunately he was left breathing.

Lindy giggled but said no more about his quirky compliment.

Holly gave him a look that said, "Don't use up all your charm in one pass, eh, old friend?"

Van motioned toward the hiking trail. "Shall we proceed?"

"Yes, let's go," Owen chimed in. *Before the rest of my foot takes up residence in my mouth.*

* * * * *

Holly allowed Van to lead the way even though she'd been through the park many times. The morning was clear and cold and would provide good hiking weather. The sky flaunted a few silky clouds, but nothing foreboding. The trees had lost their leaves, so they were no longer dressed to the nines in autumn's jewels, but the woods still welcomed her. And as always, the park was framed by the rocky bluffs she'd loved since childhood. She took in a deep breath, feeling glad she'd come with Van. Even pleased to see Owen having a good time with his date. Well, *trying* to have a good time.

Lindy stumbled, letting out the flimsiest of yelps. Owen reached out to her, but Holly squelched a grin when she saw him steady the woman as if she were his grandmother. No wonder he'd never married. But what about Owen's new determination to snag a woman? Maybe she'd have to help him along.

Their little gathering fell into a hush as they walked along.

Holly allowed the woods to envelop her. Just above them the trees linked branches like lovers lacing their hands. The sounds of the woods intensified—the jubilant trills of birds, the rush of water over stones and logs, and the rustling of small creatures under the leaves.

Van pointed to the ground and said, "'A little noiseless noise among the leaves, born of the very sigh that silence heaves.'"

"How lovely. Who wrote that?" Holly asked.

Van looked at her, his eyes glistening with what appeared to be pure delight. "It was Keats."

It was no surprise to Holly that Van could quote the work of famous poets, but it was a surprise that they both rejoiced over the same works of nature.

Lindy caught up to Holly. "Van told me about his new project, and I want you to know you're in good hands. He'll write your story with the utmost devotion. And his readers will love it."

"I think readers are going to fall in love with Holly," Van added.

"Are you finished with the rough draft yet?" Lindy asked him.

"No. I can't figure out how the story should end." Van picked up a pebble, dried it off, and studied it.

"So, Van, will you make up your own ending?" Holly hadn't spent much time thinking about a closure to her story, but suddenly it seemed important.

"I just meant I'm including the present. And since the story is continuing even as we speak, I'm not sure where to cut it off." Van tossed the stone back into the stream.

"Really?" Holly felt compelled to follow the rabbit trail of Van's disclosure. "So whatever I choose to say and do right now, this minute, could end up in the book and be read by thousands of people?" The idea was exhilarating but also surreal. She wondered if that was how reality TV stars felt, being followed around everywhere with cameras. Humans didn't do well under those conditions; they were invariably too human.

"In Van's case, tens of thousands of readers," Lindy corrected.

Van glanced back at Holly. "I'll only use these moments if I feel they're significant to the main story."

Holly picked up a stick and swiped at the grass as she strolled along. "What if I do the wrong thing?"

"Whatever you choose to do will be the way the story should be." Van smiled.

Holly stopped on the path. It meant that their date would be included in the story. *How strange.* The stick in her hands snapped in two. "I have a question. What needs to happen today to make you want to incorporate this hiking scene in the book? Does it need to be funny or memorable or life-threatening?"

Van stroked his chin. "Well, I'd ask myself questions like, 'Does this scene today add movement or substance to the plot?' Bottom line, would it keep readers turning the pages?"

Holly dropped her sticks and mulled over Van's words. She felt clueless about how to translate real life into a readable story. *Good thing Van's the writer and not me.* "So Van Keaton, the author, may show up in his own book?" She moved a tree branch out of the way a second before it would have whacked Van in the head and then steered him around the stream before his shoe landed in a water hole.

Van kept hiking, cheerfully unaware of these tiny perils and Holly's efforts to divert them.

She kept up with him, curious to hear his reply. Even Owen and Lindy hovered near them as if they, too, wanted to know what Van would say next.

"It looks like I'm going to show up in your story." Van grinned at Holly. "I hope you don't mind."

* * * * *

Owen let out a lungful of air. Van would only include himself in Holly's story if he were getting serious about her.

Holly touched her cheek to her

shoulder in a girlish kind of gesture. "Well then, welcome to my story."

"I think your work will be a tour de force." Lindy let her hands run along the lower branches. "I only wish I'd thought of it first."

Holly had never acted this way with any of her other dates. The whole scene made Owen's stomach feel tense. Made his shoes feel too tight. He hated himself for what he was about to do but felt compelled beyond reason. "Uh, Van."

"Yeah."

"Have you ever been snipe hunting?" Owen knew it wasn't his finest hour.

Holly whirled around and gave Owen her surliest expression. "Owen Quigly. You're kidding. You wouldn't *really* do that to Van."

"Do what to me?" Van's expression was as goofy as the concept of snipe hunting.

Holly rolled her eyes at Owen and then said to Van, "He intends to send you on a wild goose chase. You know, send you out with a bag and a stick to find a furry creature in the brush that doesn't really exist."

Van chuckled. "I wouldn't mind being on a wild goose chase looking for furry creatures if *you* were with me." He blew Holly a kiss.

Oh, brother. If most humans were puzzles with a few missing pieces, Van Keaton was an empty box. The couple moseyed on ahead, whispering things back and forth. Owen couldn't make out any of it. Maybe he could stir things up a bit—slip a grass snake into Van's backpack. *Naw, too infantile.* Maybe Van's real Achilles' heel was his writing. "Hey, Van, I'll bet Holly would love to read what you've written so far."

"Oh, it's not ready. Not by any means. Not even readable. Full of notes and unpolished passages. Some of it's tripe, in fact. I couldn't possibly allow anyone to see it right now in such an embryonic stage." Van gave a violent shake to his head as if it were the most abhorrent thought he'd ever had.

Holly was full of puppy-dog woe. "I realize it's a rough draft, but is there any part of it I can read? I'd love to see even the first chapter. Please, please."

Van held up his hands in surrender.

"Okay. A compromise. I will pick a chapter, edit it, and then let you read it. How's that?"

"More than fair." Holly touched Van's cheek. "Thank you."

Owen jammed his fists into his pockets. He'd only made things worse with his asinine strategies. He'd better give up before he had Van proposing marriage.

"Isn't it precious?" Lindy moved in closer to Owen. "Van and Holly look sooo sweet."

Owen rubbed the back of his neck for comfort, but there was no relief. For some reason his hands were covered with Lindy's perfume. *All this is my fault.* If he hadn't been such a coward over the years—if he'd just told Holly how he felt years earlier—maybe everything would have worked out. He wouldn't still be single, resorting to blind dates with impossibly drop-dead gorgeous females he wasn't interested in, or lowering himself to such juvenile behavior. He'd spent way too many years masking his romantic feelings for Holly, and now she was going to slip through his fingers. *No more pretending. No more excuses.*

Van and Holly laughed, and their

laughter suddenly compelled Owen to make his position known. Desperation overtook him until he bore no resemblance to the phlegmatic man of the past. His feelings for Holly, whether laughed at or not, were nothing akin to the affection between siblings. He longed for so much more than friendship. *I should just say it out loud.* "Holly?"

Owen stopped on the trail, which made the others slow down, stop, and then stare at him.

"Holly." Owen would say what needed to be said right in the middle of a double date, in the presence of God, and in the name of all that was honest and good. "Holly, I love you." There it was. Out there. For all the world to hear, especially for the one who mattered the most. He had officially leaped out of the plane and was in the middle of an emotional free fall.

Chapter Twelve

Stares from Holly, Van, and Lindy put a quiver in Owen's smile. Perhaps he'd picked a bad time to make his announcement after all. Maybe he should just run the other way. Or play dead.

"Okay, I know what's wrong." Holly tilted her head at Owen. "I forgive you for the snipe-hunting thing. I know you didn't *really* want to send Van off into the bushes where he might get a tick."

"Oh, isn't that precious?" Lindy asked. "I love it when friends make up."

"Ticks?" Van dusted off a boulder and

perched himself on top. "You have ticks here?"

Holly chuckled, offered some soothing words to Van about it being off-season for ticks, and then sat down next to him.

Owen took a seat on a fallen log opposite the couple and sighed. Good thing he wasn't in charge of the universe. Apparently he couldn't even handle a simple declaration of love. *On the other hand.* If Holly *had* latched onto the real meaning of his words, what would have happened? Would she have seen him in a new and favorable light, or would she have given him a snap on the head with a sharp stick like they were ten again? He had no idea what Holly's reaction would be, and the not knowing was driving him crazy. Somewhere amid all the frustration and helplessness, though, he'd never felt more alive than when he said those three words to Holly.

Lindy sat down next to Owen and wiggled her feet over the side of the log. "Van, I wanted to tell you I ran into one of your fans the other day. She raved about your last novel, *Land of Dreams and Drawbridges.*"

Holly tugged on Van's sleeve. "Tell us about it."

Van splayed his hand over his heart. "Well, I'm sure you've heard of the butterfly effect—the theory that the tiniest air flow generated by the beat of a butterfly's wings can affect air currents enough to eventually create a hurricane. Well, my novel relates those same effects to humans—that whatever we do and say, whatever movement we make toward good or evil, can have a powerful rippling effect around the world."

"Nicely said." Lindy clapped her hands.

"That was lovely," Holly added.

Owen endured the moment. What was it with writer types? Why did they have to turn everything into a metaphor? Couldn't a rock just be a rock? If Holly was in awe of this guy—this Cyrano de Bergerac—then Owen was in serious trouble. He had no way to compete with such panache.

For a few seconds Lindy's perfume wafted over to him on the breeze and fogged up his senses. He glanced at her. She was looking him over, and not in a way that assessed his abilities to teach

Sunday school. He wiped the perspiration off his forehead. Lindy was by any standard an intoxicating woman. So what was she doing giving him googly eyes? Surely there was a whole fleet of guys lined up somewhere, ready to sweep her off her feet. But even if there weren't any other men, he knew he wasn't the right man to do the sweeping.

"Owen, I hear you've done quite well for yourself buying and selling stocks. Is it true?" Lindy asked.

"Um, yeah, I've done all right." The question made Owen uncomfortable. "Except it's a lot of work studying the market, and I do make mistakes." Of course lately his predictions had been more right than wrong. Last time he checked he was a millionaire, but he never talked about it. No need. It would only make people treat him differently. And he liked his simple lifestyle. All he ever wanted was right here in Noel. "I'm grateful to have some stocks that are performing well right now." He laughed, but he wasn't sure why. "That's the short answer anyway."

Lindy rose and gestured down the trail. "You ready?"

Owen eased off the log and followed Lindy, even though it meant leaving Holly and Van behind.

"So, do you have any tips for beginners?" Lindy asked Owen.

"Buy low, sell high."

Lindy grinned. "I was interested in something a little more revealing." She gave him a beguiling look, and he wondered if it was a regular fixture on her face when she wanted something. It was appealing, and he figured men rarely denied her much of anything when she wore that expression.

"I'd say you should still keep an eye on the tech stocks. *However*, they all look attractive on the outset. But getting to know their ups and downs over a longer period of time is one of the keys. You'll gradually be able to see what's not so perfect. It's like staring at a diamond. At first it glistens under the lights. But if you pay attention and look more closely, you can see all the inclusions. The flaws. When that happens you should be able to make a more informed choice."

Lindy shook her head at Owen. "I don't think this is a lesson in the stock market."

"Hmm?"

"You're not a writer, but you've got quite a knack for subtext dialogue."

"Thanks, but you'll have to elaborate."

"It's when you say one thing and mean something else." Lindy gave her brow a provocative lift. "That's the short answer anyway."

"Oh." Guess there was more to Lindy than perfume and fluff.

Holly trotted by them with Van in tow. "Just so you'll know," Holly said to Lindy as she passed by, "Owen always means what he says. He's a book you can read. But that's part of his charm."

So, Holly had been listening in on their conversation.

Lindy cocked her head. "How long have you and Holly been friends?"

"Since we were toddlers," Owen replied.

Van suddenly took Holly by the hand and veered off the trail. "We'll catch up in a minute, guys." He waved Owen and

Lindy on, making it clear they wanted to be alone for a while.

Lindy sighed. "Guess they need a private moment."

Owen didn't like the sound of that. A private moment meant there'd be potential for intimate goings-on. Whispering. Closeness. And heaven forbid, kissing.

"You and Holly—I never knew friendships lasted anymore," Lindy said wistfully. "Everyone is in such a hurry these days. You know, to change jobs and friends and relationships." She reached down and swished her hands in the clear water.

"So what kind of books do you write?"

"Christian romance." Lindy gazed at him with a flicker of expectancy.

"Oh?" *Romance.* Maybe he'd better modify the conversation a bit. "And how long have you been a writer?" Owen hoped to keep his date occupied while he kept a sharp eye on the wayward couple. He sat on a rock as Lindy continued to play in the stream.

"Well, I've been writing ever since I was

a kid. I try never to brag on myself, but I will tell you this. At twelve I did write a short story that so astounded my teacher . . ."

Owen tried, really tried, to listen to Lindy, but it was difficult since Van and Holly were moving closer. They edged toward each other's lips, and it certainly wasn't for resuscitation. There was no question about their intentions—Van and Holly were going to kiss. He couldn't watch. Holly was, after all, the little Goodnight girl he'd grown up with. The one he'd built a fort with out of sticks and grass and bits of mud—mud he'd lovingly hand mixed with her. The girl he'd bandaged when she'd scraped her knee on her inaugural bike ride. *What is my point?* He'd always been a part of Holly's life, and no Nicholas Sparks wannabe was going to romance her off to Houston!

Perhaps it was time for another distraction. Owen was two seconds away from releasing a diverting holler when Lindy tiptoed over to him and kissed his cheek.

The warmth of Lindy's breath mingled with her soft hair against his skin made him lose his sobriety for a second. He stood up from the rock, stumbled backwards, and then landed not so mannishly in a stream. He scrambled up out of the cold water, his clothes soaked. "Why did you kiss me?"

"I was just trying to thank you." Lindy placed her hands over her mouth.

Was she stifling a giggle? "Thank me for what?" Owen squashed some of the water out of his jeans and coat, but his efforts were useless. He was a soggy mess.

"I wanted to thank you for saving my life." Lindy batted those huge eyelashes of hers. And then he noticed it—when Lindy talked he could see her tongue moving. *What a quirky mannerism.* The effect was mesmerizing, but not in a good way. He shook off his stare. "I know the terrain is a little wild out here, but you're in no danger. I think the most I could have saved you from are the minnows in this stream, and the worst they can do is tickle your toes to death."

"Oh." Lindy laughed. "You are *so* hilarious."

"Are you sure about that?"

"Yes." She raised an eyebrow, and her

brow meant business. But it didn't matter what her brow was up to. Or her big flirting eyelashes or any other part of Lindy. All he could think about was that snotty-nosed kid all grown up who was kissing another man.

"You saved my life because I really needed your company today," Lindy said. "You see, my boyfriend left me for another woman, and I've been alone now for almost a month."

"I'm very sorry." Even though his sympathy meter wasn't pinging off the charts after Lindy's unhappy revelation, he knew he'd come off like an insensitive boob if he tried to disentangle himself from her. Meanwhile the water's chill seeped into unmentionable places, giving fresh meaning to the word misery. He glanced over at Van and Holly. The two of them seemed anything *but* chilled as they kissed. Each other. In a sunlit meadow. Then he remembered the cell phone in his pocket. Before Owen could counsel himself against the deed, he reached into his pocket and pushed the cell phone button he'd been pushing for years.

Even at some distance Owen could

hear the tiny notes from Holly's phone playing "Somewhere Over the Rainbow."

Holly eased away from Van's kiss and reached into her pocket. When she looked at the phone, her gaze—a bit fiery he thought—darted over to him.

Owen hid behind a tree. Like a squirrel. His call had effectively broken up their cozy bubble. Life could indeed be manipulated. He wondered if Van felt that way as the master influencing his creation. It was a good feeling. No, it was a *great* feeling. Maybe he should take up writing. Then feeling like a fool, he came out from behind the tree.

Chapter Thirteen

Holly tapped her foot in the dirt. *Owen Quigly, what do you think you're doing, sneaking around, sabotaging a perfectly good kiss?* Owen and Lindy were certainly welcome to hike on down the trail without them. And why were Owen's clothes all wet? Holly turned her phone off, sent her old friend one more dark warning, and then gave Van her full attention.

Van made little circles on Holly's wrist with the tip of his finger.

Holly had a sudden urge to chuckle since the sensation felt more tickly than alluring, but since she wanted to hold onto whatever was left of the moment, she stifled a belly laugh.

"I guess you know how I feel about you."

"How do you feel, Van?"

He lifted her hand to his chest and pressed her palm against his heart. "I feel as though I've been dreaming of you my whole life."

"Oh?" His heartbeat felt impressively real and rapid, but his comment sounded more like fiction.

"I've not been the same since I met you. I don't eat much. Can't sleep anymore. But boy can I write. All because of you."

Was Van Keaton really falling for her?

"I'm glad your writing has gotten better."

He moved closer to her. "It's so much more than the writing I'm talking about."

"What *are* you talking about?"

"I'm talking about *us*."

"*Us* is a good word."

Van took her hands in his. "I'd love to know what you're thinking, right this minute."

Holly grinned. "Well, lately you've had this look like you need to tell me something."

"I do, actually." Van sighed, paused, and then sighed again. "I need to tell you that when Beatrice Monroe saw you on TV and then read my blog, she contacted me by e-mail, and I encouraged her to come to Noel to talk to you. To tell you about your mother passing away." He looked down. "I hope you're not angry with me for meddling."

"How could I be angry with you?" Holly touched his cheek and turned his head, drawing his gaze back to her. "It was the only right thing to do."

"You can't know how relieved I am to hear you say that. I've been pretty torn up about it. I mean, I could have told Beatrice not to come, and I think she would have stayed away. It might have been easier on you, not knowing your mother was dead. I honestly had no idea what to do."

"I admit, the truth has been hard to deal with, but it also means a certain amount of emotional resolution—eventually." Holly hugged her arms around her waist. "I just wish I could have said good-bye to my mother."

"Then why don't you? You should write

your mother a letter, even though she won't be able to read it. Whenever I go through hard times in my life, I journal. I put down everything in a notebook. It might be a good start for you—to find that resolution you mentioned."

"It might. Thank you." Holly thought for a moment. "I know you'll want to add what happened to my mother to your book. And I'll answer all your questions when we have more time. But for now I want to say—I feel as though I've been holding my breath all these years, waiting for my mother, waiting to live my life. As if my identity were in limbo, not really knowing who the real Holly Goodnight was—is. As if I could find a truer version of myself if I found my mother, my roots. Does that make any sense?"

"Yes, but we can watch a flower grow and thrive without ever looking at the seed." He sat on a boulder and gently pulled her down next to him.

"True." After sitting for a moment in the quiet, Holly unzipped her pack. "By the way, I bought you a gift."

"Really?"

She pulled out a packet of antibacterial wipes.

Van accepted the gift with awe. "This is the most thoughtful gift anyone has ever given me. You really do *get* me." He took hold of her hand and kissed it.

She and Van were *finally* alone, but one more question dangled in the air like an overripe tomato. "If you wanted us to be alone, Van, why did you insist on making this a double date? I don't understand—"

Van stopped the discussion by covering her mouth with his. The kiss cut off her words, but not her senses, which ebbed and flowed with sheer delight. She just hoped Owen wasn't going to spring a badger on them or pretend to have a heat stroke with all that flannel. When the kiss came to a close, her eyes fluttered open. "So, Mr. Keaton, how would you describe that kiss in your book?"

Van continued to hold her. "How would *you* describe it?"

Holly pondered the question. "Well, if we lived in the sixties I'd say the kiss was totally cosmic."

"Hey, that's good."

"Thanks."

"No, I mean *really* good. I could use it." He eased her away from the circle of his arms, yanked out a notepad from his pocket, and began scribbling on the paper.

The word *aghast* seemed appropriate. "Van, are you taking notes about our kiss?"

"Sorry." He smiled at her. "I hated to lose the moment."

"Well, I think you just did." Holly gave him a little huff and, without looking back, stomped toward the trail.

Farther down the path, Lindy appeared to be squatting in front of Owen, trying to Velcro the front of his shoe. It was impossible to ignore the fact that Lindy adored Owen. And why shouldn't she? He was a wonderful guy. Holly had always prayed Owen would find the right woman, a woman who could recognize all the wonderful facets of his personality. Perhaps Lindy was the one. But if her prayers were being answered right before her eyes, why didn't the blessing make her feel like celebrating?

Holly caught up with Owen and Lindy,

and then a short-winded Van stumbled up behind her.

"Say, Owen, did you fall in the creek?" Van put his hands on his hips. "What happened?"

"I'm afraid I'm to blame," Lindy said. "I distracted Owen with a kiss, and he toppled in."

Van looked obnoxiously satisfied.

Owen raised his chin, looking triumphant but not terribly happy.

Holly cocked her head, taking in the scene. Owen and Lindy had only known each other for what, an hour? Lindy certainly wasted no time moving in for the kill. *Now, Holly, what's with this sudden attitude?*

Van touched the small of Holly's back, and in spite of her irritation at him for his note-scribbling, she leaned toward his caress.

Owen's smile faded.

Holly dug the tip of her shoe into the dirt, making a tiny crater. She felt unsettled, but she wasn't sure why. It was like the seconds right after a lightning strike and just before the thunder. She tried to relax her shoulders, but they were frozen with anxiety. Was it Van's insensitivity? *No.* Something else niggled at her. "You guys ready to go back for some lunch? I'm famished."

"Yep." Owen nodded. "I'm starved."

Lindy shrugged. "Sure, if Owen wants to."

Van dusted off his jeans. "I can *always* eat."

So much for Van's lovesick loss of appetite.

"I'll need to stop by my house first," Owen said. "You know, to put on some dry clothes."

They all turned in unison as if in obedience to some offstage director. On the hike back toward the park entrance they made general murmurings about the beauty of the grounds and the brilliance of the morning, but their quick-stepping march revealed that everyone, including Holly, was ready to change the dynamics of the double date.

When they finally stood at the park entrance, Van asked, "Where should we eat?"

"What are we in the mood for?" Holly looked at Owen, who had his arms crossed over his chest. He had his attention fixed on Van.

Lindy pulled a packet of something out of her shoulder bag and offered it to Owen. "Want some peanuts?"

"He's allergic." Holly thought she'd come off like an overprotective mom, refusing a snack for him.

Lindy looked surprised. "Really? You're allergic?"

"Yeah, I'm afraid so," Owen said. "Thanks, anyway."

"Well, I'm a great lover of peanuts." Van smacked his lips, and Lindy tossed him the sack. "Thanks."

Lindy looked at Holly. "What else should I know about our dear Owen? Please tell me more."

"Okay." Holly grinned at her dear friend, who was now staring at her. "Owen usually wears sneakers with Velcro because he has trouble tying things. He has a crooked finger that didn't heal quite right after an accident when he was twelve. Apparently it's dangerous to juggle watermelons."

Lindy laughed.

"Let's see, he's good at chess, but he's

neither competitive nor a pushover. He likes root beer floats, hot sauce, stargazing, mushroom hunting . . . and he makes the best friend anyone could ever have." Holly felt a rush of heat, embarrassed that she'd divulged so much intimate information.

"What an endorsement," Lindy said to Holly. "I'm tempted to marry Owen on the spot."

Van busied himself scribbling on his notepad.

Holly rolled her eyes at Van, but he didn't seem to notice. She glanced at Owen, who wore one of his straight-as-a-window-blind grins and stared back at her with what she could only describe as an obtuse expression. *What is going on?* "Owen? You okay?"

"I'm fine," Owen said to Holly. "And how are you?"

"Good. I'm good." Holly grimaced, wondering if her friend was having a meltdown.

Owen cleared his throat loudly. "By the way, I've got an idea."

"Oh?" Holly said. "What's that?"

"I just thought of the perfect theme for

a Christmas tree." Owen clapped his hands, gesticulating in the most uncharacteristic way.

"What is your theme?" *Oh, dear.*

Owen looked right at Holly. "A tree covered in nothing but—teddy bears."

Holly coughed.

Van's face became the portrait of puzzlement, and he finally put away his infernal notepad.

"Ohhh." Lindy giggled as she gave her date's arm the daintiest little punch. "Isn't that just the most precious idea for a Christmas tree?"

Owen looked so miserable Holly didn't know whether to laugh or cry.

Chapter Fourteen

....

The rest of the double date passed in a peculiar blur. After a quick lunch, Holly announced she had to return to the shop and urgently needed Owen's help to set up a new window display. Van teased her about her Christmas store "emergency," and Lindy looked crushed. But owing to Holly's persistence and Owen's over-eagerness, the two of them finally made their escape.

That afternoon, after Van and Lindy had gone on their not-so-merry way and Owen had indeed given her some assistance decorating the window, Holly put the finishing touches on the display. The hay under the new manger scene was too clumpy, so she picked up the figurines, patted the straw down to make it even, and then one at a time returned the Biblical characters to the display. Lastly, and reverently, she placed the baby Jesus figurine back inside the manger. Being surrounded by all things Christmas was a daily joy for her as well as an inspiration, especially around the holidays. As her father always said, "Christmas is the greatest of all holidays since it represents the greatest of all mercies." And that was something all humans could embrace.

Suddenly, someone hammered on the shop window, pulling Holly out of her reverie.

It was Van, and he held a rolled-up wad of papers in his hand. "I have something for you," he said in a singsong voice.

"Come on in," she mouthed.

Once inside the shop Van helped Holly out of the display window and wrapped his arms around her.

"And what do you have?" Holly asked.

"Is that part of the book?" *Wow, that was fast.*

"It's still rough, mind you. But I know you wanted to read some of it."

"I do. Very much." Holly reached out for the papers. Van held onto them a second longer as if he couldn't bear to part with the pages, but then he released them to her. "I'll take good care of them. I promise."

"I hope this is what you expected."

"I'm sure it will be. I'll read it right away, and then I'll call you."

"Okay then." Van gave Holly a kiss on the tip of her nose and left the shop.

Holly put on some new Christmas music—her favorite, Josh Groban's *Noël* album—and then scooted back down inside the display window to unroll the pages. Then she stopped. A shiver ran through her. *Oh, no, no, no.* What if she hated the way Van wrote about her life? What would she say to him?

As Holly waited for her courage to build up again, her thoughts drifted back to the other half of their double date—Owen and Lindy. Why did she keep thinking about them? They made a charming couple. In fact, if Lindy were chocolate, she'd be a Belgian truffle—the imported kind with mousse. But it had been more than a little intriguing to see the interaction between the truffle and her friend. In spite of Lindy's beauty, talent, and boundless adoration, Owen hadn't seemed impressed. In fact, he apparently felt the opposite, since he'd said very little about the date while they worked on the window display. And more importantly, he'd used the teddy bear code words, which could only signal disaster.

Holly had to admit the amusement she felt was tinged with relief. But why? She wanted the best for Owen—for him to fall in love and marry. It was the same thing Owen had always wanted for her. Then why had the double date been so disjointed, so full of cross-purposes? Perhaps Owen was concerned that if either of them married, it would break up their friendship. It was a concern she'd had more than a few times.

In a moment of bravery, Holly once again unrolled Van's manuscript. He'd given her only six pages. Hmm. Van certainly didn't trust her with much of his rough draft. Holly shrugged off the disappointment and began reading at the top of page 290:

The unforeseen happened; a plot twist of heart-changing proportion arrived like a cloudburst after a long dry summer. I fell in love with the heroine. Would I become the hero in my own book? Only Holly could decide; my fate, my joy, was in her hands. Would she say yes? Would she marry me?

The pages of the manuscript fell from Holly's hands and landed on the wings of the angels. *A proposal of marriage?* Inside a book no less. Pretty romantic stuff. Was it real? Surely it wasn't a joke.

Then another dispiriting option shadowed her thoughts. Van had admitted weeks before that he might need to add bits of fictional material to the story if it started to sag in places. Perhaps the proposal was a way for Van to jazz up the story a bit. Or a lot. He could always take back the proposal later, but in the end it would still offer an avalanche of conflict and intrigue for his book.

Holly lowered her head in shame. That didn't sound right. Van was never crafty or false. So if he *did* mean what he wrote, then how would she respond? Did she love him in return? She certainly felt a growing affection and fondness for Van, but did love always follow such emotions? Surely talking it over with Van would be the wisest move, and he was only a phone call away. Holly reached for her purse outside the display window, dug out her cell phone, and pushed in Van's number.

He answered right away. "So, what did you think?"

"Did you mean it for real, Van?" Holly tried not to sound pathetic and shaky, but she wasn't used to proposals of marriage.

"I meant it for real, my darling."

Holly could imagine him smiling on the other end.

"Surprises are good, right?"

"Some are."

"And so what are your thoughts about this particular surprise?" Apparently it was Van's turn to have a trembling voice.

Now came the moment of reckoning. *What will I say, God?* "It's a proposal that is not unwelcome."

"Hmm. You sound like my attorney."

Holly chuckled. "The word *love* should not be given out lightly. When I say it I want to mean it."

"You're right, you know. Once you name a thing it's pretty powerful stuff. Take as long as you need, but . . ."

"But?"

"Please don't keep me in my agony too long."

"I'll try not to." Holly cradled the phone in her hand, wishing Van were there next to her. "Do you think we've known each other long enough? I mean, I know we've dated, and we've had lots of phone chats, but—"

"Who's to say what is enough or not enough? I know what I feel for you is real. By the way, before I ever wrote the proposal I got permission from your father."

"You did? What did he say?"

"He said he found me to be a decent Christian man, and he approved of my asking you."

"Oh?" Holly could hardly believe all that had transpired. And her father had managed not to spill the beans. Shocking. "Is that all Dad said?"

"He also said if we get married I'd

better take very good care of you or he'd come after me with a horsewhip."

Holly laughed. "Sorry, I shouldn't laugh."

"I can tell your father loves you. And I do too. In fact, if I could lay out all the scenes of my life and pick the finest, the ones that matter the most to me, I would pick all the moments we've been together."

"No one has ever said anything so romantic to me before. I have an odd question, though." She looked around, glad that no customers were milling around at the moment and relieved that her father was still working in the back room.

"Yes?"

"What happens with the story—if I were to say no to your proposal? Would you add it to the book or delete this whole part?"

"If I took it out, I would feel as though I were cheating my readers." Van cleared his throat. "So, that's it. No matter what you say, yes or no, and no matter how painful your reply might be—I will share the truth."

"I admire that." Holly touched her cheek

with the back of her hand. How had it all happened? They were so different. And yet.,,

"I admire you too."

"Oh, yeah? And what do you admire about me?"

"The whole of your life. The way you care for your father. The way you think of others. The way children light up in your presence. You dazzle everyone like Christmas morning around the tree."

"I do?"

"And you ease my poor phobic mind."

Holly chuckled. "And how could I possibly do that?"

"As you know, I have a list of quirks a mile long, and among them is a tendency to obsess about what other people think of me, which is why I gave up public speaking. But you've made me so fearless I called my booking agent yesterday and told her to start lining up engagements."

"So I make you courageous, huh? That's wonderful. I'm glad. I'd no idea I had such power."

"You're my Athena."

Holly pursed her lips. "Wait a minute,

wasn't she supposed to be the Greek goddess of warfare?"

"Yes, but Athena was also the goddess of heroic enterprises."

Holly grinned. "I've never thought of myself as a champion of anything, really. Just a shop girl. Certainly not a Greek goddess. You say such sweet things." *Irresistible things. Words as pretty as the sound of that flute of yours.*

"I'm going to miss you."

"Miss me? Why?"

Van paused. "I'm going back to Houston today."

"You're going to leave me right after a marriage proposal?" Holly's shoulders drooped. "But you just got here. Are you upset because I didn't give you an answer?"

"It's not that at all. I just figured that after the recent news about your mother, it might be too soon for you to make a decision like this. You'll need some time to search your heart. I know you'll want to talk to your dad about this—and God. I don't want to get in the way of that process. Then when you say yes—well, *if* you say yes, I'll know I hadn't coerced you into it. Although coercion is always an option."

Holly smiled. "When will you return?"

"Three weeks, but I'll call you every day."

"Promise?"

"I promise," Van said. "And really, even though my hotel room is comfortable, I always feel like I'm on vacation. I need time at home to finish the rough draft and then get some serious editing done."

"I hope you get it done quickly. By the way, you're not leaving without a proper good-bye. Are you?"

"Proper, meaning a kiss?"

"Yes."

"I think that can be arranged," Van said. "I'll have you in my arms in less than two minutes."

"Where *are* you?"

"In the sandwich shop."

Holly laughed. About sixty seconds later she met him at the front door in a rush of excitement. Was that heady feeling the beginnings of love, or was her heart playing tricks on her, knowing the dream of having a family had finally been placed within her grasp? Some part of her wanted to say yes to Van before he had a chance to drive away, but the commonsense part of her knew marriage was not to be entered into lightly.

Van encircled her with his arms.

"You act as though I've already said yes."

Van buried his face in her hair. "I couldn't help imagining it." He eased back and traced his finger along the curves of her face. "How art thou, Holly Rose?"

"Doing very well indeed."

"You won't forget me while I'm away, will you?"

Holly tugged on his collar. "Now, how could I do that?"

Van tucked her hand inside his. "Because sometimes life turns our heads in unexpected ways." He kissed her once more and then walked backwards toward his car, never taking his eyes off her. "Good-bye, my darling." After one more solemn wave, Van drove away.

Holly stepped back into the shop feeling giddy and swept away. But was she falling in love or merely aloft on a cloud lined with silvery words? Perhaps Van's idea—that they spend some time away from each other to test their relationship—had been a good one. For some reason she didn't seek out her father to give him the latest news. But why would she hesitate?

She rubbed her earlobe as her gaze rose to the ball of mistletoe. The ribbons were loose, and the Christmas heirloom dangled precariously, about to fall. She'd not yet had a chance to fulfill her dream of kissing under the family mistletoe, not in all her thirty years, and now was not a good time for her dream to fall apart. Holly grabbed a stepladder.

Chapter Fifteen

Van looked in his rearview mirror. Holly had gone back into the shop before his car was out of sight. Not a good sign. He certainly wanted to leave his proposal in the hands of Providence, and yet tipping the scales in his favor sounded promising too. He would enlist Holly's dearest friend to help his cause. Fortunately he knew just where Owen lived. The guy worked from home, so he was sure to be there.

When Van pulled up to Owen's house, he was surprised by what he saw. The home appeared well built and situated ideally in a lush valley, but the structure was rustic and small. He wondered what the guy did with all the extra cash he made in the stock market.

Van walked up to the porch, knocked on the door, and then had some serious second thoughts. Maybe the guy didn't like him well enough to promote his cause. He waited a moment longer while negative scenarios proliferated like rabbits. No one answered the door. Good. He should let it go. Now. His clever idea for soliciting romantic help from Owen suddenly seemed ludicrous. Just as Van turned to leave, the door opened. No one but God heard his groan.

"Hi, Van." Owen crossed his arms. "What's going on?"

Van coughed. "I just wanted to, you know, ask you something."

"All right." Owen opened the screen door. "Do you want to come in?"

"I don't have the time, but thanks. I'm on my way back to Houston."

"But I thought you just arrived." Owen stepped out onto the porch. "Does Holly know you're leaving?"

"Yes, she does." Van took in a long,

deep breath. "Listen, I know we don't know each other well, but I already feel as though I can trust you."

A flicker of something unreadable lit Owen's expression and then disappeared. "Thank you."

"So I wanted to ask you a favor."

"All right. Depends on what it is, I guess."

"Fair enough." Van looked at his shoes and then back at Owen. "I proposed to Holly today."

"Excuse me?"

"I proposed."

"Marriage?"

"Is there any other kind?"

Owen took a step closer to Van, his frame looming over him. "And did she say yes?"

Van swallowed. "She's going to spend some time thinking and praying about it. And, of course, talking to her father and friends, I'm sure. Since you're her oldest friend, I thought you could help me out by—"

"By convincing her to marry you?" Owen sat down on a bench.

"Well, maybe you could just mention my various qualities. The good ones, that is. Remind her of all the advantages there are to marrying me." He waved his hand. "Never mind. You don't know me all that well. But maybe you could champion me a little. I love her, Owen. I only came to Noel in the hopes of writing Holly's story. I never meant to fall in love." Van ran his fingers through his hair. "I realize that phrase is worn out, but it's as true as if I'd been the first person ever to say those words."

"You seem sincere." Owen twiddled his fingers.

"So, may I count on you for your support?" Van cringed, thinking he sounded more like a man on the campaign trail than a man in love.

Owen paused. A long pause. So long, in fact, the man must have been about to decline his request.

Should he have spent more time getting to know Owen before trying to get his approval? He'd hoped that setting Owen up with Lindy would garner him some points, but then again, Owen hadn't seemed all that enamored with Lindy. Like the publishing business, love was unpredictable. Who knew what was going to be a blockbuster or a bomb?

Unfortunately his foray into matchmaking had been the latter. But perhaps Owen was at least grateful he'd made an effort. "You've hesitated so long I'm thinking maybe you don't approve of me."

Owen rose from the bench. "I'm sure you understand I have to think of Holly first. She seems to care for you. But I'm concerned about her happiness. *Long-term* happiness. So if you think you can give her that, I'll try to be fair in my remarks."

"I would always do my best to make her happy, but of course there are no guarantees in this life."

Owen frowned. "For someone who has a gift for words you suddenly sound awfully businesslike. Or maybe *noncommittal* would be a more accurate term."

Van shook his head. "I love Holly. I always will. It's just that life is full of—irregularities."

"Meaning?"

"No matter how hard we try to make other people happy in this life, they may choose unhappiness. I can only tell you how *I* will feel. What *I* will do."

Owen seemed to bristle at his comment. "It's in Holly's nature to choose joy, so I doubt that problem would ever come up."

Even though the day was cool, sweat trickled down Van's shirt. "Do you think you could—well, I'd hoped you might—"

"I won't twist Holly's arm if that's what you're trying to say."

Van put up his hands. "Not quite the words I would have chosen, but—"

Owen pointed his finger at Van. "I will give you this. Both of us want the same thing for Holly. We want her to be happy all the days of her life. I will agree to this—to do everything in my power to make that happen."

Those weren't the words Van had wanted to hear, but he guessed they were all Owen was going to offer. "Thank you." He reached out to Owen.

They shared a firm handshake, but something dangled in the air between them. Was it a challenge? Van doubted it. Owen was probably just acting like Holly's big brother—watching out for her. *Then again.* What if Owen's feelings for Holly went beyond friendship? He *had* spoken her name with such passion. But if that was the case, Van couldn't feel sorry for Owen since he'd had so many years to make up his mind. He'd had plenty of chances to propose.

After sliding behind the wheel of his Lexus, Van dismissed his worries and plugged in his vocabulary CD. In his rearview mirror he could see a kid—who must have been one of Quigly's neighbors—trying to pull a load of bricks in a red wagon across the meadow in front of his house. To the boy's credit he kept pulling, but it became obvious the wagon wasn't going to budge another inch. It was one of those situations that could easily double as a life lesson. *Great.* Van hated those teachable moments even more than he hated bad book reviews. And those pesky life lessons usually popped up when he did something wrong. *Am I out of sync here with Holly? Trying to force something You haven't ordained?* He'd learned over the years—and usually the hard way—that life whirled along better when he let God lead the dance.

Van took another look in the rearview

mirror. Owen had come to the kid's rescue, but just as he reached down to help the boy, the wagon toppled over on its side, spilling the load of bricks all over Owen's feet.

* * * * *

Holly awakened on the couch with a snort. What time was it? She glanced at her cell phone. 6:10 p.m. Hmm. Had the doorbell rung? She rubbed her head and neck, trudged to the front door, and found Owen standing on her porch. "Hey, Quig."

Owen didn't give her the standard greeting or elbow rub; he just stood there staring at her. Finally he said, "I'm here to invite you to dine at my house. A celebration dinner."

"Oh, yeah?" Was he going to help celebrate Van's proposal? How could he know so soon? "What are we celebrating?"

"Life." Owen grinned.

Holly shook her finger at him. "You know, you've been acting kind of funny lately."

"Moi?"

"Yes, *moi*." Holly narrowed her eyes at him. "And speaking of funny, why did you ring my phone when we were on our hike? It was like you'd never seen me kiss a guy before."

"Dinner will be served in my gazebo tonight." His hand made a flourish as he dipped his head. "I'll pick you up at seven. Good?"

Holly realized he wasn't going to answer her question. But he would later—she would make sure of it. "Okay." Before she could pelt Owen with more questions, he headed down the front path back to his car. Why was he limping?

As she shut the front door, guilt trickled in. Was dinner with Owen kosher while she considered a marriage proposal from another man? But it was only Owen, the man who was like a brother. Van knew well that Owen was her best friend; he knew they spent time together. She had accepted no ring from Van, made no promises—except to consider his proposal—and yet she felt mutinous!

She drummed her fingers on the door. *Owen is like a brother to me.* And he had always thought of her as a sister. Holly slid down to the floor and placed her head in her hands. *Au contraire.* She suddenly realized that the new look in Owen's eyes wasn't the gaze of a brother.

Maybe the timing of the dinner would work out after all, since she should talk to Owen about the proposal. If she *did* choose to marry Van, they would need to discuss how marriage might change their friendship. *Oh, my. Oh, my. Oh, my.* What would life be like without Owen? Would they be reduced to passing each other on the streets of Noel and merely saying hello? That sounded like torture. Unthinkable, really. Why couldn't Owen have been born a woman? Then there'd be no complications surrounding their friendship, no appearance of impropriety. But Owen wasn't a woman. He was a man. And he had that funny look in his eye.

Then Holly remembered the crazy vow they'd made when they were twelve—a pledge to marry each other if they hadn't found love by age thirty. The oath flooded back to her in great detail. They'd been in Short Bottom Cave, talking about nothing and everything as usual, when Owen got down on one knee—an idea he'd gotten off a TV sitcom—and slipped the toy ring on her finger with a solemn vow. She embraced the pledge that day, saying the words back to him. It had been so silly—and yet.

Holly went to her bedroom, opened the bottom drawer of her jewelry case, and after poking around in a jumbled mess of old costume jewelry, found the ring. It was brown like dirt with a clear plastic stone perched on top. She chuckled.

Well, she promised to go to Owen's for dinner, and go she would. Maybe she'd just "forget" to freshen her deodorant or brush her hair. That would give Van a fair advantage.

But no matter how Holly rationalized her prospective dinner with Owen, she still felt guilty. She put the ring back in the drawer and sighed. Why was it women emerged from the womb with a supply of guilt ample enough to last a lifetime? Holly thought it was a reasonable question.

Chapter Sixteen

Holly kept her word by not tidying herself for dinner. For Van's sake she would look as grungy as possible. She looked in the bathroom mirror. Hmm. Disintegrating makeup, crumpled pantsuit, and tufts of hair going in assorted directions. Yep. Pretty mangy.

The doorbell rang, and even though it was just Owen at the door, she felt nervous. All because of that look in his eye? Oy! She swung open the door. Owen Quigly stood before her dressed in the nicest-fitting and most ridiculously handsome tuxedo she'd ever seen. "What *are* you doing wearing that thing?"

The light in Owen's eyes dimmed, and Holly felt awful. In fact, she felt as softhearted as a rock—a big ol' stub-your-toe-and-holler kind of rock. "I'm so sorry, Owen. You just took me by surprise. You look—*very*—nice."

"Thanks. And you look beautiful."

Considering her scruffy appearance, Owen had to be lying, but his words made her smile anyway. "So, we're going to your house for dinner?"

"That's right."

"Since you went to so much trouble getting all dressed up maybe I should go and change."

"You're perfect."

Holly grinned. "Okay." She stepped outside and locked the front door. "Do you mind if I ask why you're all decked out?"

"You'll see." Owen offered her his arm.

"I've never known you to be so mysterious, Mr. Quigly." Holly stole glances at him as they made their way down the front sidewalk.

"Maybe there are still a few things you don't know about me."

"Impossible. I've known you since we were both feeding mud to each other. There isn't anything I don't know about you."

"There's one thing. And you'll know it tonight." Owen opened the car door for her and she slipped inside. Hmm. Van might not be so forgiving if he knew about the tuxedo and the secret.

Owen turned left on Highway 59 and drove out to his home on the meadow. Holly had always loved his house—a cozy little place made of rough timbers, a steel roof, and a wraparound porch. Owen led her around the house to the backyard.

A large stone gazebo—one Owen had built himself—was lit with a bazillion white Christmas lights. Holly gasped. "You know I'm a sucker for twinkly lights." A fire was lit in the outdoor rock fireplace, and it crackled and sputtered pleasantly. Inside the arbor, a table had been covered with linen and set with fine china and crystal. "Where did you get all of this?"

"My granny gave it to me years ago. It's been in my attic. I never had a reason to use it—until now."

"I wish you would tell me what the

special occasion is." She raised an eyebrow.

Owen pulled out a chair for her. "All in good time, my dear." He covered her lap with a quilted blanket. "I don't think you'll need this, but just in case."

Apparently God was in collusion with Owen concerning his special plans, since Holly could never remember such a warm fall evening in Noel, and so close to Thanksgiving!

After she'd gotten settled comfortably at the table, Owen brought out baked salmon and wild rice with roasted butternut squash on the side. She wanted to say how shocked she was that he wasn't serving her food out of a can or spread from a jar, but she curbed her tongue. It might not be the best time for one of her snorting laughs either, so she said demurely, "I didn't know you could cook."

Owen filled her goblet with chilled Pellegrino. "Cooking channel." A slice of lime floated to the top.

"You've made it all look—irresistible."

Grinning way too much, Owen gave the blessing.

They ate heartily but more quietly than

usual. Holly kept sneaking glances at Owen as she took sips from her glass. The evening was not what she'd expected. As they finished the last of their entrées, a breeze came through the gazebo, blowing her napkin onto the floor.

Owen rose from his chair, came around to her side, and picked up her napkin. "You dropped this." With a sweeping motion he flung the napkin outward like a seasoned waiter, slipped it carefully back on her lap, and then let his hand linger on hers.

"Thank you." Holly looked up at him. Had his dark eyes always sparkled? Had his red hair always curled over his forehead like that? The depth and perplexity of those queries overloaded her senses. Her thoughts fuzzed like a TV losing its satellite signal. She fumbled with her utensils until her fork took a flying leap, flipping up, up, and away.

With remarkable reflex, Owen caught the utensil in midair. His expression turned earnest with a hint of mischief. He leaned down to her ear. "You seem a little undone this evening, Miss Goodnight."

The airflow from his whisper tickled her ear. "No, it's the breeze. It's being unpredictable this evening, don't you think?"

Owen raised back up. "Is that so?"

"And there might be a butterfly or two." Holly let the words escape in the air before she could catch them. She wanted to laugh but couldn't. Perhaps she had a momentary clog in her laughing ducts. She wanted to give his arm a friendly jab, diffuse the intensity of the moment, but she couldn't do that either. What was happening? Their repartee had never taken such a provocative turn. Could friendship become something new after decades? Or had her feelings been maturing all along, and she hadn't realized it? "Dinner was wonderful. My stomach welcomed it with open arms."

Owen laughed. "Good, because I forgot to make dessert."

Holly sputtered out a chuckle. "This is plenty sweet." She rubbed her earlobe.

"You always do that, you know."

"What?"

He leaned down to her again. "You always play with your earlobe when you're reflecting on something. When there's a decision to be made."

"I guess I do."

Owen came so near that she thought he might kiss her cheek.

Holly turned toward him, which brought his face only inches from hers. Something stirred, something more than agreeable. Warm, lovely feelings encircled her, drawing her closer to him. She could feel his breath on her cheek. Their lips were so close.

"Holly?"

"Yes, Owen?" She licked her lips.

"Your hair is caught on my tuxedo button."

* * * * *

Owen cringed. *Oh man, how smooth was that?*

Holly blinked, looking puzzled. With a light touch she gingerly untangled her hair from his button.

He sat back down, and the wood groaned out his frustration. Why hadn't he kissed her? Instead, he'd taken an escape route. Holly had looked so receptive. She certainly wouldn't have slapped him. But what if she'd pulled away with a look of disapproval in her eyes? Disappointment? It would have been unendurable.

"I'm afraid my hair is a gnarly mess, Owen. I'm sorry."

Someday he'd have to stop playing the role of the coward and just tell her how he felt. Maybe the moment could still be redeemed. "I have an idea about your hair. Give me a minute." Owen went back into his house and rounded up some shampoo, conditioner, and two bathroom towels. He dropped them into a bag, filled a pitcher with warm water, and then carried everything back out to the gazebo, praying the mild weather would continue and hoping Holly hadn't fled to the hills.

"What in the world are you up to now?" She chuckled.

Owen took hold of her hand. "Do you trust me?"

"I do, Quig, with my life."

"Then you can trust me with your hair." He took his bag of surprises and a chair down toward the stream. "Follow me."

Holly did, and when he motioned for her to sit down, she obeyed.

"Okay, lean your head back on this rolled-up towel."

"Are you going to wash my hair?"

"Yes."

"Owen, please don't feel obligated because I said my hair was—"

"I do not feel obliged or forced or pressured." Owen put his hands on her shoulders. "It's okay to accept help. Then others can know the joy of giving like you do."

"But—"

"Shush, please." Owen dug the shampoo out of his sack.

She shook her head but grinned.

"You warm enough?"

"Amazingly—yes."

Fortunately he'd found the perfect spot where they were surrounded by a cluster of cedar trees. A little nervous, Owen plunged forward with his plan. He'd never been very romantic or spontaneous, but for Holly he would try anything. If he could teach himself how to solve a Rubik's Cube or play six games of chess simultaneously then he could surely come up with a creative way to show his affections. After he poured some warm tap water over Holly's hair he began to massage in a little shampoo.

To his satisfaction, Holly let out a moan. Then she opened her eyes. "Have you been watching *Out of Africa*?"

"No, but I like that movie."

"And are you going to tell a story like Meryl Streep?"

"I don't think so, but I'm hoping you're enjoying this."

"I am." Holly shoulders relaxed in the chair. "You bought coconut shampoo. Mmm. I feel like I need a grass skirt."

Owen grinned. In all the years he'd known Holly, he'd never touched her in such an intimate way. The connection felt pleasurable and stirring, and he had an overpowering urge to kiss her. But timing was everything, and he was determined not to blow it. When Owen had finished shampooing and conditioning her hair, he poured more warm water over her dark locks. "Nice?"

"Very."

Owen dried her hair thoroughly with another towel.

Her eyes fluttered open again. *"That was a first."*

"I hope—I pray it was a good first."

"It was."

"Still warm?"

"Very." Her word came out in a faint whisper.

Owen leaned down again. His mouth hovered over hers. The time had come to say the lines he'd memorized—the ones he'd held in his heart all of his adult life: "Nothing in the world is single; all things by a law divine in one spirit meet and mingle. Why not I with thine?"

Holly smiled. "That poem is so beautiful, Quig."

He winced when she called him Quig, since it was the nickname she'd started using when they were barely out of sippy cups. "I have to give credit where credit is due. The poetry came from Percy Shelley, but the heartfelt way you heard it was my touch." Owen stayed near her face. So close, and yet he still didn't consummate his feelings with a kiss.

Holly took his face in her hands. "You've never quoted poetry in your life, except when Mrs. Jerkins forced you to in the fifth grade. But why quote poetry to me now? Now that another man has fallen in love with me?"

Owen knelt down next to her. "Remember when we were little and we'd play by my granny's spring and you said, 'This water never stops coming out of the ground. I can't imagine it ever drying up'?"

"Actually I do remember saying it."

"I must have felt that way about us, thinking the spring would always be there. I got way too comfortable with us, always believing you'd be around. Couldn't imagine such a nice thing ever drying up. You've dated other guys before, but you've never gotten serious."

"Or they never got serious about *me*."

"Thank God."

"Please tell me something." She gave his sleeve a tug. "Are you feeling obligated somehow? You know, that vow we made as kids? Are you—"

"Can't you see it, Holly. In my eyes? This has nothing to do with the promise we made as kids."

"I do see something I've never seen

before. I just don't know what to do with it."

"Well, *I* do." Owen didn't wait any longer as he lifted her into his arms and kissed her.

Holly didn't hesitate in returning his affection. In fact, the intensity of her kiss surpassed all his imaginings. It was a kiss he could get lost in. After years of pondering and hoping for such a moment, she was finally in his arms, and nothing had ever felt so good. He moved his kisses to her temple and then down to her neck. He whispered in her ear, "Isn't this better than rubbing elbows?"

"Light years beyond." Holly chuckled. "It made my lips go numb."

He pulled away to look into her eyes, to see the Holly who had become so much more than a friend. "I love you, Holly. I've loved you all my life. And I don't mean like a brother or a dad or a nice uncle."

She straightened his bow tie. "My dear Owen. So this was your secret?"

He nodded.

"That explains why you told me you loved me out on the hiking trail."

"It wasn't the best timing to make a confession of love."

Holly shook her finger. "And that's why you were acting so strangely."

He caught her finger and kissed it. "I gotta tell you, watching you with Van became agonizing. Much more painful than the time I got trampled by Luther Burdock's miniature horses."

She touched his cheek. "You should have told me how you felt."

"I sensed that you didn't feel the same way, and because I didn't want to lose you as my friend, I convinced myself that what we had was enough. When I first talked about not getting married years ago, and even recently when I said I was hoping to marry, well, I was just waiting for you to come around—to see me differently. But these are the ramblings of a coward."

"You are the finest man I've ever known."

"Finer than Van Keaton?" Owen hated himself for asking such a pointed question.

"You must think I'm so fickle. The way I'm carrying on with you both."

"You're not capricious, but I'd sure like

to know if you kissed Van with such fire." Owen lowered his gaze. "Oh, wow. Guess I deserve to be slapped for that one. Forgive me."

"Of course I forgive you." She looked at him. "But remember all of this is so sudden. I need some time." Holly gently eased out of his embrace. "I should have told you. Van asked me to marry him."

"I know."

"How could you possibly know about that?"

"Van dropped by my house before he left for Houston. He asked me to put in a good word for him. I wasn't sure what to say. I didn't tell him how I felt."

"He really did come by—to ask you to do that?"

"He did." Owen crossed his arms. "Look, Holly, I'm not going to convince you to marry that pipsqueak, no matter how clever or witty or *literary* he is. Sorry, I take back the pipsqueak part."

Holly chuckled. "So, are we arguing?"

"If we are, it'd probably be the first time."

"Funny to argue—over love."

"I think Keaton would call it *irony.*"

Holly shook her head at him.

"I have an idea." He took a step closer to her.

"You do?"

"Why don't we dance?"

She put up her hands. "But don't we need music?"

"Maybe." After Owen led Holly back to the gazebo, he reached over to a metal box and flipped a switch. Soft jazz poured over them like rainwater flowing down from the hills. "Let's get you toasty again." He threw several more logs on the grate and poked at them until the fire was blazing.

"You've thought of everything this evening." She joined him in front of the fireplace.

Owen lifted Holly's hand up to his shoulder and then placed his hand on her waist. "Shall we?" Leading the way, Owen got them swaying together to the music.

"I never knew you could dance."

"I can't." Owen spun her around and then whirled her back to him again. This time he held onto her more closely.

She tilted her head, looking him over. "You've got that look in your eye again, Mr. Quigly."

"I need you to do something for me, Holly. It's just this one little thing I need from you."

"And what is that?"

"I need you to marry me. You're the one. You always have been. I adore you, Holly Goodnight. I did the moment I set eyes on you."

"But I was wearing a diaper."

"I was too." Owen shrugged. "But I could tell we were meant for each other even then."

"How could you tell?"

"The way we smacked each other with our toys."

"Ahh, the stuff of true romance." She snuggled against his shoulder.

Owen guessed Holly had no idea how much he cared for her. He would even give up a free lunch with Warren Buffett just to hang out with her. "I finally told my parents how I felt. I called them up in Montana."

Holly looked up at him. "What did they say?"

"They said, 'What took you so long'?"

She smiled.

"Look, I know I'm confusing you, Holly,

and I know my timing is messed up. Especially now, with everything that happened yesterday. But I couldn't hide what I felt any longer. To not speak up while Van—well, I know I'll regret that silence for as long as I live." A breeze rustled Holly's hair, and he brushed the strands aside. Then he lifted the quilt off the chair, wrapped it around her, and pulled her to him. "You know, numbers have been my thing all my life—not words. But this one is easy. You are a wonder to me, and I can't imagine my life without that wonder."

"Owen—"

He leaned down to kiss her again, but Holly pressed her fingers over his lips.

"Forgive me. But as long as Van still thinks I'm considering his proposal, I can't do this." She looked away. "In fact, I shouldn't have allowed you to kiss me at all. It was wrong of me."

"I'm sorry." Owen released her. "It does feel a little like trickery on my part. You thought your best friend was going to feed you some dinner, and a guy doing a really bad impersonation of Casanova showed up instead."

Holly grinned. "I knew something had changed between us—and I chose to come anyway."

"I have to know. This kind of affection between us—had it ever crossed your mind all those years?"

Holly sat down and clasped her hands together. "Once in a while I had wondered what it would be like."

"You did?" Owen softened the music and sat down next to her. "There is one more thing I need to say. If you did marry Van, I have this distinct feeling he wouldn't want me to spend time with you. Especially if he knew how I felt. And I couldn't blame him."

"Yes, I had wondered about the changes we'd have to make." Holly pressed the back of her hand against her forehead. "I don't know what to say. You deserve an answer, but I feel so lost right now."

Owen had never been an overly emotional man, but at that moment he knew what a broken heart would feel like. More than anything, though, he wanted to do the right thing. He would let her go for now. "I'll take you home."

"I guess that would be best." Holly shivered.

Owen took off his jacket and slipped it around her shoulders.

"Thanks." She kissed his cheek.

Owen would drive Holly back to her house, and all would appear to be just as it was. And yet nothing would ever be the same again. One word, though, one word from her, and everything could change. *When the time is right, God, please let that word be yes.*

Chapter Seventeen

Holly climbed into bed, her emotions a mess of panic, confusion, and euphoria. Life had become all things complicated. Sleep was unlikely. If she were to drift off, she doubted there would be any more nightmares about her mother. Her dream world would be riddled with a different kind of torment—decision. Strange to go her whole life without any marriage proposals and then receive two in one day! The earth felt tilted on its axis. One wrong move and she felt as though she would fall off the planet.

She punched her pillow and then

hurled it across the room. It smacked into a lamp, nearly knocking it to the floor.

Either way she went, someone was going to get hurt. To break Van's heart would be painful. To break Owen's heart seemed inconceivable. How could love cause such chaos? For Van she felt fondness, attraction, and great admiration for his accomplishments as a writer. But were those emotions really connected to love? Owen represented friendship, loyalty, and a newfound appeal. More honestly, it was a sincere passion.

How would she ever survive the decision-making process? She had a ferocious urge to try her father's habit of binge eating. She could drown herself in ice cream topped with hot fudge, whipped cream, and maraschino cherries. But as rhapsodic as the prospect might be, the bottom line meant her bottom line would no longer fit into her jeans, and she certainly wouldn't respect herself in the morning.

It was one of those moments when she longed to have a mother to talk to. Someone who knew about love, someone who could give her advice from a woman's point of view. But she loved her father dearly, and since he was always so full of common sense, she picked up the phone. Pacing the floor, she recounted every detail of the story to her dad, and afterward he offered her what she'd expected: understanding and love. But he didn't tell her what she should do.

"Thanks, Dad."

"Anytime, Cricket." He cleared his throat. "You know, either way you decide to go, you have my blessing. But just so you won't wonder about it later—I'm rooting for Owen."

That made Holly smile. After she hung up the phone she dropped back into bed, feeling loved but still without any absolute answer. She picked up Van's new novel off the bed table, *Land of Dreams and Drawbridges*, and turned it over to read what some big-shot author had written about it: *"A deeply moving portrayal of sacrificial love within the confines of war, poverty, and human frailty."* Wow, what an endorsement. Holly felt honored to be loved by a man who could write so beautifully and receive such praise for his work, and yet she knew that even the finest seal of approval on his art had nothing to do with love.

She set the book aside and reached for *Emma*, a Jane Austen novel Owen had picked up for her at the library. It was the only Austen novel she hadn't read, but she had seen the movie some years earlier. Then it hit her—*Emma* was the story of two friends falling in love. Wasn't it Emma and Mr. Knightley? How could she have missed Owen's hint? Very sneaky of him.

That's it. Mistake or not, I'm calling my best friend. Holly slipped on her super-ratty but super-comfy bunny slippers and padded into the kitchen to make herself some jasmine tea. She picked up her hot brew, sat on the floor in the corner of the kitchen, and called Owen on her cell phone. He answered right away.

"Owen?"

"Yeah?"

"I'm sorry to call so late."

"Doesn't matter. You know that."

"Yeah, I know. Thanks."

"Having trouble sleeping?" Owen asked.

"Yeah."

"Have you tried your jasmine tea?"

Holly took a sip from her mug. "I'm drinking it now."

"Good."

"Are *you* having trouble sleeping too?"

"Yeah."

"Can I guess why?"

"Well, there's this girl, you see. I'm in love with her. And I found out I won't be able to live without her. But let's not talk about me. What about you? Why can't you sleep?"

Holly pushed her mug aside. " 'Cause I'm scared."

"You have good reason to be. People make wrong decisions all the time. It's one reason the divorce rate is so high. That and the fact that people don't know how to *stay* married. Commitment sounds good on paper until people have to actually do it."

"So, what does my best friend say I should do?"

Owen paused. "What does your heart tell you?"

"I don't know."

"What do you think God would have to say?"

Holly shrugged. "I'm not sure."

"Well then, you're in a real pickle, my friend."

She rested her head in her hand. "Do you remember the time I ate a gigantic pickle on an empty stomach, went for a ride on your tire swing, and then spent the rest of that day throwing up?"

"Oh yeah, I remember it. You got sick all over my new high-top sneakers."

"Oh dear, I did, didn't I?" Holly chuckled. "And then Owen Quigly stayed right by my side the rest of that Saturday."

"I didn't mind."

"It's always been that way." Holly sighed. "If you were no longer a part of my life, something inside of me would die."

"I feel the same way."

"Pray for me, Owen."

"I have been—for your whole life."

"Thank you."

"So, do you think you can sleep now?" Owen asked.

"No."

"Me either."

"But it was nice to hear your voice."

Owen took in a deep breath. "One

word from you and you'll be able to hear that voice the rest of your life. Even when you go to bed at night."

"Now I'll never be able to go to sleep."

"Maybe that wasn't fair."

"'All's fair in love and war,'" Holly said.

"Who said that?"

"I have no idea."

Owen chuckled.

"Goodnight."

"Goodnight, Holly Goodnight."

She smiled and folded up her cell phone. The tea had gone cool, so she set her mug in the sink and went back to bed. Before pulling up the covers she glanced down at her old bunny slippers. They were worn threadbare, and yet she couldn't bring herself to throw them away. Hmm. Was she guilty of doing the same thing with her love life, wanting only what felt old and comfy? Was she leaning away from Van's love simply because it felt new and risky while Owen was all things familiar? Someone who could never *abandon* her?

Holly wrestled with these latest accusations against herself until her thoughts fell again to the loss of her mother. She recalled Van's idea about writing a letter. It had been a good idea, one that might help with closure as well as give her insight into her dilemma. She wouldn't be able to sleep anyway. Holly got out of bed, pulled out some paper from her writing desk, and began a letter to her mother.

Dear Mom,

I'm so sorry I never got to meet you. I want you to know that for whatever reason you left me all those years ago on the steps of The Little Bethlehem Shoppe, I forgive you.

The gentleman you left me with adopted me, and he turned out to be the very best of fathers. I hope that brings you comfort.

To be honest, there were lots of times I was confused and heavyhearted when I thought about my past. And then when I heard you died before I could ever meet you—well, it is a sadness that will take a long time to heal. I missed the mother-daughter times we could have shared. There were so many. My first baby tooth

hidden under a pillow, the moment I learned to ride a bike, my first softball game, and the day I came to know the real meaning of Christmas in my heart.

I would have told you about my very first crush, my first kiss, my best friend, and finally, the two marriage proposals that came on the very same day. You could have gasped with me, and then you could have given me a mother's wisdom. I'm not sure what you would have said. Maybe you would have told me that my love was like a bright star and that it had always been anchored in the sky for all to see. I had just never bothered to look up.

Your daughter, who will always love you,
Holly Rose Goodnight

"Good-bye, Mom." Holly folded the letter and slipped it into an envelope, hoping God would help her let go of her mother without ever forgetting her. At that thought, tears threatened, and she reached up to pinch her nose as she always did. But how foolish was it to always keep the tears from flowing?

Perhaps the ability to cry was a gift—to be able to release the pain when words weren't enough. So all the emotion she'd held inside, the tears she'd been afraid to release, came out in profusion.

In the middle of her emancipation, a thought came to her—if people needed her, really needed her constant help, then no one would ever abandon her again. Was that afflicted notion at the root of all her good deeds? If so, she really had come undone. *God, may all my small acts of kindness be without strings. Let them fly free as well.*

Some time later, after she'd dried her tears, Holly climbed back into bed, reached into her night table, and pulled out the compass Owen had given her. She turned it over in her hand, studying it. *Lord, just as I leave one maze I feel as though I've entered another, and this one is even trickier. I know You want me to choose well in marriage, so I am really open to some divine navigation.*

Holly snuggled under the covers, thinking of Owen and praying about Owen. And then, much later in the night, choosing Owen.

Chapter Eighteen

The bedside alarm went off, and Holly slammed her hand on the buzzer. Morning already?

The phone rang. Just before she slammed that too, Holly glanced at the caller. It was Van. The choice she'd made the night before came back to her, and even though she had great peace about it, she had no idea how to tell Van about her decision. She sat up in bed, patted her face, and then picked up. "Hi."

"How is my love?"

"Just waking up." Holly wiped the sweaty hair out of her face.

"Someday soon I'll be the one waking up next to you."

Holly felt speechless. His statement was full of presumption, and yet he said the words with such devotion it was hard to be angry.

"Holly, are you there?"

"Yes."

"You sound so far away."

"I'm right here. How was your trip? Did you make it home okay?"

"I didn't make it very far."

Holly gave her face another pat or two. "Where are you?"

"I'm at a hotel in Bentonville. I drove a couple of hours toward Houston, and then I suddenly remembered that my publicist had set up a book signing for me at the Hometown Bookshop here."

"Really?"

"After church this morning, do you mind meeting me there at noon? *Please* tell me you can."

Holly took in a deep breath. "I can. I'll see you at the bookshop in Bentonville."

" 'Bye, my darling."

"Good-bye." Holly hung up the phone. She would have given him the news then, but she felt he deserved an explanation in person. And since he was writing her story, she would have to get used to talking to him despite their broken relationship. How hard was that going to be? He would still need to interview her and give her updates concerning the progress of the book. And if the book sold well, what if there were a movie? She doubted such a thing could happen, and yet there was no way to know how far the story would go. What if their lives were linked for years to come?

Holly sank back under the covers, wondering how her simple, small-town life had gotten so complicated. After a long groan and an even longer prayer, she followed her usual routine of showering and eating breakfast. Then she slipped into a navy dress and matching coat.

Holly was on the road soon after Sunday morning services, making her way toward the Arkansas border. When she arrived in Bentonville she pulled into the parking lot of the Hometown Bookshop and then promptly froze solid. Why hadn't she practiced what to say? She got out of her car, thinking she had a few seconds to spare to gather her wits, but Van quickly met her outside and swept her into his world as if it were her world as well.

"We're running a little late," he whispered into her ear and then turned to an older woman who stood near him. "Pauline, this is Holly Goodnight."

Pauline, a woman who obviously worked for the bookstore, gave Holly's hand a vigorous shake. "It's so nice to meet you. We've heard a lot about you, Ms. Goodnight."

"You have?" The woman's tone was full of nuance. What had Van told her?

The woman smiled. "We're so honored to have Mr. Keaton here. There's already a crowd waiting for him. If you'd like to follow me, we have a special place for you."

Special place? "Oh, that's okay," Holly said. "I don't really need—"

"That's perfect." Van smiled at Pauline. "Thank you for taking care of Holly."

Van placed his hand on the small of Holly's back and moved her toward the center of the bookstore. There was indeed a gathering of people waiting for him, and behind a podium stood an entire wall of Van's latest novel, *Land of Dreams and Drawbridges*.

"Did someone place a bottle of water just inside the podium?" Van asked Pauline.

"Yes, of course."

Van raised an eyebrow. "Bottled water *only*. Cold, right?"

"Yes, just as you requested."

"And what about the introduction? My assistant e-mailed it to you weeks ago."

"Yes, Mr. Keaton, we have your intro." Pauline raised her chin a mite. "In fact, I have it memorized."

Van gave Pauline a tiny salute. "Excellent. Thank you."

Holly's face heated up as Pauline ushered her to the front of the room and offered her a chair that faced the audience. Would those in attendance think she was his wife?

A hush settled over the audience as Pauline stood behind the podium and cleared her throat.

After a long introduction, resplendent with Van's many accomplishments, the crowd gave him a generous round of applause. Van then strode to the front of the crowd and took his place behind the podium.

"Thank you for coming today." Van's gaze swept over the gathering. "I'm grateful to each and every one of you for your interest in my work. Whether it's curiosity, ambivalence, or even disdain. I'll take anything I can get."

Chuckles trickled through the audience.

"Before I read an excerpt from *Land of Dreams and Drawbridges*, I'd like to make an announcement."

What kind of announcement? Holly ran her hand along the folds of her dress and waited. She felt a hiccup coming on but managed to stifle it.

"I'm excited to say the release of my new book has been moved up. It'll come out in September, just in time for next Christmas. The title will be"—Van paused, caught Holly's gaze with a knowing smile, and then said to the audience—"*Once Upon a Christmas Eve*."

Van had kept the title such a secret that Holly was surprised he'd blurted it out among strangers. But it was impossible to question his disclosure, since he'd chosen such a lovely title.

"*Once Upon a Christmas Eve* is the true story of Holly Goodnight, who was abandoned as an infant on the front step of The Little Bethlehem Shoppe in Noel, Missouri, on Christmas Eve. Albert Goodnight, the owner of the shop, adopted the baby. Holly grew up, and she's with us today. May I introduce Holly Goodnight." Van gave a grand flourish toward her as if she were a featured car on a showroom floor.

Someone in the crowd whispered, "I've seen her on TV. Poor thing."

Holly smiled at the crowd but felt like crawling under the book table—for the rest of her life. But how could she complain or be embarrassed? She agreed to have a book written about her life.

Van took a sip of water. "While writing Ms. Goodnight's story—which I'm carrying through to the present—I myself became part of this work of creative nonfiction as I interacted with Ms. Goodnight and her father and friends in Noel. And then the most extraordinary and unexpected thing happened. Something—" Van's voice broke. He paused and looked away, as if holding back his emotion. "The writer, Van Keaton, fell in love with the heroine, Holly Goodnight."

Chapter Nineteen

The store went silent. Everyone looked from Van to Holly and then back to Van, waiting for a reaction. Or further explanation. Or anything that would give them permission to breathe again.

Van pulled out a black velvet box from his pocket, and happy noises erupted from the crowd.

Oh, no. God, please, no. Not in front of everyone. Holly's heart skipped a beat. She could hear the blood rushing back and forth in her ears.

Van turned to her. "I wanted to ask you now, since I couldn't wait another minute.

You are and always will be the love of my life. Would you do me the honor of becoming my wife?" Van knelt down in front of her.

"I do love you." *But.* Before Holly could formulate the rest of her sentence Van cracked opened the little box, and a large marquise diamond sparkled in front of her. For a second she felt mesmerized by the adoring glow in Van's eyes, the crowd's excitement, and the swelling emotion of what was surely the most embarrassing and yet romantic moment of her life. But her decision had been made, and it included Van only as her biographer, not as her husband. She should have practiced her speech.

Before she could utter one word of articulate protest, Van slipped the ring on her finger, and the audience broke out into a mind-numbing applause. Was she going to be physically ill? *Dear Lord, have mercy on me. What have I done?* She hiccuped.

Some of the people on the front row shook Van's hand while others yelled congratulations. After a few minutes everyone settled down enough that Van could read from his current novel.

While Van spoke eloquently to the crowd, Holly dissolved into a pool of wretchedness. How would she ever squirm out of her predicament? She shouldn't have said she loved him, but they were the first words that came to her. She did, in fact, care for Van, even loved him in a way, but it wasn't enough—at least not enough for a lifetime. The dilemma they found themselves in, though, hadn't been only of her making. Van had deliberately cornered her in front of a roomful of strangers, twisting her around his little finger. With that thought in mind, she got more and more irritated at him.

After Van finished his reading and his Q&A with the audience, it was time for him to sign books and chat with his readers.

Holly backed out of the limelight. Van didn't seem to notice, and that was best. She was relieved, since it would give her some time to think. What would she say to him now?

An attractive young blonde stepped up to Van's book table. "I just read *Land of Dreams and Drawbridges* and loved it. Would you sign my copy?"

"Of course, and I'm glad you enjoyed it." Van accepted the book and began signing his name on the title page.

The woman pressed her hand over her bosom. "It was sooo romantic and beautifully written. But you gave it such a tragic ending. Do you think this new book you're working on will have a happy ending?"

Van smiled. "I'm doing my best to make certain it does."

The woman lit up in his presence, glistening like a disco ball.

Holly had to admit she understood the woman's attraction. Van looked handsome and scholarly in his camel-hair blazer. Perhaps she too had been awed by Van's prestige and bravura and connection to a world that was anything but ordinary. Hmm. Had she even asked him enough questions about his life, his beliefs, his dreams? Even though Van had claimed to like Noel, would he have eventually asked her to move to Houston?

Perhaps she really had been dazzled too much by the shimmer on the surface. Holly twirled the diamond ring on her finger and, without gazing at it, weighed her own character and found it wanting.

The young blonde glided away from Van with a look of bliss. In fact, each customer in line who visited with Van shuffled off looking satisfied. It was obvious he had the gift of bringing joy to people through his charismatic personality and his stories. It was hard not to admire such talent. When Van had made it through the long line and signed every book the store set in front of him, he was left beaming at the table. Holly wasn't sure if it was from all the adulation or the engagement. Probably both.

Van rose from the table. "Darling, how about some Starbucks? It's nearby." He pulled her to him and kissed her forehead. "By the way, you look charming in that navy dress. Like twilight, the blue hour—remember?"

Holly smiled at him. "I remember." Even though she was upset with Van for placing her in such an awkward situation, the last thing she wanted to do was hurt him. She still had no speech, no perfect way to end their relationship. Perhaps she was just too human to be inside the pages of a book.

* * * * *

Van escorted Holly out into the sunny day, but no amount of late autumn sunshine or crisp air could bolster his dwindling hope. What had he been thinking, putting Holly on the spot in front of so many people? Easy answer. He had so feared her refusal that he'd allowed himself to resort to underhanded and manipulative tactics. He had as much integrity as the sole of a shoe.

As they approached Starbucks Van opened the door for Holly. He bought their usual beverages, and then they settled into cozy chairs in the back. The merry expression Holly usually wore had gone missing, and he knew why. "I'm sorry I did that to you."

She touched his arm. "I thought it was romantic. However."

"*However*, what I did to you was unforgivable." Van took off his glasses and rubbed the bridge of his nose.

Holly's chin quivered. "I forgive you."

Van stared into his cup but didn't take a sip. "Do you know why I brought you here?"

"Because you love good coffee?" She smiled.

"I've always believed that no bad thing could ever happen in Starbucks. So I—"

"Van."

"Yes?"

"I want us to stop pretending. We need to—"

"Holly, please." Van's eyes stung with tears. He put his glasses back on. *Lovely. Now I'm crying.* "I have no excuse for my behavior, except somehow I thought it would change your mind. I see now those were the sentiments of a fool. Or maybe just someone who was blinded by desperation. I've never fallen in love before. I'm totally smitten. But I can see there's no amount of flute playing or clever language that will change your mind."

"You really did sweep me off my feet, you know." She gave his shoulder a squeeze. "It was like being caught up in this beautiful hot air balloon, drifting along on some breathtaking ride. But up there I couldn't see things clearly."

"And now you do?"

Holly nodded.

He stared at Holly's hand, the one clasping his shoulder. He took comfort in her touch and yet grieved over it, since that intimate connection would be taken from him. "You know, my editor has read some of the first draft of this new book, and she says it will take me where I want to go as a writer. They expect my sales to double. And *you* did that for me, Holly. You turned my career around. What will I do without you? You're my muse. My love."

Holly rested her head on his arm, and when she lifted it back up, her eyes were damp with tears.

Van pulled a handkerchief out of his pocket and dabbed at her cheeks. Then he slipped his laptop out of his bag and turned it on.

"Are you going to write all this into the book—*now*?"

"All my life, I've sort of lived for myself. I've never been terribly courageous. I would like to do the right thing for once. So without being overly dramatic, I'm going to write myself out of your story, out of your life."

Van typed as he said the words. "Even as I dried Holly's tears and she said her good-byes, I already saw her at a distance like the last rays of a sunset. I saw her years being played out in Noel." Van paused to control his emotions. "As the seasons came and went, she would embrace every wonder. She would see blessing in sacrifice, joy in simplicity, and she would receive tender affections from every life she touched. And most of all, Holly would grow old with her dearest friend and greatest love—Owen."

Van couldn't remember a time when the pain of being alive felt so acute.

"That was beautifully said, Van. I wish it could have ended happily for everyone." She leaned toward him. "How long have you known about Owen? That he was more than just a friend?"

"I went to his house in hopes he might support my proposal. He may have told you."

"He did."

"Well, after our brief talk I finally concluded that either Owen disapproved of me in general or else he'd fallen in love with you." Van turned his computer off and slipped it back into his bag.

"And how did you figure out which one was the truth?"

"Maybe it was the impassioned way he said your name."

Holly smiled. "I see."

"There's just no way to ask you this without sounding petty, but what is it that made Owen *the* one? I know you and I don't have a special handshake. We didn't grow up together or have a history. And I know I'm a high-maintenance, paranoid germophobe who's—well, you know my foibles."

She took a slow sip of her latté. "Maybe love is sort of like the wind. Who can really know where it comes from?"

"Are you sure *you're* not the writer?"

Holly chuckled.

He wished that something so well said wasn't so painful to hear. "I wish you both well."

"And I pray you'll find joy. Van, you're very resourceful. *And* you're charming and dear. Someone is out there—just waiting to love you." Holly chuckled.

"That sounds cheesy, but I don't mean it to be."

"I know." Van tried to drink his coffee, but he was more weary than thirsty. "You're right. I'll eventually move on—if I don't I'll end up on the street, pilfering through Dumpsters. Well, maybe not that. Too many germs." He knew his grin wasn't very convincing. "Just let me look at you for a moment, Holly Rose. Guess that should be the last time I call you Holly Rose. Wouldn't be right otherwise." He straightened his shoulders and brightened, determined not to bring her any more grief.

Holly rested her head on his shoulder.

Van circled his arm around her. To hold her felt so good. Even now, with no hope for a future.

"I wanted to thank you for your help."

"My help?"

Holly eased away. "Even though you didn't intend for it to happen, you brought me to a crossroads with Owen. If it hadn't been for you we may never have moved forward. I wouldn't have seen the course that had already been set for my life. And while I'm pleased that you're writing my story, it's meant so much more than that. All those interviews and talks—they genuinely helped me come to terms with my past. It has all meant so much to me, Van. Thank you."

"You're welcome." He shook his head and smiled. "I hope it's all right if I send you occasional e-mail updates about the book."

"I'll always be here for you—in that way."

Van knew well what she meant. They would never again be together in such a familiar manner. From now on, all contact would need to be in the name of business or friendship.

She slipped the engagement ring off her finger, handed it to him, and kissed him on the cheek. "I don't want to leave you here like this."

"I'll be okay." He nodded. "We *both* will."

Holly rose to leave, and he watched her go, allowing himself to take in the finality of the scene. The glass door slowly closed behind her. She didn't look back, but then he hadn't expected her to.

Van leaned his head on the table. Tears came. He didn't care who was watching him. What did it matter?

After a few minutes, his cell phone came to life. He glanced at the caller—Lindy. She was probably disappointed about Owen not calling and wanted to cry on his shoulder. Feeling a sudden bond with her, he answered the phone.

Chapter Twenty

....

Holly opened the car door as she breathed a prayer for Van—that he would recover more quickly than he ever thought possible and that he would find a great love of his own.

On the long drive home, thoughts of Owen could no longer be kept at bay. The look of affliction on his face when she'd walked away the night before caused her even more pain. Her best friend was out there somewhere, still waiting for her answer. She couldn't ease Van's suffering, but she could put one man out of his misery. She could make one happy ending. And she knew just how she would do it.

Owen. How she loved him—not because it was safe, but because it was real. Why had she waited so long to discover what was already there? God had been listening all along. *She* was the one who hadn't been paying attention to the resounding trumpet of love! No more denial and nonsense. The time was now.

Holly pulled into Noel knowing just where to find Owen. On a Sunday afternoon he was always at home reading a good book. But after ringing the bell, pounding on the door, and then peeking in the window, she realized her certainty about his whereabouts was faulty. Where had he gone? Disappointment trickled into her spirit along with panic. Had he changed his mind about her? Was he so wounded from her response to his proposal that he'd left town for a while? Didn't sound like Owen. Could he have gone to the shop? It was closed on Sunday, but then again, he did have a key. It was worth a try.

Holly drove into town, parked on Main,

and ran up to The Little Bethlehem Shoppe. Even though the sign read CLOSED, she tried the door. It was open. The moment she stood inside the entry she saw legs coming out from under the bottom of a tree—Owen's legs. Relief washed over her.

"We're closed," Owen hollered.

She walked toward him, her shoes clomping softly on the wooden floor.

"Holly?"

"Yes." She opened up the branches and looked down at her dear Owen. "How did you know it was me?"

"Something about the way you walked across the room. Neighborly footsteps, but maybe a little sneaky too."

Holly smiled at him. She hoped—oh, she hoped—Owen hadn't changed his mind, but as she searched his eyes, she could see the love all over his face. "What are you doing here on a Sunday?"

"I was at home trying to read, but I couldn't concentrate, so I thought I'd come in the shop for a while. It's peaceful here, you know, puttering around. And this place is so filled with memories—so full of you—that, well, being here makes me feel closer to you. And that's always a good thing."

"Mmm. Words don't get any sweeter than that."

"Was there something on your mind—in particular?" Owen sounded hopeful.

"I did want to talk to you." Holly could barely hold back her emotions.

"Is it something I want to hear?"

Holly released the branches and strolled around the tree. She could have jumped up and down and screamed, "Yes, I'll marry you." But perhaps something so celebratory and so sanctioned by God deserved at least a romantic prelude. "Well, I have a new theme idea for a tree, and I was excited to tell you about it."

"Oh?" Owen sounded disappointed. "That's all?"

"Well, it's the best theme I've ever come up with. First, we'll start with a tree that looks flocked. Faux, of course. And then we'll decorate it with bouquets of gardenias, tulle, and white ribbons."

"White sounds promising." Owen came out from under the tree. "Tell me more."

"Well, the tree will be so beautiful it'll become the talk of the town."

"And why is that?" Owen stepped closer to her.

"Everyone will say, 'It's about time Holly and Owen put up a wedding tree. In fact, we don't know why they didn't think of it sooner.'"

Owen took her into his arms. "It *is* the best idea I've ever heard."

Holly traced her finger along his face, studying him in a new way. "I can't believe I've been looking at you all these years, but I'd never really *seen* you—until now. How can that be?"

"Well, life is full of mysteries, and apparently our love is one of them."

"So we're right up there with the Devil's Promenade and Big Foot?"

"Maybe." Owen glanced up. "Well, look at that. We're standing right under the mistletoe."

"So we are. And it's about time we made full use of it." Holly tilted Owen's chin toward her lips for a kiss she hoped he'd remember for a long time to come.

Epilogue

....

That same year, on the eve of Christmas, in a chapel nestled in the Ozark Mountains, a wedding was about to begin.

Ivy Quigly, Owen's mother, smoothed Holly's bridal gown and then adjusted her floor-length veil. "Now, don't you look just like a princess?"

Holly hugged the woman, grateful to be on the receiving end of Mom Ivy's generosity and her gift for mothering. "And thanks for the lace gloves. They're perfect."

"Well, you had to have something old."

Mom Ivy patted Holly on the cheek. "The music is about to begin, dear."

Holly turned to her father and latched onto his arm.

"Are you ready?" he whispered.

"Are you kidding, Dad? I am *soo* ready."

He chuckled. "What a glorious day this is. I'm going to have grandchildren at last."

"Daaad." She jiggled his arm.

The guitarist began to play "The Wedding Song," and they both straightened.

"Here we go, Cricket," her father said.

Together father and daughter started that famous march up the church aisle.

The stone chapel—which had floor-to-ceiling windows and a majestic view of the woods and mountains—had been the ideal choice for the ceremony. Holly glanced up at the rafters and saw the Christmas ball full of mistletoe. Her father had tied the keepsake just above the spot where she and Owen would seal their vows with a kiss. She grinned, thinking how many times Owen must have stood beneath that very mistletoe, and how she never knew he was the one—to kiss, to marry, and to love for a lifetime.

As Holly passed each pew, the townspeople of Noel gave their nods of blessing—Miss Plumtree, Sandra Westin and her boys, Vincent Hagerdey and his wife, and most surprisingly, Van and Lindy, snuggled side by side. Holly had no idea how Van's life story would go, but she prayed it would have a happy ending.

Holly squeezed her dad's arm as they continued up the aisle. Standing at the front, smiling at her, was Owen Quigly. *That is,* my *Mr. Quigly.* How she loved him.

Just outside, among the oaks and hickories and pines, snow began to fall as though angels were sprinkling white confetti. A few gasps rippled through the crowd. Snow on her wedding day. *Just how beautiful is that?*

Holly remembered the gift of the compass and breathed a prayer of thanksgiving to God, the divine Navigator of her soul. The path had been lit and love was all about them, falling down like the snow, pristine and full of wonder.

About the Author

Anita Higman is the author of more than two dozen titles, including fiction, nonfiction, children's books, and plays. Anita's romance books include *Love Finds You in Humble, Texas* and contributions to *Ozark Weddings*, *Larkspur Dreams*, *The Love Song*, and *Castles in the Air*. Her published mysteries include *Another Stab at Life* and *Another Hour to Kill*. Anita is a member of ACFW and the Christian Humor Writers' Group, and she has been recognized for her involvement in literacy programs. A Texan for the past twenty-six years, Anita has coauthored an award-winning book about her home state, *A Tribute to Early*

Texas. She lives with her husband near Houston.

www.anitahigman.com